THE APOCALYPSE MECHANISM

BY J.M. RICHARDSON

Winter Goose Publishing

Winter Goose Publishing
2701 Del Paso Road, 130-92
Sacramento, CA 95835

www.wintergoosepublishing.com
Contact Information: info@wintergoosepublishing.com

The Apocalypse Mechanism
COPYRIGHT © 2012 by J.M. Richardson

First Edition, August 2012

Cover Art by Winter Goose Publishing
Typeset by Victoriakumar Yallamelli

ISBN: 978-0-9851548-7-5

Published in the United States of America

*To my beautiful wife Melissa
and daughters Audrey and Elle*

Chapter 1
June 4, 2006

James P. Beauregard sat in his den silently admiring the grandeur of the antique décor of his Chartres Street home, death on his mind, and death in his hand. Though the entire house was bathed in the darkness of a typical New Orleans night, he was still able to observe the finely crafted furniture, oil paintings and beautifully polished oak construction between the faint luminescence of the streetlights outside and the sporadic flashes of lightning. He would miss it, or would he? Do the dead miss anything, or simply blink into nothingness?

The torrent of rainfall had a soothing effect, yet created an unrivaled feeling of depression in James, and though he had lived in Louisiana for his entire thirty-five-year existence with typically rainy summer weather each year, he had never overcome this feeling. Perhaps if he had not been chronically alone, nights like these would not be as dreary.

James sat in his favorite chair facing the expansive, unlit fireplace, which seemed to yawn mockingly in pity at his mundane existence through the beautiful black wrought-iron screen. *My God*, the fireplace seemed to say. *How did you let yourself become what you have become? I remember when you were ambitious, quick-witted, and ready to hold the mirror spitefully in front of the world to show her just how wrong she was about herself. You were among the top in your field. Now look at you. You're a sniveling, self-pitying drunk who can barely make it to work on time on account of a hangover.* James simply shrugged, admitting it to himself.

The oak floor sprawling before the fireplace was stained in its original burgundy-red color, accentuated by masterfully crafted early nineteenth-century imported rugs. According to family tradition, when James's great-great-great-grandfather, Gaston Beauregard, purchased the mansion in 1872, his father entered the confines only once, claiming that the color resembled the crimson-stained ground on which he had ordered so many young men to their deaths.

The lightning flashed once again, followed by God's timpani resonating through the stormy sky. The temporary flash revealed the radiance of the deep red 1830s wallpaper, crowned with raised gold fleur de'lis patterns. The entire wall to his left was covered in bookcases adorned with dozens of rare classics, histories and documents. In the corner to the left of the bookcases was a tall glass case with a wooden frame, which housed such priceless items as letters written home by his great-great-great-great-grandfather, whom James frequently referred to as *The General,* and a wooden, velvet-lined box, which housed two 1857 Colt Army, cap-and-ball revolvers, one of which was missing.

James's hand trembled as he lifted the bottle of Basil Hayden's bourbon from the late eighteenth-century coffee table before him and tilted it to pour himself another drink. Placing the bottle back on the table, he lifted the glass to his lips and closed his eyes as he took in the aroma of the warm cedar undertones. He loved this brand of whiskey, and as the smooth bourbon slid down his throat he felt the warmth of it spread from his esophagus to his belly, and beyond. There was nothing like the burn of a good whiskey. Basil had become James's one true love. Basil was the only one he could depend on.

Savoring the flavor and warmth of his drink, he tilted his head back and for a moment his tensions and dark memories seemed to melt away. He opened his eyes, his sight immediately trained on the gorgeous, antique crystal chandelier hanging from the ceiling above him. Even its beauty could not offset the gloom of the darkened room that engulfed it. It simply cast a sparkle-ridden shadow on the far wall each time the lightning flashed through the window. Despite another sip of bourbon, the depression returned.

James returned his head to its natural position, tilting it uncomfortably from side to side as he listened to the vertebrae pop. He then fixed his gaze upon the large painting above the fireplace mantle. He felt his eyes soften with admiration and respect. The painting was positioned directly above the officer's saber being displayed below. The torso-up portrait of the man seemed to leap forward from the canvas. The gold in the stars upon the shoulders of the gray uniform shimmered as if the paint itself were made from gold.

A brief grin formed on James's face as he remembered he had wanted to dress that way for Halloween as a kid. His mother had made him a little Confederate general's uniform and bought him a plastic replica of a saber. "Don't hit anyone with that sword," she would say as he ran wildly playing *swashbuckler* or something. "That includes the dog!" His mother had even combed his hair from left to right with the part on the left side, just like in the painting. The finishing touch was a thick brown mustache and a little inverted triangle of hair drawn just below his bottom lip. "How precious," she'd marveled as little James ran off to terrorize the family German shepherd.

There was a roar of thunder and James was brought back into his dreadful present reality. His fingers traced the deep grooves of the masterfully carved armrest of his favorite chair. He loved the ornateness of the eighteenth-century masterpiece. *It really is a beautiful chair. It would be a shame to ruin it by the deed I'm about to commit,* he thought.

James's attention again shifted to the painting. "What would you do, General?" he asked the figure. "Certainly you've dealt with feelings like this. All those young men you sent into the slaughter. Some were no older than fifteen, if I recall."

But the man in the painting did not respond. James simply nodded his head and chuckled as if the General were a therapist who simply looked at him like he was crazy. He picked up his glass and imbibed the remainder of its contents as his smile morphed into a wince and tears began to roll down his unshaven cheek.

James lifted a picture of a woman and a boy and brought it close to his face so that his alcohol-dulled eyes could focus. She was beautiful, the bright sun causing her dirty-blonde curls to glow on that spring day. Everything was perfect—the picnic, the deep green of the grass and trees in Audubon Park, the zoo. The ten-year-old boy in the picture smiled without a care in the world as he clung to his mother from the back with his arms around her neck. His brown hair and brown eyes were obviously inherited from his father. Then there were flashes of twisted metal, darkness, police strobes. Back to reality.

"I'm sorry," he sobbed. "I remember our vows. I swore to love and protect you, but I couldn't. I'm so sorry!"

James's grip loosened as the framed photograph plummeted to the floors between his feet. He half expected shattered glass, but surprisingly, the picture remained intact. Did it matter anyway? James remained hunched over, sobbing violently into the palms of his own hands.

Another drink.

He tried to pull himself together. *Don't be such a Nancy*, he thought, drying his tears with his sleeve and reaching for the bottle of whiskey. James poured the last of the smooth, fiery liquid and lifted the glass to his lips.

As he ran his hand across his goatee, he reached for the remote control to his rather elaborate stereo system and began to browse through the extensive collection of CDs in the changer. *Pantera? No, too heavy. Skynrd? Too . . . Alabama. Classical? Bach. Johann Sebastian Bach. This was perfect. The Brandenburg Concerto No. 3* was one of his favorites.

James tried to turn up the volume but nothing happened. "Damned batteries!" he shouted, violently jamming down on the button. Finally, it began to work. He turned the volume up slightly and slumped back in his chair, revealing a rare smile.

As the melodically perfect waltz tickled his eardrums, many questions filled his head. *Chin? Mouth? Temple?* James couldn't help but grin that the temple would be perfect. It was a place that brought people closer to whatever god people believed in. James found humor in the notion that if his body were a temple, it would not be unlike the Athenian Parthenon. Structurally, though badly weathered, it was still holding up, yet inside it was almost completely gutted of anything resembling beauty, substance or holiness.

The clicking sound seemed almost a part of the Bach piece emitted from the stereo speakers, and like the music, the clicking was welcomed and beautiful. As the noise was produced again and again, James regarded it as a bringer of peace to his troubled soul. He decided to look down at the object in his hand that was causing such a calming sound.

The 1857 Colt Army was exquisitely crafted with dark, blued metal parts accentuated by beautifully lacquered mahogany grip. The initials

P.G. T.B. were engraved on the left-hand side of the barrel, a gift from Jefferson Davis, the president of the Confederate States of America, himself. James pulled the hammer back, rotating the cylinder, and producing that all too warm clicking sound. He then held the top of the hammer tightly with his thumb, gently squeezed the trigger, and carefully let the hammer safely back to rest against the next round. James savored the sound as he repeated the process again and again, wondering who would come into ownership of the majestic and commanding weapon.

"Now I'm ready," he sighed, pulling the hammer back one last time. Slowly, James brought the barrel of the gun to a vertical trajectory, and then even more slowly brought the muzzle to a rest against his temple. Steadily, he tightened his right index finger, putting tension on the gold-plated trigger.

The ringing of the phone from the end table to his left startled him from his trance-like state enough that it almost angered him. He had never been that close to actually going through with it, and the sudden, untimely phone call could have made him jerk his finger, sending his brain matter raining down upon the expensive rugs. Then, he started to wonder if it mattered. After all, he did have his mind made up to put a revolver ball through his head.

"Who the hell could that be?" James squinted at the number on the caller ID. "A 203 area code? Where the hell is that?" More importantly, whom did he know there?

James decided not to answer it, but he was also curious and opened his black leather address book that lay beside the phone. He knew there was a list of cities and their area codes somewhere between the measurement conversion guides and the list of toll-free numbers to major hotel chains.

His finger slid down the page as his eyes scanned the area codes listed on the right. Finally, his finger stopped on 203, and then traced the dotted line back to the city list on the left side. "New Haven, Connecticut?" he puzzled. "Yale!" almost getting excited. That call could have been the dean of the Yale history department about the guest lecture he wanted to give there on ancient engineering. *At six-fifteen? That's seven-fifteen in New Haven! Aren't all facilities closed?*

As James continued to stare at the telephone and ponder the meaning of a call from Connecticut, the phone began to ring again. *Maybe things could be looking up.* Slowly, as if the receiver were going to electrocute him when he touched it, he moved his hand closer to the phone, lifted it from the cradle and silenced the ringing.

"Hello?" James's tone tripped with confusion.

"James," the man's hefty voice on the other end spoke, winded, "how's it hangin'?"

"Who is this?"

"James, I know I've picked up this damned Yankee accent, but tell me you haven't forgotten your best buddy!"

"Timothy Horn." James uttered the name in a monotone fashion, muffled undoubtedly from the bourbon.

"Please, you're getting me all teary-eyed from your overwhelming excitement to hear from me after two years. It's quite touching."

"Cut the shit, Tim. What do you want?"

"Hey, Jimbo, I know we didn't exactly part on the best of terms, but tell me you're not still upset at me."

"You're a lying, cheating dickhead son of a bitch."

"I missed you, too, buddy," Tim fired back. "Look, I was sorry to hear about Abigail and Max . . . I would have come to the funeral, but—"

James cut him short. "Tim, I appreciate it, but I thought I told you to cut the shit."

"Fair enough, James. Look, are you drunk?"

James stared at the empty bottle of Basil Hayden's, the Colt in his hand still cocked and ready. "Not too bad," he replied, slurring his speech ever so slightly. "Is there a reason you're calling me, or did you just want to give me that warm and fuzzy feeling I get when I talk to you?"

Timothy did not speak for several seconds. "Tim, I'm hanging up. I'm busy. Goodbye."

"Jim, I need your help."

James stopped short of setting the phone back into its cradle. "Gambling? Jail?"

"Of course not. I need your expertise. We've found something. Ancient texts, depictions, artifacts." Tim was getting excited. Clearly, he wasn't joking. He was like a child.

"My expertise? You're the big brain—Mister backwoods Baton Rouge boy gone Yankee Yale big-dick," James said.

"No, James. This is unprecedented. This is unique. This is groundbreaking. This is *your* field, chief."

"What do you want from me, Tim?"

"There's a ticket waiting for you at New Orleans International. Yale's tab—first class. Your plane leaves in two hours so you have to hurry."

"This may be a dumb question, but where, exactly, are you sending me?"

"It's been too long. I need to see you in person." Timothy's tone lightened. "Two hours. Oh, and leave the booze at home. It's free in first class."

There was a click, and Tim was gone.

James rolled his eyes and stared at the floor for a long time. "Drama queen." His tone was annoyed. "Connecticut? Really?"

James struggled to his feet using the arm of the chair for support. He reached for the remote control, turned to face the stereo, and pressed the *power* button, but not surprisingly, the stereo did not turn off. He began violently pressing the button and striking the remote on its side, as if that would do some good.

"Damn batteries!" he said, trying it a few more times. All in one motion, James threw the remote control down on the chair, slowly lifted his right hand and fired the Colt, sending the volley into the heart of the stereo system, launching sparks through the air and abruptly bringing the Bach masterpiece to an end. He then carefully placed the weapon on the table, stumbled forward a bit and headed upstairs to pack his suitcase.

Chapter 2

All was quiet in the darkened valley around the young man as he made his way down the stone-paved avenues bordered by once towering walls. He gazed upwards into the sky and silently praised God for such heavenly beauty in the millions of stars and the moon that lit the cosmic canopy above.

This was only his fifth time to visit this holy place. He was still awestricken at the sheer importance of the sight. As a child in Tehran, he remembered his father talked of it often and he would beg him to tag along on one of his pilgrimages. His father would always say that he was not yet ready, but would take part in this holy mission when he was old enough.

He looked out across the eroded hills and mountains that surrounded the valley and marveled at its beauty. *How many thousands of men have died in this place? Tonight, it is calm, but soon there will be shrieks of terror the world over, and God will have his vengeance.*

The young man began to lose sight of the valley as he descended an ancient set of stairs that led deep into the mount. He had to hold on to the iron rails to keep his footing; thousands of years of weathering and foot traffic had worn away the stone steps so that little friction remained for his sandals to grip.

When he had gone as far down as the stairs would carry him, he began squinting his eyes and moving his head from side to side, scanning the earthen walls around him. This was more difficult than he imagined. Though this was his fifth time to visit the site, he had never been down here, nor had he ever attended the ritual. The moon did not cast its pure beams into the recesses of this shaft.

His eyes adjusted to the darkness a little. He moved through the shadows, further into the tunnel before him. The priest had instructed that no torches were to be lit. The young man wondered if this had some symbolism within the faith or if the instruction was to prevent the government authorities from investigating. He imagined that they would not be very happy with what they found happening at a national monument if they did investigate.

The young man stood there in the darkness of the earthen tunnel, fumbling around through his garments where he found a plastic, cylindrical object. He bent the object at a forty-five degree angle as if he were breaking a twig, and the item returned to its original form, glowing a bright neon green. He squinted his eyes a little at first as his pupils began adjusting. His caramel skin seemed to turn a deep olive color when mixed with the green light. His snow-white robes and turban almost seemed to emit their own light in reflecting the light of the glow stick.

He held the glow stick in front of him as far as he could reach, and stepped forward. His lips moved as he counted in Farsi no louder than a whisper. He walked very slowly. Unable to see very much further than his own feet, each step was unsure. Would there be another set of steps? Would there be a pitfall? Would there be some imperfection in the height of the boards that created the walkway beneath his feet?

The walk seemed to take forever. The further he moved into the bowels of the mount, the stronger the scent of smoke became, yet he could see no fire. "Six hundred and ten, six hundred and eleven, six hundred and twelve," he counted, and then stopped as he had been instructed. He turned to the right and moved to the wooden rail that prevented tourists from leaving the walkway. Extending his glow stick beyond the rail as far as he could, the young man saw a shape take form in the rock wall about five feet away—a large crack-like opening.

Is this it? Could this be the entrance? He studied it for several moments. He had taken the appropriate number of paces, and the aroma of burning timber was as strong as ever. This had to be the place.

He carefully climbed over the handrail and stood on the edge of the walkway. He then probed below with his foot in order to judge the distance he would have to step down. Surprisingly, the stone floor of the tunnel was only about two feet below, so he brought his other foot down below the walkway, turned and began moving closer to the crack in the wall.

He could tell that it was about seven feet tall and three feet wide—a tight fit, but possible to enter. The smoke, he noticed, now seemed to pour from the opening, so he bunched a piece of cloth from his white garments, holding them over his mouth and nose with his left hand, while his right hand clutched the crucial glow stick. With the light extended to his right, the young man began to fit his slender body into the crevasse.

He inched his way deeper into the opening, beginning to feel like the sand crabs he had observed scurrying along the beaches of the Persian Gulf as a boy. But the terrifying confines of this place quickly brought him from childhood bliss back to the realities of the present. As the passageway made a sharp turn to the left and then back to the right, he began to realize why no one had ever found this place, save for the few that belonged to his order. Geologists must have revered it as a simple natural flaw in the rock structure. Archaeologists probably thought of it as a rupture in the tunnel wall that occurred during its creation. Whatever the case, no one would look at the deep chasm as a passageway to a hidden chamber. The smoke was getting thicker. The glow stick illuminated it, making it more difficult to see past his own nose. He blinked his dry, burning eyes as he coughed out what he could not filter with the cloth. Yet, he began to hear a sweet melody that took his fears and apprehensions away. He felt uplifted in the eyes of God. He could hear the muffled chanting and prayers of his brethren, and around the next corner glowed illumination that could only come from the sacred fire.

Chapter 3

"Don't you hate it when your butt goes to sleep? I mean, it's bad enough when your foot or even your hand goes to sleep, but *pins and needles* in the ass are just a pain in the . . . well, ass," James chuckled to the aging African-American man two barstools to his left. The man simply cast an irritated look in James's direction.

"No, really, do you know what I mean? My flight has been delayed for two hours since I got here. I don't even like to fly!" James continued. Once again, all he got was the *go to hell* look from the squat, elderly man.

James turned his head back to the forward position and locked his eyes on his drink. *It's a shame these airport people have no idea what good whiskey is. Jesus, I've reduced myself to Jack Daniels at the airport bar.* With that, it was time for another cigarette. Lifting the half empty pack from the slightly less-than-clean bar surface, he opened the flip top and extracted another sinful pleasure, bringing it to his lips. With his textured stainless-steel Zippo in hand, he masterfully flipped back the lid, striking the wheel in a brilliant flash of white-hot sparks, but producing no flame. *What a waste*, he thought. *All that show-boating and it didn't even light! Damn it, out of fuel . . . no matter.* He then set to searching his pockets for his spare Bic.

James caught himself admiring his pants while patting his legs for the familiar bulge of a lighter. The black Italian suit was always a hit with deans and presidents of other colleges and universities. Reaching into the left inner coat pocket, he found his kelly-green Bic. Quickly, he began striking the flint repeatedly as if this would be the last cigarette he would ever smoke. As the bright flame appeared, James touched the end of his cigarette to it, sucked on the devilish orange filter, inhaled the noxious fumes and blew the gray fog into the air almost with a sigh of relief.

Yes, I look good, he observed as he ran his hand across the sleeve of his coat. Taking another hefty gulp of his Jack Daniels and a drag of his cigarette, James fixed his eyes on the mirror behind the bar. The man that stared back at him and seemed to imitate his every motion was not James Beauregard, grandson of a wealthy businessman and descendant of a famous general. He wore a black Italian suit just like James but only slightly resembled him. This man had not shaved and the stubble was beginning to connect the long, brown sideburns to the goatee around his mouth. His short, brown hair was combed down and spiked in the front but had not been fixed since early that morning, and was beginning to look ragged. Bags were beginning to form around his dark brown eyes. He was wearing a beautiful sky-blue shirt, but it was badly wrinkled and the bleach-white collar was unbuttoned with the gold and blue necktie loosened. This man did not look good.

Oh, hell, he thought. *I'm not impressing anyone, especially at Yale. Why am I even going? Is this just some sick joke? Is this another way for Tim Horn to torment me? These uppity New England jerk-offs won't take me any more seriously than this guy sitting to my left!*

"That's enough!" James's train of thought was gone. In fact, it had been derailed, killing all passengers aboard. James directed his attention to the elderly man in his periphery. The man had a look on his face as if James had just been caught sleeping with his wife. *Ooh, wrong picture to paint, James.*

"What? Did I say all that out loud?" James said, feeling like he was losing his mind.

"What the hell you talkin' about?" the man replied.

James didn't know what to say. He simply had no idea what was going on.

"You keep tappin' that lighter on your whiskey glass and it's drivin' me absolutely shit-nuts!" the man spouted off. "You've obviously got problems and you need to lay off that juice."

"I'll take it under advisement," James shrugged off the encounter.

"No, I'm serious. You are in bad shape. You're dressed like you're goin' to a job interview somewhere, and I have a feelin' they ain't gonna like what they see."

"What, are you a shrink? Are you my life coach?"

"No. My eyes ain't what they used to be, but I know a jackass when I see one."

"Whatever. And no, I'm not going to a job interview. I'm going to meet with some colleagues at Yale. Ever heard of Yale?"

"Oh, I see. You think I'm some poor, dumb nigga from the ninth ward on my way to Chicago to hook up with my peeps."

"No, I never said—"

"I got my bachelor's degree from Xavier, my master's from UNO, and I run my own shoe store on Canal Street."

"I'm very happy for you." James sounded condescending still, but tried to work his way out of this hole. "And I never implied that you were a poor, dumb . . . you know."

"You may not have implied it, but you were thinkin' it. That's for damn sure!"

"Mister UNO master's, you have no idea what I was thinking. You don't know anything about me! So why are you judging me?" He took another sip.

"Probably the same reason you were judging me." The old man paused as if to calm himself and regroup his thoughts, then continued his statement with renewed ferocity. "Y'know, I ain't no big-shot professor like you think you are, but in my sixty-five years I have learned somethin' about sociology. Everybody judges everybody. Few have the courage to do it openly."

"I was not judging you." For a moment James thought he felt his nose grow a few centimeters longer. He kept his composure, however, and braced himself for the inevitable *bullshit*.

"Bullshit!" The man looked offended.

James tried to hide the uncontrollable grin growing upon his face by taking another healthy gulp of whiskey.

"Everybody judges," the old man continued. "When we see an Arab-looking man walk through the airport, we secretly think, *this raghead is gonna blow this damned plane up*. When we see an Asian girl in a college classroom, our minds go straight to high SAT scores. A Hispanic is automatically Mexican and works in construction. A homeless man is a drunk, a rock singer is a pothead, a Jew is good with money, and I'm the po', dumb-ass nigga from ninth ward flyin' up to Chicago to hook up with my peeps."

"Yeah, and sometimes we're right."

"That attitude is exactly what I'm talkin' about. You think you're at the top of the food chain—a master of the universe. And yes, sometimes we are right with our assumptions. I'm right about you, and you know it. You could be a master of the universe if you weren't so damned scared."

"Scared? What the hell do I have to be scared of?"

"You're scared of everything! You're scared of flying in that plane, scared to quit drinkin' and smokin', scared of the black man sittin' next to you, scared of life and scared of death! We judge because we're scared."

"I think you're way off," James said, rolling his eyes. He then took another drink, trying to mask that the man was uncomfortably on-target.

"This ain't you, I can tell," the man kept babbling in more of a fatherly tone while gesturing at James's appearance. "You could be that master of the universe if you wanted to. But you've done dug yo'self into a hole, and you're the only one that can get yourself out."

James was really beginning to get uncomfortable now, frantically reaching into the pack of Camels for another cigarette and lighting it. He thought about every burning word the old man had said. He thought about his wife and child. Rage was beginning to peak, and as he was about to release every tension that had been accrued over the course of the night, he harnessed it and suppressed it into a single, quiet phrase. "Yes, I know."

"Then straighten up and go do something good for mankind at Yale." The man stood up from his barstool, finished his glass of water and trudged out of the bar muttering something under his breath. James wasn't sure what it was but he had a good idea, distinctively hearing the word *asshole*. Even the bartender began to keep his distance.

Suddenly, the PA system clicked on at the nearby gate. The Delta employee behind the counter began calling for flight 1093 nonstop to New Haven. *Let the fun begin*, he thought, and steadied himself to walk for the gate.

Chapter 4

The chants were getting louder as the young man drew closer to the end of his rocky corridor, and what sweet music they made. It was as if the blessed melody was physically pulling him closer to his brethren and salvation.

As young Khalim inched his way to the end of the passageway, his heart sang with joy at the sights, sounds and smells of the vast chamber that surrounded him. He looked upwards toward a ceiling that he could barely see through the smoke. It must have been some one hundred and fifty feet high, concave, natural, and sloped downwards to four walls that had been expertly carved smooth, forming four perfect ninety-degree corners. The room was enormous—at least nine thousand square feet by his judgment—and seemed to glow a dull orange color, reflecting the light of the fire.

Khalim observed the one-hundred-or-so men spread across the room, all dressed as he was, bowing, praying and chanting with their eyes closed. Before them raged the sacred fire rising upward in praise of mighty Ahura Mazda. The flames crackled and the wood hissed as if to join in the congregational praise of God. Khalim felt the heat radiating onto his skin—as though the warmth of God was cleansing his spirit.

On the other side of the sacred inferno was a great stone platform raised above the rest of the cavern floor. Upon the platform stood a massive stone altar. Glowing the same hue of orange as the walls, covered in the dust and dirt of a millennium. Khalim wondered how long it had been there along with everything else. He knew that the Pharaoh Thutmose III had fought battles in the valley above, and that was nearly four thousand years ago.

Khalim looked even further than the altar, and as his eyes caught sight of the man who stood there praying and chanting with the rest, his soul felt uplifted and joyful. His priest, Adimah Marah, stood before the altar chanting and praying in unison with the rest of the order.

There before him lay open the Avesta, its ancient pages seeming to outshine the flame of the sacred ritual fire. Khalim's heart trembled in reverence of his priest and mentor as he folded his hands and began to pray with the others.

The young man bowed his head and brought it back upright in the sacred rhythm, quietly reciting in Farsi the praises of Ahura Mazda. His eyes were closed in deep prayer as his skin and soul absorbed the warmth of the fire and his ears took in the sounds of the flames and chants.

The young Persian man lifted his head and opened his eyes to allow them to explore further past the altar and the priest. He could see nothing in the background. It was as black as the tunnel he had traversed earlier. Yet he couldn't help but feel that something definitely waited in those shadows. Then, with the raising of the priest's hands, all was silent in the subterranean temple.

"Ahura Mazda be praised!" Marah exclaimed in Persian.

"Send us our savior and destroy all evil!" the congregation responded in unison.

There was a deafening silence in the chamber. No one moved, coughed or sighed. The priest scanned the faces of the worshippers, and a slight grin of affection appeared on his face when he saw young Khalim. Each and every man in the cavern watched Adimah Marah's every move, waiting for the rest of the ritual to begin.

"We are the last of our kind—the true keepers of the faith," the priest continued. "We have been chosen by Ahura Mazda to oversee and carry out the prophecies of the Gathas."

Khalim began to feel almost unworthy of this honor. *Why have I been one of the chosen few? Why has Ahura Mazda chosen me?*

"This fire is symbolic not of destruction, but of the cleansing power of God!" the priest exclaimed, extending both hands before the fire that raged in his forefront. "Soon, this fire will be much greater than we see it here. This fire will touch each soul, each tree and each blade of grass. It will destroy Angra Mainyu and all of his evil that resides on earth. Our world will be pure and good again! That time is upon us now!"

All at once, the congregation's voices rose in joy and praise. The roar lifted above the flames and seemed to shake the chamber to its foundations. Then the priest raised his hands once more and silenced the crowd with not a word.

"Those of you young new members of our order, welcome. You will be the last to step within these walls. There will never be any more of us than there are now. The timeline has been fulfilled thus far and the signs have come to pass. Over the thousands of years, two of the saviors have been born within our order. We have seen Aushedar! We have seen Aushedar-mah! Now the third and final savior has been born to us from a virgin. He is descended from Zarthosht."

All was silent. The worshippers were in shock. They had not imagined that this would be the day that all was to be unveiled. They waited, riveted, eager to hear what was to be said next.

"I am the Saoshant!" the priest roared, filling the room with his word.

Each worshipper immediately dropped to his knees. Young Khalim's spirit was soaring. *He is the Saoshant? God be praised! No wonder I felt such a connection to him!*

"And now I reveal to you the method of Mighty Ahura Mazda's purification of the world. This is what brings about the end!"

Adimah Marah lifted an unlit wooden torch from beneath the altar, walked down to the sacred fire, and plunged the torch deep within the flames. Upon retracting the torch, its end blazed with the light of God. He then slowly walked back far behind the altar into the shadows. Khalim could see the blazing torch descend to an object as high as the priest's waist. As flames began rising from the top of the object, he could see it was a square container of oil. Yet the flames did not remain there—they traveled further into the shadows revealing that this was a long rectangular aqueduct of oil. Khalim then watched the fire split left and right at perfect ninety-degree angles, traveling away from the point of origin. Once again, they sharply made another ninety-degree turn, traveling deeper into the shadows.

Slowly, the dark area behind the altar illuminated and the flames ignited more oil in the background. Khalim could not believe what he was seeing. A look of shock and terror filled his expression. *This is the method used to carry out the prophecy of Zarthosht?*

Chapter 5

Why the hell does this always take so long? Why can't we just get it over with and get into the air? James seriously thought about getting off the plane and going home.

From the time he got onto the plane to the point of takeoff always seemed to take forty-five minutes. It was the anticipation of those horrifying first several minutes of the plane's ascent that churned his stomach more than the actual takeoff. Then there was the idea of being a few miles above the earth's surface for a few hours trapped in a ninety ton steel box filled with thousands of gallons of jet fuel.

First class flying was a must. The drinks were free, there was more legroom and one didn't have to wait in line for as long. There were downsides, however. Waiting in line was replaced with waiting inside the *death box with wings*. The minutes began to double in length and James thought that he would never take off. The Boeing 767 began to make an awful noise as it inched away from the gate. Sitting in a window seat on the right side of the plane, he could see that there were two or three other planes waiting for their signal to roll onto the main runway. "Shit," he said as his jet moved into position behind the next in line.

His stomach began to squeeze and churn its toxic contents as the roar of the engines peaked and the plane began to move. The movement began slowly, then within an instant the 767 reached a thunderous speed, blurring everything James saw from the small first-class window.

He quickly closed the window, held his breath and tightened his already knuckle-whitening grip on the ends of the armrests. Suddenly, he lifted the shade on the window again and reluctantly gazed out at the blurring lights in the near distance. Dabbing the sweat from his shiny forehead, he turned slightly to the left to see the young man next to him staring with eyebrows seemingly permanently fixed in a raised position. The wide-eyed glare reaffirmed exactly what James was already thinking. *It's time for a drink.*

He could already hear the squeaking of the cart's wheels growing closer. He hadn't had a drink in an hour and longed for that familiar burn in his esophagus and stomach.

"Can I offer you something to drink?" the brunette flight attendant asked, smiling as widely as she could with her dimples punctuating the corners of her mouth perfectly.

"Sure, Kelly," James replied, observing the shiny faux-gold nametag positioned just above her left breast. "Make it a Jack and Coke. And get my friend here whatever he wants," he continued, gesturing to the young man to his left. "Put that on my tab."

The flight attendant giggled, placing her right hand over the center of her chest. James half expected that she wouldn't get the joke, and was pleased at the woman's surprising level of intelligence. It wasn't that he thought all flight attendants were stereotypically dumb. He simply had first perceived her as being a little dim. *That guy was right. We all judge.*

"I'll have a water," the kid said to Kelly. He then turned his attention back to James. "I'm Dave," he introduced himself, extending his right hand.

"James," he followed suit, clutching the young man's hand.

The flight attendant handed Dave a small, twelve-ounce bottle of water and then looked to James with her painted-on smile. "It will be a moment on your drink, sir," she assured, walking back to the service area.

"So, are you headed back home, or are you from New Orleans?" James asked his new traveling companion, already knowing the answer.

"Going home," he replied. "I'm starting summer session at school in a couple of days."

"Yeah, I noticed you had a Sigma Tau shirt on." James motioned at the faded fraternity shirt. "Yale?"

"Yeah, I'm in my third year of pre-law."

The flight attendant, Kelly, strolled gracefully down the aisle, carrying the blessed spirits that James had ordered. "Here you are, sir," she cheerfully handed him the twelve-ounce Coca-Cola, a small cup of ice, and what James called a *midget bottle* of Jack Daniels, then she walked away.

"So, you know they're going to make you clean up your care-free appearance once you start at some law firm," James mentioned motioning to the young man's shaggy hair, cargo shorts and flip-flops. He didn't know why he had just said that. Sometimes alcohol removed the filter between his cognitive process and his mouth.

The jovial smile on Dave's face vanished as if someone had just tickled him and then immediately punched him in the face. "Well, I don't think I'll have much trouble finding a job but they'll definitely make me clean up," he said, eyes transfixed on the bottle of water in his hand.

"What do you mean?"

"My dad is a senior partner at McHenry, Scruggs and Cheatam in New York. My grandfather, Joseph McHenry, was a founding partner."

"I've heard of that firm. Every time I turn on the TV they've got an advertisement for some kind of class action law suit against chemical companies for causing some rare form of leukemia in their workers."

"Yeah, that's them. I'm being groomed to follow in my father and grandfather's footsteps. They had my college picked out before I was born."

"That sucks. So you didn't want to be a lawyer growing up?"

"Growing up, yes. That's all I knew. That's all they talked about. But by the time I was in high school I became interested in biology. Really, I wanted to be a marine biologist."

"I know exactly what you mean," James uttered the words as if fixed in a trance. It sounded as if David McHenry was recanting James's entire life story.

James reached for his second Jack and Coke of the trip, lifted it from the folding tray before him and began to touch it to his lips. In an instant, his hand and drink rose uncontrollably above his head before he could taste the nectar within the confines of the plastic chalice. He panicked more than a bit as he felt the whole of the plane shift up and down as it moved through very rough air pockets. He gripped the armrest as tightly as during takeoff with his left hand and brought his drink back down to the tray.

"Dude, it's just turbulence," the young college student grinned as James tried to catch his breath.

"Dude, I don't like to fly," he shot back, realizing after the fact that he had just been very rude to the undeserving young man. "Sorry."

"Hey, don't mention it." The young man seemed to shy away from his obviously disturbed neighbor.

James thought back to twelve years ago, sitting in a local bar in Baton Rouge.

"Do you want me to get you a nipple for that beer?" the tall, well-dressed man shouted across the restaurant as he strolled toward the table from the restroom. His shiny black wingtips resonated the sound of fine leather soles as they came in contact with the brick floor. James always thought he looked like an ancient Roman with his thick, black hair curling about his head in quasi-Caesar fashion.

"It's not going to drink itself!" he continued, drawing closer to James and his other drinking partner.

"What are you talking about, Timmy?" James replied, grabbing the German import and drinking it faster, trying not to seem like he was.

"You're nursing the hell out of it!" Tim grinned.

"I can take care of myself," James said, grabbing his beer again and drinking a little of it while extending his right middle finger in Tim's direction.

Tim scooted his chair closer to the table, reached for his India Pale Ale and gently backhanded the shoulder of the other man at the table. "Matt, can you believe this son of a bitch is gonna try to get a professorship at Tulane in the fall?"

"Really? You didn't tell me that." Matt looked shocked as he reached for his pack of Marlboro Lights 100s. Matt was beginning to show signs of intoxication with a brown stain from an earlier stout adorning the front of his white button-down. His expression turned from shock to happiness as his already friendly smile grew to each of his light brown sideburns. "That's awesome. I hope you get it."

"I appreciate it. I hope I get it, too," James nodded his head in acceptance of Matt's support.

"But why Tulane, Jimbo?" Tim seemed to scoff at James's university selection.

"You're getting your PhD this semester, too. You know damn well that LSU won't hire you as a professor if you got your doctorate here," James replied sharply.

"Yeah, I know. But why Tulane? You're at the top of your class. You could go somewhere like Colombia or Yale," Tim argued further.

"I don't want to go up north somewhere. I love the south. Plus, I can reopen the family home in the Quarter and live there." James took another gulp of his beer.

"I forgot about the house, you lucky bastard. God, I can't believe how long it's been since you inherited it," Matt turned his eyes toward the ceiling as if to ponder how quickly time had passed. He then moved his face level with the other two men and smiled. "Every year we used that house to party during Mardi Gras."

James couldn't help but grin. They had some fun times in that house. The memories of Mardi Gras in his family home with his fraternity brothers were, not surprisingly, fonder to him than the memories he had with his mother and father there. There was too much screaming and fighting. He remembered not being able to fall asleep at night as a child because of the commotion.

"Yeah, fun times. But I seem to remember y'all breaking something in that house every year." James tried to smile, rejoining the festive moment.

"Speaking of lucky bastard, you have to remember that this asshole also inherited his dad's stock in the company," Tim almost interrupted James. There was no smile on Tim's face. It was as if the idea was appalling. "I still can't believe that he left it to you after all the two of you had been through."

James was in the middle of a sip of beer. He eyed Tim without moving his head and slowly brought the bottle from his lips to the table as a menacing frown grew on his face.

"You know why he left it all to me. We all do. But what fucking business is that of yours? If you ever mention my father again, I'll kill you," James threatened, his facial expression assuring that he was quite serious.

"It'll never happen again, chief." Tim pushed slightly back from the table, his face feigning humility.

There was an uncomfortable silence at the table for a moment, though the restaurant bustled all around them. No one wanted to make eye contact and no one seemed to want to break that silence. The evening remained in a delicate balance. One wrong move or word could send it crashing down. Matt, however, had no shame. He was the daring one. He knew he could always rely on his quick wit to change the mood.

"Well, I guess we won't get invited back down to the house for Mardi Gras once Abigail has a hold of it. You're definitely pussy-whipped," Matt remarked, breaking the silence.

They all burst into laughter. The bad air surrounding the table began to melt away.

"No, I don't think naked, loose women running around the house is quite Abigail's style," James grinned.

"But tell me you're not going to miss it," Matt said, gesturing toward the atmosphere of the room.

"Miss what? This is Baton Rouge. I'd only be moving back to New Orleans," James refuted.

James couldn't help but think about it, and the more he did the more Matt's words made sense. Although Baton Rouge and New Orleans were only approximately seventy miles apart, they were two very different places. There were similarities, such as elements of Cajun and Creole culture and rich history. But mostly, they were different.

One might drive or stroll through the oldest and most historic areas of New Orleans, like the Garden District or the French Quarter, and actually still sense the old aristocracy. The homes range from lavish late nineteenth-century Victorians, to beautiful Creole antebellum gems, to colonial era Spanish-style treasures. It is as if the ghosts of the olden days still roam the city, searching for a fleeting glimpse of what they knew New Orleans to be. Sugar and cotton are her bones. She has Africa, Europe, and the Caribbean in her veins. James dreamed of her every moment he was away.

Baton Rouge had a different identity. This is a city of politics and of Huey Long. Long's capitol building overshadows the old antebellum capitol building as his statue laughs in the face of any state politician who dares challenge the corruption that he instilled in the fabric of Louisiana politics. Plantations line River Road, symbols of the city's permanence over the years. She is a melting pot of Deep South and Cajun culture, and everyone wears purple and gold.

James was going to miss LSU Tiger culture. Ancient live oak trees covered the beautiful campus, and lined the historic Highland Road that ran through the middle of campus. Long, gray Spanish moss hung from those trees, supplying that classic south Louisiana ambiance. The clock tower stood like a sentinel and the fraternity houses looked like antebellum homes rich in sugar cane wealth.

James gulped down the final ounces of his lager, and set the empty green bottle back within the condensation rings it had been forming on the stained wooden tabletop just as the waitress approached. He gazed down at the *Around the World* card before him as he pondered which beer he would be sampling next.

"Guys, it looks like I've got five left," he observed, pointing to the remaining beers on the list.

"Have you been sneaking in here without us?" Matt accused laughingly. "I've got, like, twelve, and lightweight over here has around seventeen," he motioned toward a scowling Tim Horn.

"What can I say? I'm a professional," James chuckled.

"I should say! You got your nameplate on the wall of fame nine times," Tim motioned toward the wall at the far end of the restaurant. It was covered with hundreds of tiny rectangular brass nameplates, one for each person who had completed the sixty-beer *Around the World*.

"Yeah, I hear that you get more than just a nameplate after your tenth completion, and I'm five away. Besides, if I move back to New Orleans, this may be my last time, so it's got to be special," James smiled. He then lifted his gaze toward the patient waitress. "I think I'll knock out another one of these third-world countries. Red Stripe, please—with lime."

"After this, are you coming out with us to Tigerland?" Matt inquired.

"I can't." James showed the regret in his facial expression. "I've got to meet up with Abigail later and I think she would prefer me half-ass sober for a change."

"Don't be such a pussy," Tim scoffed. "Tell that woman you're going out with the guys!"

"Have you seen Abigail?" Matt raised his eyebrows. "If my girl-friend—"

"Ahem!" James feigned clearing his throat.

"Oh yeah, fiancée," Matt corrected, "looked half as hot as she is, I'd tell you guys to beat it, too."

"Whatever," Tim fired back. "A good woman would be waiting at home for whenever her man got back—regardless of what time it is—and be ready to put out at the drop of a hat."

"Now it all makes sense!" Matt shouted, as if to have had an epiphany.

"What?" James asked curiously.

"I always wondered why Timmy here has never had a serious relationship as long as we've known him. I thought it was the aftershave."

Matt and James burst into a frenzy of laughter as Tim gripped his beer like it was trying to escape. The expression on his face was priceless. There was mostly embarrassment with a touch of aggravation.

"Laugh it up, fuckers," was all Tim could manage to repeatedly utter without looking at either of his ridiculing friends.

"Seriously, guys," James began to speak through Matt's and his own laughter. "Abigail, or no Abigail, I can't go out with you tonight. I've got to get up and put the finishing touches on my thesis, and you guys should be doing the same."

"You still haven't told us what it's about," Matt said enthusiastically. "We've been asking you for weeks. It seems like you've been so secretive about it"

"Alright, I'll tell you." James looked down at the table. The waitress came by and set down his Red Stripe. He removed the lime from the top of the bottle, squeezed the juice into the beer and inserted the rind. He placed his index finger into the top of the bottle and turned it upside-down, allowing the rind of the lime to float to the bottom end, and then turned it upright.

He took a healthy gulp of his Jamaican-made beer as he gazed at his friends. Their eyes were transfixed upon him in anticipation. It didn't make any sense. It was as if Matt and Tim had five of the six winning numbers of a lottery ticket, and were waiting for the sixth to see if they would soon be millionaires.

"My thesis is on ancient technology," James uttered, taking another sip of his beer, "with special emphasis on the reasons that the learning, thinking and innovation of the Roman Empire didn't continue in Europe after the fall of the Western Empire."

"Come on, James. It's been done before!" Tim said condescendingly as he sipped his beer.

"Tim . . ." Matt eyed him in contempt.

"What? It has!" Tim stated again.

"You're kind of being a dick," Matt shot back.

"You see, this is why I didn't want to say anything," James shook his head in disgust. He took another drink of Red Stripe as a scowl formed on his face. "You've always got something negative to say."

"We're talking about your doctoral thesis, here!" Tim defended. "Every history professor at LSU—no, any high school history teacher will tell you that when Rome fell, Europe splintered and the less advanced barbarians took over. It's the dark ages, James. It's not just historical theory. It's regarded as fact!"

"All history is theory, Tim," James corrected. "Opinion and bias, backed with sources and evidence. Did you live in the dark ages? Did you see it happen? All we have is archaeology and a few vague ancient texts."

Tim fell silent. James had a point.

"I'm not just recanting what other historians have been saying for ages. I don't agree with the popular theory on this," James stated.

"Then what are you arguing?" Matt was intrigued.

"What if the reason for the dark ages was something much more deliberate?"

"You mean the dark ages were planned? It was on purpose?"

"Exactly. The Greeks built the Parthenon. They were masters of geometry, philosophy and math. Our modern education system is partially based on theirs. They conceived theatre productions that used only machines."

"The Romans continued to innovate. Their architecture was unprecedented. Half of the buildings in any major city from Berlin to Los Angeles bear some kind of feature that the Romans or Etruscans invented. Their principles of military strategy exist in modern warfare today. They invented the odometer for measuring milestones along their roads. There are functioning Roman aqueducts in Spain. What about Hadrian's Wall in northern England? Clearly, the splendor of Roman thought reached all corners of their domain. They have even found what appears to be an ancient computer dating from Greco-Roman antiquity."

"The Antikythera Mechanism," Tim said softly.

"What's that?" Matt seemed confused.

"It's supposed to be a small machine. They found it in 1904 at the bottom of the Aegean Sea. They think that it was a mechanism for keeping up with the days, months and years," Tim explained.

"Throughout history, there are few instances where some new idea or innovation was not borrowed from another culture," James continued. "In most cases, writing and language, agriculture and technology were all borrowed. You find the pointed Islamic arch in medieval European cathedrals. You find Chinese black powder being used by eighth-century Arabs. Religions split from religions. Judaism, Christianity and Islam. Hinduism and Buddhism. There are ancient Hindu myths involving an original paradise of creation, original man and woman, eating from a forbidden tree and banishment into the world. Every language from the U.S., across Europe, through the Middle East to Bangladesh is related under the same canopy."

The other two men said nothing as they listened to James get truly excited about what he was telling them.

"So if we know that Roman invention and ideas were introduced to the European masses, why did they not survive despite the fall of Rome? Why did architecture relapse into a few churches and a bunch of mud huts? Why did people cease to learn? Everything is borrowed. Why were only language, military and religion borrowed?"

"The Visigoths and Vandals destroyed Rome and all it stood for. Germanic tribes overran the country," Tim explained.

"The Visigoths *adopted* Roman culture, tradition and religion. They were the ones who kept Christianity alive," James refuted. "Why were only a few things kept?"

"Are you suggesting that someone purposely kept the people of Europe in the dark? Are you talking about a conspiracy theory?" Tim spoke in disbelief.

"Is it that hard to believe? Throughout the dark ages there was little intellectual thought, art, invention or education. But the Muslims did learn and invent. Most of the rest of the world did, too. Europeans started learning from Muslims again through contact during the crusades. Even then, the Catholic Church shunned new scientific thought as heresy. Even Galileo retracted some of his ideas at one point, and he was still found guilty of heresy just for saying that the Earth wasn't the center of the universe. Amazing what a threat of burning at the stake can do for common thought and consensus. Before that, they did away with pagan beliefs through manipulation. They let some beliefs be kept, like dressing up like ghouls on All Hallows Eve, and demonized others. The history of western civilization is a conspiracy."

"Ladies and gentlemen, we will be starting our descent here in a few minutes. Things may get bumpy so make sure you have your seatbelts fastened and your trays in their upright positions. We will be landing in New Haven in about half an hour." The captain's announcement startled James from his trance as the sudden turbulence filled him with dread.

Perfect. More turbulence. It would be a tragedy to crash before I have a chance to stand in front of Tim Horn again.

Chapter 6

The sweat rolled down James's ghastly white face as he frantically added speed to his staggering walk toward the fresh air of the airport concourse. To him, the tunnel leading away from the dreaded 767 may as well have been a mine tunnel—dank, heavy-aired, and prone to collapse. Upon entering the better-circulated concourse, he straightened his back, dropped his leather briefcase to the bluish-gray carpet below, and closed his eyes while tilting his head back and breathing in deeply through his nose.

After a moment, he turned to gaze back at the dreadful tunnel from which he had just emerged, and realized that in his haste to exit the plane, he had been the first person off. A wave of embarrassment overcame him as he watched a number of fellow passengers filing out of the passageway holding their noses and covering their mouths in disgust as they leered at him, knowing that he was the perpetrator who had made the last twenty minutes of their journey a living hell. Among the passengers exiting the plane was James's young travel companion, David. He had a look on his face of repulsion that had been conquered by laughter.

"Dude, what did you eat? You stunk up the whole plane with your little puking fit," David grinned as he approached James, who was still basking in relief about getting off that plane.

"I'm sorry," James apologized, hanging his head in embarrassment, yet grinning. "I told you I don't like to fly, and I don't like turbulence." James had never had the strongest stomach.

"It's okay, man. I've been depressed about leaving New Orleans. That smell brings back fond memories of Bourbon Street," David joked, causing James to laugh and, perhaps, feel a little better.

The airport was buzzing around them. Dozens of people were seated at gate A11 awaiting the boarding call for Flight 1709 to Chicago. There were men and women in business suits impatiently checking their watches and e-mailing business associates through their notebook computers and smart phones. There were college students devouring cholesterol-laden hot dogs from a nearby airport deli. There were parents trying desperately to recapture their wayward young children who were running and screaming among people attempting to maintain some sort of composure in the face of such annoyance.

While he really didn't care for flying, James liked being in airports. There was something about the sights, smells and energy of the airport that appealed to him. In spite of the constant mob of people bumping into him in a hurry to get to their gate and the painful experience of going through security, it was an oddly happy place. Like being awoken by a bullhorn from a very good dream, James was brought out of his airport bliss by the terrible residue in his mouth—bourbon whiskey with red beans and rice, blended with stomach acid. Red beans and rice was his favorite meal. Though it smelled heavenly while being prepared and eaten, it never smelled as good as leftovers. *Those poor people on the plane*, he thought. *All that garlic, onion and celery! No wonder it smelled so bad!*

The only thing on James's mind now was finding an all-purpose convenience store in the airport. He scanned back and forth among the restaurants, sunglass shops and magazine vendors until he saw what he was looking for. He made his way, followed by his young friend, through throngs of people hurriedly strolling up and down the main walkway.

They entered the store complete with magazines ranging from *Modern Bride* to *Penthouse*, a wide array of candy, a cooler filled with twenty-ounce bottled drinks, and more Connecticut souvenirs than one could ever hope for.

James darted directly for the cooler full of drinks, yanked it open and grabbed three bottles of water. He twisted the cap from the top of one of the bottles and began chugging while David stood watching.

"Hey," David said with a smile as James continued chugging, "you're pretty good at that. Can you teach me to do that with a can of beer?"

After the last few ounces of water were sucked into his mouth,

James gasped heavily as he glared silently at David. "Maybe when you're older."

While in line, James began looking over the rather wide selection of chewing gum and breath mints, trying to decide what would best fit his ruined pallet. As he reached for his selection, David spoke once again.

"So, what's the mission?"

"Excuse me?" James seemed taken aback. *Mission? Strange choice of words.*

"Mission," David repeated. "Your business," he said with still no acknowledgement from James. "What are you in town for?" he said finally, much slower as if he were speaking to a foreign man who spoke little English.

James shook his head rapidly and abruptly, as if awoken from a trance. He set down on the counter two unopened bottles of water, an empty bottle, and a jumbo pack of cool-mint gum. The young lady simply leered at him, complete with an expression that seemed to say *Uh-huh!* as she rolled her eyes. While she began scanning the items, he dug into his back pocket for his wallet.

"I'm meeting a . . . colleague," James choked out the word he never thought he'd utter in conjunction to the name Tim Horn, turning his head toward David.

"Which company?"

"Yale."

"You're a professor?" David's eyes grew much larger.

"Yeah, at Tulane. Does that surprise you?" *Of course it would. How many professors have you ever met in this kind of condition?*

"Well, I've never seen a professor drink before."

"Son, we all drink. Besides, I'm from New Orleans. Hell, when I was an undergrad, I'd go up to The Chimes and drink with my professors."

James paid the red-head behind the counter with a ten-dollar bill and walked away without his change, his young friend just behind him. He then handed David one of the bottles of water as he opened the third, hoisted it to his lips and gulped down half of the contents. David silently drank his water and grinned as he watched the alcoholic professor fumble with the package of gum, becoming slightly frustrated as he had difficulty opening it.

"Well, thanks for the water, Professor."

"Doctor," James corrected.

"Sorry. Dr. Beauregard. It was nice to meet you. Good luck with . . . whatever you're in town for."

"Thanks. It was good to meet you, too. Good luck with school. And don't worry, you'll figure out what it is you truly want out of life."

David smiled with a nod of acknowledgement, turned and began walking toward the door to the baggage claim. James grew sad to see the young man go. He was bright with a brilliant future ahead of him. He closed his eyes as tears began to well up. The young man reminded him of himself at that age. He knew how David felt, yet also felt guilty that it had been easier for him to find what he truly wanted to do with his life. He wondered what it would be like if David were his son. He knew he would give him the means to follow his own aspirations. He thought of his own son. How would he have turned out? Would he have turned out like this fine young man? Would he have been rebellious? Would he have gotten mixed up in drugs? Would he have become an alcoholic?

James then took hold of the handle of his briefcase and began walking toward the baggage claim door.

He looked around to see if his young friend was still waiting for his bag. The conveyor belt had not yet begun to deliver luggage to the dozens of impatient travelers. Perhaps he would see David once more before parting ways. He scanned the area in vain, as David must have been traveling with only his carry-on bag.

Suddenly, the conveyor belts began to run, rolling suitcases, roller cases and duffel bags onto the larger metallic conveyors. James grumbled to himself, his arms crossed. The third suitcase that popped out of the subterranean luggage vault was his. James brightened up. *Maybe this day is looking up*, he thought. He grabbed his suitcase and rolled it along toward the exit.

He wondered how he was going to get to the school or if Horn was even there. It was then that he noticed a man in a black suit, white shirt and black tie standing near the exit door. The twenty-something-year-old man was a sight straight out of a movie with his messy spiked hair and sign that had a person's last name on it. As James drew closer, he saw that the sign bore the name *Boregard*.

A grin formed on James's face as he shook his head. He had to remind himself that he was in Yankee territory now. How would they know how to spell a name like that if it were simply read to them over the phone while giving them instructions on who to pick up and where? Most people up here had probably never seen a name like Beauregard, never mind the fact that it was the name of a famous general. He doubted that history books in the north even mentioned the name of the man who gave the order to fire on Fort Sumter, starting the American Civil War.

James strolled up to the man, uttering not a word. The two men made eye contact, which did not stray. It seemed that the moment lasted several minutes. It was as if they both were about to produce brass knuckles from their pockets and have a scuffle right there in the airport.

"Dr. Beauregard?" the young man said, his eyes never losing contact with James's.

"Yes."

"Please come with me."

James followed the young man through the double automatic doors to a black Lincoln limousine waiting just outside. The driver stowed his passenger's baggage in the trunk and then walked back around to open the door for James. He felt like he was about to get in and sit next to a mob boss to report how the racket down in Brooklyn was going. *Am I about to get whacked and dumped in the river?*

Other thoughts began to overcome. He suddenly realized how crucial and important this trip and this meeting with Tim Horn were.

They had gone all-out with the first-class ticket, the limousine and probably a nice hotel room, all at Yale's expense.

"Hey, do you know where we're going?" James finally inquired of the driver.

"Yeah." There was a youthful cockiness in his voice.

"Are we going straight to the school?"

"No, I'll be picking you up in the morning for that. Right now we're going to the hotel."

"Yeah? Which one?"

"The Omni. President's Suite."

"Hmm . . . nice . . ."

Chapter 7

James abruptly opened his eyes and immediately panicked. He was expecting to see the ceiling and its ornate French-style crown molding in his French Quarter home. But this ceiling was foreign to him. For an instant, he did not know where he was. Had he gotten drunk at the piano bar again and mistakenly stumbled into the wrong home? Where were the owners? They'd kill him if they found him. Or was this a one-night-stand? He uneasily turned his head to the right, dreading the image of an unsightly beast curled up next to him, and then sighed in relief that no one was there.

As the phone that had initially awoken him continued to ring, he realized where he was. His room at the Omni Hotel was luxurious. Its beautiful furnishings were all in tones of garnet and gold from the bed-spread and drapes to the upholstery of the chairs. The garnet and gold accentuated the deep red finish of the cherry-wood desk and tables. He was in New Haven. Had the alcohol clouded his head that much? It ached a little, and the room still rotated slowly.

He sat up in his king-size bed, realizing he was totally naked beneath the covers, and reached for the telephone that was perched on the nightstand to his left. He picked up the receiver and put it to his ear.

"Hello?" he uttered in the classic slow, hung-over manner.

"Jesus, I thought you would never answer," the man on the other end said, seemingly agitated.

James immediately knew who the man was. It was the limousine driver from the previous night. Last night was a bit of a blur but he somehow remembered the chauffeur, sneering at the thought of the cocky young man.

"Rough night. What do you want? It's . . ." James paused to glance at his expensive Omega wristwatch, "almost seven a.m."

"Sir, your meeting at the university is in an hour. That's all I know.

I have a job to do, and I'll be outside your hotel in forty-five minutes."

Then he hung up. James had not even the chance to rebut. He knew there was a reason he didn't like that driver. "What an asshole!" James placed the phone back down onto its cradle.

He slid off the comforter and sheets, and touched his feet to the floor. Slowly, he hoisted himself upright, becoming a little dizzy as the room spun more quickly. As he made his way around, he observed a trail of the clothes he had on the night before leading from the closet to the bed. *At least I hung up my suits and put my clothes away first*, he thought, making his way to one of the room's windows.

He drew the curtains, half expecting the usual pain of his pupils rapidly contracting in adjustment to the sudden burst of light through the windows. Instead, James was surprised to see that the windows were tinted, and beyond them was a radiant sight—Yale University.

It was no match for the live oaks and Spanish moss of LSU, but it was quite breathtaking in its own right. From his tenth story room, James looked down to see New Haven Green directly below, with its criss-crossed pathways and three magnificent churches. He had been to Yale before, but had never noticed how many churches the university had. From his room, he could see Dwight Chapel and Battell Chapel in addition to the three on New Haven Green.

Yale truly had some beautiful old buildings. Structures like Sterling Memorial Library, Welch Hall, Lanman-Wright Hall and the Calhoun College complex all seemed to be cut from the same seventeenth-century English architectural fabric. The lavish use of curves and strong lines was tell-tale English baroque style. There were even a few accents of Gothic architecture in some of the churches and clock towers dotting the campus. They had steeply pitched roofs, slender towers, stained glass, and pointed arch windows. Medieval-style battlements lined the roofs and tall chimneys shot up across campus, so obviously mimicking London. *Exquisite*, James thought to himself.

Forty-five minutes later, James was strolling through the lavishly decorated lobby of the Omni and out the door exiting onto Temple Street.

The surprisingly cool New England breeze caressed his body as he stopped to check his appearance one last time in the semi-reflective window of the hotel. Despite the recent whiskey binge, his look was immaculate. His hair was fixed in the usual fashion, but unlike the night before, his face was smoothly shaven and his goatee was trimmed. He admired how well the expensive navy-blue suit was tailored to his body as he tightened the navy and gold necktie and straightened the collar of his white shirt.

When he turned, there was the driver he had the unfortunate chance to meet the night before, leaning against the same limousine and wearing the same attire. James knew the driver and car were not there when he exited the building. He had turned for a brief moment to face the window, and when he turned back, the driver was there. *This is like a bad dream*, he thought, ducking into the back seat. The driver shut the door, walked around to the driver's side, got in and set the limousine into motion.

"How far is it?" James inquired of the driver.

"Not far. It's just a few blocks away on York Street," he replied into the rear-view mirror.

James found himself once again admiring the beauty of the campus and the buildings. It was not his beloved LSU, but it was stunning, nonetheless. Just as he found himself entranced in admiration, he was abruptly halted as the car came to a stop in front of the Hall of Graduate Studies, which housed the History Department.

"Thanks for the ride." James swallowed his pride enough to smile at the driver as he stepped out of the car.

"Don't mention it, bro," he replied sarcastically as he rolled up the automatic window and sped away.

Bro? James shook his head as he made his way toward the entrance to the semi-gothic style building. *Who the hell does he think I am, one of his idiot frat brothers?*

As the limousine rolled away and he was forever done with the annoying splinter of a driver, he smiled, turning to the monumental stone façade before him. It was as a Gothic cathedral with its decorative pillars and massive pointed archway entrances. A cathedral of academia, no doubt.

His heart fluttered and his neck quivered, suddenly and inexplicably nervous. But why? Surely, he was not that uneasy about seeing old Timothy Horn. Perhaps it was the mystery of what he could be about to see, or that he was in the presence of such scholarly greatness and history. He shook off the feeling and straightened his tie, putting on a stern, professional face, and then entered.

Chapter 8

"Where can I find Timothy Horn?" James asked the receptionist in the massive lobby of the building.

"Dr. Beauregard?" the middle-aged woman smiled.

"Yes, ma'am."

"They're expecting you, sir. Walk down the main hallway," she stood up, pointing down the hall without breaking eye contact, "and make a right. It will be the fifth office on your right."

"Thank you," James winked at the blushing woman as he confidently walked in that direction, carrying his briefcase.

The sound of his leather soles on the polished floor echoed like thunder. It reminded him of some important lawyer in a movie making his way through the courthouse to a courtroom where he was going to save the life of some wrongfully accused murder suspect. The sound made him feel official, even special. They had contacted *him*, of all people in the world, to be an expert in whatever they had discovered.

As he turned the corner down the hallway to the right, he began scanning for the fifth doorway. About forty feet further down the hall, he found the fifth enormous oak office door. His stomach began to churn with anxiety as he anticipated who and what was behind the entrance. Anxiety rushed in over the thought of coming face-to-face with Tim. There was the prospect of a career-changing archaeological find. There was nervousness of Yale hotshots analyzing his knowledge with every bit of scrutiny they could muster. With a deep breath and a closing of the eyes, he knocked, and the echo that it produced raised the level of his nerves to a new discomfort.

The door opened, and there to greet him was none other than his nemesis. "Jim! You made it! How are you?" Horn extended his hand and addressed him as would a long lost friend. It was the kind of greeting that was reserved for a friend that was actually happy for the reunion.

"Horn," James could only muster the name. He considered not shaking his hand, staring at it for a long while before eventually grasping it. He momentarily cursed his polite, southern upbringing. Tim smiled into James's eyes.

"Come on in." Horn ushered him into the sprawling office, which was much larger than he had thought.

It was everything he had expected in an office belonging to a high-ranking member of the Yale History Department faculty. The walls were a deep, rich mahogany with darkly stained antique furniture and black leather upholstery. There were volumes of books on the shelves and antiques in glass cases and on pedestals throughout the room. There was Greek pottery from the Doric period, Hellenistic busts and an Egyptian Hieroglyph-laden tablet from the Middle Kingdom.

"Jim, this is Dr. George Husser," Tim announced, pointing his entire hand in the direction of an aging man behind the desk. "He's the Dean of the History Department—this is his office."

"Dr. Richard Gaines, professor of ancient history," he continued introducing the others in the room with the same hand gesture. "Dr. Isabel Larson, Dean of the Archaeology Department; Dr. Christian Lockheart, Director of Roman studies; and Dr. Noelle Broussard, professor of geology. Everyone, this is Dr. James Beauregard, the most brilliant historian at Tulane."

James nodded politely to all of the scholars in the room. He recognized a couple of the names from books they had published in their respective fields. But his eyes remained fixed upon Dr. Broussard, though she seemed to pay him no attention. There was a mystique about her. Her gorgeous golden eyes were perfectly complimented by her long, wavy dark brown hair, mysterious eyebrows and olive hue. Her white button-down blouse wonderfully accentuated her figure, as did the black pin-striped skirt.

Tim sensed James's attraction, and cleared his throat. "Jim, I'm sure you recognized this from the name, but Dr. Broussard is from Louisiana. She grew up in Baton Rouge, as a matter of fact."

James broke from his trance and extended his hand to Dr. Broussard. "A pleasure, ma'am," he regained a level of professional manner as she shook his hand lightly and grinned.

"Dr. Beauregard," Husser suddenly broke his silence, "your credentials precede you. Bachelor's, master's and PhD in ancient history from LSU," he read from the sheet of paper before him. "Well-respected professor at Tulane University, author of a number of books on everything from ancient mythology to historical conspiracy theories and, of course, CEO."

Wow! James cringed a bit. *What did they do, run an FBI background check on me?*

"Yes, sir," James smiled. "What can I say? I'm a mogul."

He scanned the room to check the reaction to his sarcasm. It was just as he had expected—nothing. Only Horn and Dr. Broussard seemed to snicker covertly. The rest of the stuffy Ivy-League quacks seemed impervious to wit, their noses high and eyes piercing.

"Yes, and you come very highly recommended by your friend, Dr. Horn," Husser continued, gesturing and smiling in the direction of Tim.

"Ah, yes," James's smile weakened quite a bit as he moved only his eyes in the direction of Horn, "and what a great friend he is to have recommended me."

Horn knew that the statement was wrought with facetiousness, yet he smiled anyway. He half expected James to open from his mouth a torrent of hatred, but also knew that he would not damage his appearance of being professional in front of Yale professors.

There was an uncomfortable silence in the room after that point. It seemed that everyone in the office caught on to James's opinion of Timothy Horn. Everyone wished that they could say something to break the tension, but somehow could not, despite the obviously grand circumstances under which these great minds were assembled. So the man who brought forth the feeling of tension decided to release it.

"So where is it?" James cut to the chase.

Husser gave him a look of perplexity. He looked at James like a dog looks at its master when he utters a funny-sounding word like *li-*

quor or *garage*. He was clearly caught off-guard, but after a moment or two, he understood what James was inquiring of. His facial expressions changed from the usual stern scowl of an Ivy-League elitist to that of a giddy young boy who was just told that they were going to get some ice cream. James giggled a bit as he watched the short, round man with hair only around the sides and back of his head trip over his own feet as he scrambled around the desk as quickly as he could.

He excused himself between James and Horn, recklessly bumping into both of the men as he made his way across the spacious office. James shivered excitedly. Dr. Broussard could see it in his facial expressions. He knew this was going to be some groundbreaking discovery that would change the world's perception of history. Everyone stood their ground as only James inched closer to the table where Husser was standing. They had already seen it. The suspense mounted as he awaited the moment when Husser would unveil it. And then he did.

"Voila!" Husser yanked away a black sheet to reveal what James could tell from afar were several square or rectangular objects lying flat upon a black velvet cloth. He had to get closer. Frantically, he rushed across the room until he drew nearer, and could tell what the objects were. Then his look of excitement turned to perplexity.

"Pictures?" He glared at Dr. Husser, confused and perhaps with a level of disappointment. "Where is the map to the Holy Grail? Some ground-breaking discovery?" He scratched his head. "Where is the cross on which Jesus was crucified? The body of Jimmy Hoffa? The first Pez dispenser?"

"James," Horn interrupted uneasily, "you have to *look* at the pictures."

James immediately felt ridiculous. *That may be the biggest brain fart I've ever had*, he thought. A look of humility came over him as he tried to salvage a little of his credibility. Perhaps it was the fact that he hadn't slept much lately. Or maybe it was the hangover or jetlag. In any case, he turned silently back to the photographs on the table, shaking his head and grinning embarrassedly.

At first glance, he wasn't sure exactly what he was looking at. There was a lot of dirt and rock with brown, gray and black colors blending with one another in a way that almost seemed to camouflage the focal point of the picture. It was a tablet of what seemed to be the finest granite, expertly carved from some quarry and chiseled with a text as precise as he had ever seen. It was large. James noted from the tape measures placed around it that it was approximately six feet long and four feet in width.

As he looked at the next two photos, he first thought they were different shots of the same tablet. They were not. He squinted, moving his face closer to the photo, noticing that they varied in length and the text was not the same.

"Who discovered these?" James asked the group as he studied the tablets further.

"I did," Dr. Broussard spoke confidently.

James looked up. He gazed across the room to see her standing like a pillar of professional ardor. She was proud of this find. Her face exuded sternness, or even discontent. She probably felt that James had disrespected her school and the find. Yet, this did not mask her radiance, and he was stricken, smiling uncontrollably.

"A geological study?" James looked perplexed.

"My team and I were studying the history of eruptions of a volcano. We found them as we were taking core samples."

"So you just ran into something hard on the way down through the layers?"

"No, the country's government requires that we rule out the possibility of archaeological finds before we are allowed to take samples. You can't even dig a post hole for a stop sign without doing it. They had their own dig team on hand, as did we."

"But if you conduct an excavation beforehand, won't that damage your evidence."

"It would, but usually we don't have to do that."

"What do you mean?"

"We used a sonar imaging device to detect whether or not there were any irregularities in the layers below. An irregularity would indicate an object, in which case the archaeologists would excavate."

"And let me guess . . . there were irregularities."

"Which *did*, in the long run, damage our study," she shrugged.

James looked back at the tablets, trying to determine if he had missed anything. The manner in which they were cut from the quarry was not peculiar, nor was the text, save the fact that it was beautifully done. He could not figure out what all of the excitement was about.

"What do you make of the text?" Dr. Husser asked excitedly.

"Well," he replied, shaking his head in deep observance, "it's Ancient Greek. If you're asking me to translate, I'm a bit rusty. I can make out some things about wrath and fire, but that's about it. It's hard to tell the dialect. Corinthian, maybe? Where was it found?"

No one answered. There was an uneasy quiet in the office. It seemed that no one wanted to answer that question. Was it secret? Was it illegal? James waited patiently at first. But as the silence continued, he looked up from the pictures and toward the group, imploring them with his cutting gaze.

"Southern Italy. Mount Vesuvius," Horn broke his silence.

James turned sharply, as if surprised. He looked at Horn with an unwavering shock over the answer mated with undying hatred of the man who uttered it, and said nothing. His eyebrows rose as he tried to make sense of it in his head. But it was only an initial shock that faded into realization that this was not really uncommon.

"Okay, gentlemen," James paused, "and ladies," he smiled with a false request of pardon for excluding them. "This is not that special."

"Why," James slightly mocked the collective intelligence of the group, "do Greek and Roman letters, architecture and deities have so many similarities?

"Because," Dr. Gaines sighed, feeling offended, "the Greeks colonized parts of Italy."

"Exactly! Extra credit points to Dr. Gaines. Come on, folks, you're some of the top scholars in this area. You should know this."

"But, Pompeii? Naples? These were not Greek cities. Upon their founding, they weren't even originally Roman cities," Dr. Gaines offered rebuttal.

"Not true. The Bay of Naples was a trading hub, and the Greeks and Phoenicians before them would have had the opportunity to exert tremendous influence on the area. Naples was originally the Greek city of Neopolois—fifth century BC hell, the Greeks even thought the thermal vents at the base of Vesuvius were an entrance into the underworld of Hades."

"Dr. Beauregard," Dr. Larson spoke for the first time, "we know all of this. And we can see how one may see this evidence as irrelevant." Her stone expression turned to compassion and understanding. "We also know that you've gone through a lot recently, and we express our deepest regret. But please don't dismiss this find until you've seen everything."

"What do you mean?" James puzzled.

"The translation of the text," she replied.

"Of course," he lowered his head in shame. *Another brain fart.* "Lay it on me."

Dr. Husser reached calmly into his left inside coat pocket and slowly produced a folded sheet of paper. He glared at James with renewed giddiness. As he unfolded the paper, he broke eye contact with the uncouth southerner and adjusted the eyeglasses that rested upon the bridge of his nose, and began to speak.

"God's creation has fallen into disrepair. Mankind has fallen from grace. Heaven has fallen into despair. Time is drawing near that all will be purged and all will become pure again. Let the world be warned that the prophecy of Zathustra shall be fulfilled and mankind will quiver before the wrath of Ahura Mazda before their fiery destruction. Only the key that lies with God's son will save him. DCLXVI."

Not a word was spoken for several moments. The Yale faculty stood emotionlessly eyeing James, who lifted his head and gazed back to them in awe. His lips were not closed, nor did he blink. His eyes betrayed his secret thoughts of utter confusion. His mind raced with notions of possibility found within the realm of improbability. He took the copy of the translation from Husser's hand, reading it over and over with light whispers under his breath.

"It makes no sense at all," James finally spoke. "Prophecies, Vesuvius, tablets, Greeks . . . , Ahura Mazda!!" he exclaimed as his lowered head shifted from side to side.

"Now you see why we asked you here," Horn said calmly, as a smile crossed his face. "Nothing adds up. So many random historical elements, eras and cultures . . ."

James was stunned. He could no longer make eye contact with anyone in the office. His mind was elsewhere, constantly tapping every bit of information he had ever learned to try to reconcile the unmatching pieces of this puzzle. He wondered how it could ever be more confusing.

"But there's more," Dr. Broussard spoke. James was awakened from his thoughts. He looked up, imploring her to speak, yet begging her not to add to the confusion.

"The tablets were not found near the surface as if buried by the shower of ash with the rest of Pompeii," she began. "They were much deeper, found very close to the base of the volcano."

"Our team first excavated through a layer of ash, then of metamorphic rock—cooled lava," Dr. Larson interjected. Dr. Broussard frowned, cutting an unnoticed nasty look at Larson.

"Yes, I'm familiar with metamorphic rock," James rolled his eyes.

"Then a layer of ash again, before getting into much older layers dating back thousands of years; millions in some areas. After examining the nature of the irregularities, compacting and folding inward of the layers, we are convinced that these tablets were once housed within a . . ." she paused for a moment.

"A cavern," Dr. Broussard finished the statement excitedly. Her joy-lit face beamed with pride. Dr. Larson fumed. She said nothing but crossed her arms, scowling.

"And tablets were not the only objects found in that cavern, Dr. Beauregard," said Dr. Husser.

"What do you mean?" James was overwhelmed.

"There are other photos that you haven't seen," Husser pointed to the table.

He turned to the table once again, and moved his eyes from left to right, scanning across the pictures of the tablets and beyond. There were indeed more pictures. James picked them up, and sorted through them in disbelief and bewilderment. Strangely-shaped, corroded metal objects, broken but fascinating. As he rifled through the photographs, his eyes began to widen, and then he spoke in a voice dripping with disbelief.

"Are these . . . what I think they are?" he gasped, his eyes never leaving the photos.

"We don't know, James. We were hoping you could tell us," Horn said calmly and casually.

James's hand uncontrollably covered his gaping mouth and he almost began to look nauseous. He looked up and sharply glanced around the room. His body trembled and his knees became weak. He leaned on the table for support while the rest of the faculty grew concerned, sort of reaching out their fingers, but retracting them, unsure of whether or not they were to run to his assistance.

"Please excuse me," he said finally, finding the stability to straighten himself. "I need some air."

He stumbled out of the room, closing the door behind him.

Chapter 9

Young Khalim sat motionless and silent in the only chair within his fellow worshipper's home. His eyes would not move. They were transfixed upon the fire he had earlier built in the crude hearth before him.

It was an unusually cool night for the summer. Perhaps the world had gone cold with fear in anticipation of what was to come. *It will not remain cool for long,* he thought. *Soon, this fire will spread and the world will burn with the delight of purification.*

He looked deep into this fire, his retinas aglow with the imprint of the light it emitted. His legs extended outward from beneath his white robes and his feet were planted flat on the dusty floor. His head rested upon his open right palm, propped to the side with his elbow on the armrest of the chair. He had the look of innocence and of malevolence; friend and foe.

So many things swirled through his mind. He thought of the Shaoshant—he was actually there! The prophesies were coming to fruition. There were thoughts of the duty he would have to perform. He thought of how proud his father would be of him. But mostly, he thought of what he had seen only recently. He had never been prepared for that surprise. It certainly was not what he had expected, yet it made perfect sense to him now.

Khalim pondered on how glorious it was that evil would soon meet its match. It would be wiped from the earth with a swift flame of destruction. And how soon it would come! He smiled. *Only one week left? After thousands of years, it is finally here! The evil of man will be gone forever.* He thought of how many would lose their lives, agonizing and writhing amid the destruction. Then his expression changed from smiling and joy to that of sorrow. He wondered if he should feel sorrow for evil man or if he should loathe them. He directed his eyes to the far corner of the room and the assault rifle propped on end. He stared at the weapon for a long while thinking of how deserving mankind really was of such pain.

Is this what Ahura Mazda wants? Does he want pain and suffering? Is that the price to pay for purification? Certainly, man has felt this wrath many times over the ages and yet has not learned from the experience. Perhaps man's fate has not been fully decided. We shall see soon enough.

Chapter 10

The hotel bar at the Omni was dimly lit, washing over the beautiful dark red stain of the bar, the stools, the tables and other high-quality wooden furniture in the room. It was a relatively large room for a hotel lounge, yet sparsely populated. James could hear a dozen or so businessmen and professors from around the country inaudibly discussing their stock portfolios and lecture content. They all had bad hair and heavy aftershave, sipping dirty martinis and getting the night started before they hit the strip clubs. Overall, he liked this place. It was low-key and private. Furthermore, he frequently caught himself admiring the impressionistic and Victorian-era art prints that gave the room a splash of color.

He also liked the bar. Its red-stained base and rails were nicely accentuated by the smoke-gray granite top. Paired with the hundreds of cocktail glasses hanging from the rack overhead, the true beauty and focal point of the bar was the bottles set before the mirrored wall behind the counter. James was impressed by the selection of spirits this lounge had. There were very few low-end brands, and all manner of liquors from around the globe. Anything that one could desire, from the expensive and obscure for the true connoisseur, to the mid-priced and well known for the first-class wannabes, to the flavored liqueurs that college girls and divorcées drank while trolling for rich businessmen.

"Your friend, Dr. Horn, told me I might find you here," a female voice uttered to the left of his table. The voice startled him a bit, as he had not really expected any visitors this evening. He turned his head and smiled slightly to see that the beautiful geologist from earlier that day was in the process of sitting at his table.

"And what a great friend he is to send you looking for me," James replied, smiling at the thought that Horn knew better than to seek him out personally.

"Somehow, I got the feeling that you two have had a rough history,"

Noelle smiled, detecting the sarcasm. "Why don't you guys get along?"

"I'd rather not talk about it," he admitted, losing his smile and lowering his head.

"I'm sorry," she quickly realized she had overstepped. One could see a look of regret upon her face. She had offended a seemingly nice, yet odd man that she had only so recently met.

The silence lasted for several seconds, but seemed like minutes. James would not look up from his drink, and Noelle tried desperately to reestablish eye contact and favor. She was beginning to give up hope, contemplating leaving. She had almost made up her mind to, when her opportunity arrived. The waitress, a young lady with light-brown curls in a ponytail, strode up to the table with her black-tie regalia. Pad and pen in hand, she inquired as to what Noelle would be drinking, as James lifted his head and his gaze. Noelle looked into James's eyes, silently seeking approval and permission to stay.

"What are you having?" she smiled at him, as if to forget her opening blunder.

"Macallen eighteen-year-old," he smiled, drank the remainder in his glass, and motioned to the waitress for another, using the ice-filled vessel.

Noelle smiled at him, then to the waitress and said, "Bud Light will be fine," sending the waitress away to get their drinks.

"Not a scotch woman?" James grinned across the table.

"When I was in college, I dated a guy that loved scotch," she began to open up to the professor. "He would keep just about every premium brand that you can think of in his apartment. He used to persistently try to get me to drink some with him."

"Why?" James was interested.

"I don't know. We really didn't have that much in common. Maybe he felt like we'd have something else we could pleasantly do together besides sex."

James was a little stunned at the comment. He wasn't appalled by uncouthness, just a little shocked that she was that comfortable around him.

"So one day, he convinced me to try some Glenlivet."

"Good stuff. How was it?"

"It tasted like sewage smells."

James couldn't help but laugh, not just at the humor in the tale, but at the relief that he, and probably she felt now that the ice was officially broken. This came just in time, as the new drinks arrived at the table.

"I threw up all over his couch," she continued to laugh out loud. "We broke up the next day. I guess the incident was symbolic of our relationship."

"Well, at least you hate scotch for the right reasons," James had calmed his laughter, yet still smiled uncontrollably. "Most people get a sip of some nasty blended brand, decide that they hate the taste and never drink scotch again. But, Bud Light? All these exotic beers that they undoubtedly have behind the counter and you have a Bud Light?"

"What can I say? I was raised at Tiger football games and tailgate parties. It doesn't matter what kind of beer is on hand. What matters is the secret ingredient—good people and laughter."

"I'll drink to that," James raised his glass, lightly tapping it against Noelle's elevated bottle. They drank a couple of sips in silent celebration as they looked deeply into one another's eyes.

"So," Noelle set her beer back upon the table, "I have a question."

"Fire away," James smiled.

"Husser mentioned you are a CEO," she smiled inquisitively.

"Ah, yes," he smiled and nodded his head. "You're wondering how a college professor is also a CEO. Long before I was born, my grandfather started a publishing company that specialized, and still does, in the academic—textbooks, journals, etc. It wasn't long before the name became widely respected in the publishing world and they were making a fortune. When he died, he left his majority interest in the company to my father . . ."

"Who left it to you," she interrupted.

"Yes, but it wasn't that simple. My old man was all work and no play. He treated my mother and I like employees and drank heavily. As an only child and the sole heir to the empire, I was being groomed for a future in business."

"Obviously, you had other interests."

"That was the problem. While my dad was trying to teach me about stocks and dividends, I'd rather be reading about the treasures of the pharaohs and the lost city of Atlantis. My mother left when I was a senior in high school. She came from money, too, so she did fine alone, but she died less than a year later," James's tone turned into a somber one.

Noelle was beginning to see a picture of what made this man tick. She knew there was something that ailed him emotionally. There was pain deep inside and it fascinated her. She leaned in over the table, her chin on her fist, gazing into his big brown eyes.

"I figured things would get better once I started college. I joined my father's old fraternity, did my basic classes, and began my road toward success. The trouble came when my father got the letter from LSU congratulating me on declaring my major."

"Business Administration?" she said sarcastically, trying to lighten the mood.

"Funny," he smiled slightly, "but no. History. Dad was enraged. He threatened me with cutting off my funds and bringing me home to live with him. I guess he would have forced me to work for him until he passed the torch to me."

"So what did you do?"

"Business Administration."

Noelle giggled a little as she sipped her beer. "So how did you end up as a history professor, anyway?"

"Two years into college, my dad got sick and died shortly after."

They both took on a more somber expression. Somehow, Noelle knew it would come to this type of turning point in the story and dreaded it.

"He left it all to me—the house, the antiques, the stock, everything. And I changed my major; got my doctorate. I married my college girl-friend, moved into the house, had a child, and now I teach."

"How do you juggle that with the company?"

"I own sixty-three percent of the stock. I appoint the board of directors, go to a few meetings to vote and I frequently show up to approve or disapprove an author or two. They usually listen to my advice in that area, since I know half of these assholes personally. But it's not hard—I just delegate most of the administration of the company."

"If you don't mind me asking, how did your father die?" Noelle felt uneasy about the question.

"No, I don't mind . . ." James gulped his drink. "Cirrhosis of the liver. So you can tell, I'm sure, how hard I'm trying not to become my old man," he continued, then drank the rest.

"Was there ever a time when you weren't so cynical?" Noelle shook her head, speaking before she had time to think about what she was saying.

"Oh, yeah. I was fine, even after Dad died. Leave it to a drunk . . ." he alluded to some other event, and then stopped short, pausing to shake his lowered head.

"I'm sorry. I didn't mean to . . ." Noelle once again found herself remorseful of her choice of topic. They had all been briefed on his recent tragedy by Dr. Horn.

"No, you're fine," James smiled a little. "I'm sorry, too. There's no way you could've known."

There they sat, once again staring at each other. They said nothing, and didn't need to. Eyes can say more than words sometimes, and their eyes spoke volumes. Noelle's conveyed sympathy, warmth and admiration. She admired that he had endured so much loss and pain and still maintained at least some form of dignity. James's eyes told Noelle that he was lonely and thanked her for her open heart and open mind.

"So, about earlier today . . ." Noelle broke the silence as she smiled deviously.

"Oh yeah," James returned the smile, "I was wondering when this would come up. How did the uppity bastards take it?"

"Let's just say that they were a little taken aback," sarcasm dripped from her words.

"Well, at least I let them know that this is one academic who is not going to drop to their knees and worship them as the gods of academia just because they're Yale faculty," he sneered.

"Yes, well, all worshipping aside, why did you run out of there like that? Weren't you interested in working on this find?"

"Of course it interested me. Hell, a little too much!"

"Meaning?" Noelle puzzled at his statement.

"Meaning I thought I was about to have a panic attack!"

"Over an archaeological find?"

"All of it. I was tired of those arrogant sons-of-bitches in there analyzing me as an outsider. I kept getting looks from them like I was some kind of backwards, inbred hillbilly! Then, with all of the evidence . . . just none of that makes any damn sense."

"Well, I assure you that it makes more sense to you than it does to me. I have no clue what all of that stuff in the translation meant." Noelle shook her head and paused as if to contemplate carefully what she was going to say next. "Are you ready for more confusion?"

James looked at her in bewilderment. How could this get any more complicated? He braced himself, and then gave a nod to continue.

"I'm sure you're familiar with carbon dating," she continued.

"Yes, of course."

"The pieces of wooden beams you saw in the pictures were dated at somewhere between the fourth and third century BC," she explained.

"Okay, so far, so good," he listened attentively.

"But the other plant life that was buried by the same seismic event was dated to have existed during the first-century AD, meaning that the eruption that compacted the cavern was likely the—"

"Same eruption that destroyed Pompeii," he interrupted, placing his face woefully into his hands for a brief moment. He looked distraught and deep in thought as he motioned for the waitress to bring another round.

"Are you okay, James?" Noelle looked worried.

"Yeah, it just doesn't add up. Greek presence in the area doesn't bother me. But Greek tablets found in an Italian cavern speaking of wrath, Apocalypse, Zathustra and Ahura Mazda do."

"What does it all mean? What is Zathustra?" Noelle was confused.

"Are you familiar with Zoroastrianism?" he asked as Noelle shook her head. "There once was a prophet named Zoroaster, or Zathustra, who founded perhaps the oldest known monotheistic religion. It's an old Persian religion. It's older than Judaism, and in fact it seems that a lot of Zoroastrian beliefs influenced Judaism and Christianity."

"What do you mean?"

"In the Zoroastrian Avesta, or their holy book, there are descriptions of creation similar to the Old Testament. There's a story of a flood that wiped out human kind with the exception of one holy man and his family. There's even a savior called the Shaoshant that will herald the destruction of the evil world by fire and lead the righteous home to Heaven. Sound familiar?"

"And let me guess, Ahura Mazda is God."

"Precisely. And Angra Mainyu is the equivalent of Satan."

"So when did this religion die out?"

"It didn't," he uttered to Noelle's surprise. "It's still practiced on every continent but Antarctica. It doesn't have a huge following, but there's still a nucleus of believers in Iran. The religion was founded in Persia. Not surprisingly, Zoroastrians in Iran are heavily persecuted by a majority of Shi'ite Muslims there."

"So the people that carved these tablets were Zoroastrians?" Noelle made the connection.

"Yeah, it appears so, but two things don't make sense. First, these writings were not made by normal Zoroastrians. They had to have been some sort of fundamentalist sect within the religion. And second, what are Persian Zoroastrian writings doing on a tablet in Greek text in Italy?"

"I'm concerned with the connection to the eruption of Vesuvius," Noelle pondered. "My education says *coincidence*, but my gut says otherwise."

"I'm not sure I follow." James was lost on the concept she was trying to convey.

"We found ancient Greek tablets speaking of destruction inside an imploded cavern at the base of Mount Vesuvius. What does that mean? And what the hell were all those other things found buried near the tablets?"

"Beams and what seemed to be . . ." he paused, as if to receive the epiphany that Noelle was alluding to.

"Yes?" Noelle implored impatiently.

"Gears . . . axles . . . springs . . ."

Noelle was speechless. She simply lifted her fresh beer to her lips and took several large swallows as she watched the wide-eyed James Beauregard contemplate the implications of what the find meant.

"Gears?" Noelle finally said.

"Yes, they looked like fragments of rather large bronze gears, corroded by time," he couldn't believe what he was saying.

"So what? Are you saying that there was a machine in my cavern?" she asked in disbelief.

"I don't know. Maybe."

"What kind of machine?"

"Not sure. But I can think of a place where we can figure it out. You up for a trip home?"

"Oh god, really?" she did not expect that from his mouth. "I've known you for half a day and you expect me to get up and just go off on vacation with you?" she half smiled, more enticed than she would admit at the moment.

"Sure, why not?" he shrugged, the scotch reducing his inhibitions in proposing such a thing. "You're not teaching any summer sessions are you?"

"No, but . . ."

"Then what's stopping you?" he smiled widely. "If you change your mind when we get there, you can just drop in on your family in Baton Rouge."

"I haven't seen them in a while," she bit her lip, seriously thinking about it. She stared into the brown glass of her beer bottle as if it were a crystal ball that would give her the right answer if she looked hard enough. "Screw it," she finally said and smiled.

James called for the tab and they left the bar.

Chapter 11

For the second time in two days, James Beauregard was riding in a fly-ing metal casket. This was the highest frequency of air travel that he had ever experienced. The only exception was making connecting flights, especially during his travels to various parts of Europe, Turkey, North Africa, Japan, and Latin America. Other than that, if he had to travel domestically to promote a new book, he tended to take the train.

He preferred to take the train for other reasons, as well. Views of the countryside from the air were great, albeit terrifying, but there was the constant chance that there would be cloud cover along the way, making it impossible to enjoy one of the only positive experiences in air travel. Trains, on the other hand, allowed him to see the countryside in all of its splendor, as if he were driving himself, but more relaxing. He didn't have to worry about stopping for gas or paying attention to the road while he marveled at the scenery, and he could drink all he wanted without worrying about the threat of causing an accident and killing a family.

James began to feel the tears well up in his eyes with that thought, as he took another sip of his drink. This was one of the things he hated the most about the tragedy. At any place, at any time, a single, seem-ingly harmless thought could creep up and send him into an emotional frenzy. Even worse was when some asshole tells an insensitive joke or even mentions something in passing that will trigger the same effect.

The feeling of suddenly plummeting a few hundred feet immedi-ately took his mind off of his morbid thoughts, and sent his body into a symphony of uncontrollable reflexes. His abdomen tightened, his eyelids clamped, his grip contracted sharply on the end of the armrest, and he had a sporadic urge to vomit, which he promptly fought back. When he opened his eyes, the first thing he saw was Noelle's gleaming smile.

"You okay, James?" she inquired softly. "It's just a little turbulence."

He paid no attention to what she said. He was so entranced with her. He began to wonder why she came with him. They had met less than twenty-four hours earlier. In this day and age, who goes with a stranger on a 1,700 mile trip based on hunch and theory? What if the whole thing turned out to be nothing? They had not even discussed the logistics of sleeping accommodations. Where would she stay? With him? In a hotel?

She was still smiling at him. "You want to tell me why we're headed back to New Orleans? Are you trying to sweep me off my feet by flying me out to a charming, romantic city, and wining and dining me so you can get into my panties?" She batted her eyes and smiled coyly and slightly mockingly. "You know, I've been here before."

"Is that all it takes?" James smiled back as Noelle giggled girlishly.

"There's a special exhibit at the Tulane museum," he regained a touch of seriousness. "I'm ashamed to say I haven't actually been to it yet."

"You're not going to tell me what the subject of the exhibit is?"

"Nope. It's a surprise," he smiled. "But hopefully, it will give us some insight into what you and your team have found."

Chapter 12

The yellow minivan taxi, laden with two passengers, easily made its way down the darkened and seemingly deserted downtown streets of New Orleans. Normally, throngs of people were swarming down the streets, meandering between the towering CBD high-rise structures, drawn to the bustling nightlife meccas at Harrah's Casino on Canal Street, at the elegant fine dining restaurants of the warehouse district or at the packed bars of the French Quarter. James stared out the window of the cab as Noelle stared at him, and then turned her gaze back to the desolate sights beyond her window.

The taxi crossed Poydras Boulevard, passing the towering high-rise corporate hotels, and then crossed Canal Street into the Quarter. Noelle marveled at the majestic old customs house to the left. "It's been so long since I've been back," she said, regret in her voice. "I'd almost forgotten how much I love this state . . . and this city."

James smiled, but said nothing. He could not imagine ever leaving. The city and its unique culture had nurtured him and his individuality since birth. He had jazz in his veins and voodoo in his soul. He had been incubated in a sweltering Creole biome—another world in this swampy little corner of the United States.

"But . . ." she paused, as if to stop short to avoid offending James.

"But what?"

"Where is everyone?" she nodded toward the window as they passed the beautiful St. Louis Cathedral, flanked by the twin Cabildo and Presbytere buildings on either side, and accentuated by the splendor of Jackson Square before it.

"What do you mean?" he said straight-faced, and looked in that direction. "Oh, well, most people are, I'm sure, on Bourbon Street punishing their livers," his sarcasm kicked in. "Jackson Square kind of dies down after dark, except for the fortune tellers that prey upon drunken passersby."

"Yeah, I'm sure. But most of the parking lots are right back there," she turned and looked out the back window of the cab. "They're pretty empty. I know this isn't Bourbon Street, but I should at least see people walking through here on their way to all the bars and strip clubs."

"Yeah, well, it's funny how the wrath of God can change all of that in a single day," he scoffed.

"Oh, come on!" she smiled. "It's been a while since the hurricane. A year in late August. Everything's back to normal."

"Ha!" James scoffed again. "You really believe that?"

"I never see anything on the news about it," she replied candidly.

"That's because the media and the American public have the attention span of a two-year-old," he fired back. Noelle could tell that he was getting irate, and this was a sensitive subject. "It ran its cycle."

"Look at 9/11. After it happened, everyone in this country came together. There was a lot of *are you okay* going around. Lee Greenwood made more money in the year after the attack than he did his entire life. Patriotism was at an all-time high, and that's what this country needed. But five minutes later, everyone would rather fight amongst themselves and blame their shitty lives on somebody else."

Noelle was stunned. She didn't know what to say. "Well, everything looks normal," she got out as she looked around at the Quarter.

"This is the city's main tourist attraction and source of revenue. Do you honestly think the city gives a shit about the poor areas? You go take a look at the lower ninth ward. One in fifteen houses is rebuilt and reoccupied. Major businesses have left town. Housing prices and rent in the Quarter have gone out of control. Average working stiffs are getting shot outside of their office buildings. There are plenty of people who still haven't rebuilt even in Metairie."

"Why? Didn't they have insurance?"

"Of course they did. But there were so many damaged houses that none of the insurance companies wanted to pony up the money. It was already paid out in the form of bonuses, and when the unexpected happened, they got caught with their pants down. Insurance companies don't care about helping people rebuild. They care about their dividends—their profits. They found every loophole they could to not pay people's claims. Things are not normal around here." James shook his head in disgust.

The rest of the trip was silent as the two of them rode down Decatur Street and took a left on Ursuline. On Chartres Street, they arrived at their destination—the regal old Beauregard Mansion.

It stood guard over the lonely French Quarter street like the general of its namesake. Retrieving her luggage from the back of the taxi, Noelle could not take her eyes off of the beautiful Greek-revival home with its unique Creole flair. Its gold-painted stucco was trimmed in white, including the four lanky columns in the front. They passed silently through the wrought-iron gate in the front, and climbed one of the two semi-circular staircases leading to the upper-level front door. It was stunning.

"You know why these old antebellum homes have two stairways in the front?" James asked his guest.

"No, but I know why the front door is all the way up here," she answered. "In case of flood. The river is right over there," she pointed out to her right.

"Correct," he smiled. "And the double staircase was to keep men from looking up the dresses of the ladies on the way up the stairs. A men's side and a women's side."

Noelle could never have dreamt of staying the night in a place like this. She had been to plenty of antebellum homes in her life. She was from Baton Rouge. Yet, she had never had the chance to stay in one. Most of them were unable to accommodate overnight guests. They were museums, complete with authentic period bedding and furnishings. She wondered if it would be spooky to stay in a place like this. She also felt embarrassed that she had never been to this part of the Quarter. She went to college in this town, but it seems that she had confined herself to the areas of the old colonial city that had the highest number of bars. This part of the French Quarter had more homes, shops and museums.

James opened the heavy door with an ancient creak, and revealed the radiance of the home's interior. It took Noelle's breath away. She dropped her bags onto the blood-red wooden floor boards and gazed, mouth opened, at the panoramic view. There were paintings and sabers adorning the walls, antique hutches filled with fine china and artifacts from a long past era covering the entire expanse of the home.

"Your room is down the hallway," James broke the silence, amused at how entranced his new friend was with the home he often took for granted.

"Thanks," she smiled politely as she picked up her bags and walked briskly in the direction James had pointed. She made her way down the hallway as she watched him checking his answering machine for messages.

"No, not that one!" James tried to stop her, but she was already pushing the door ajar.

It only took a moment for him to arrive at Noelle's rear, and when he did, he found her to be staring silently into a room that she knew he would never willingly allow her to see. Its dark, midnight-blue walls were covered with cut-outs of the planets and stars. There was a model space shuttle hanging by wire from the ceiling. Positioned around the small single bed in the center of the room were a toy box and various toys against the wall on the floor.

"I'm sorry," Noelle stood silently and motionless with her hand placed gently over her mouth. She could not begin to express to James how sorry she was for intruding. She simply gave him a look of deepest apologies, watching him with his head lowered and his thumb and fingers clutching his tightly shut eyes.

"It's okay," he consoled the clearly shaken woman. "Let me put your bags in the guest bedroom." He lifted her luggage, and took them to the room just across the hall, pushing the door open, and laying them on the floor just inside. "A drink?"

He led her back through the house, stopping at an ornate old cabinet, reaching inside and grabbing a bottle of fine bourbon and two glasses. Noelle followed him to the door leading out to the back veranda.

Immediately, there was a smell of roses and other fragrant flowers filling her nose as she stepped onto the large porch. The old pavers in the courtyard below were slightly colored green with moss or algae. The small, black iron fountain in the center spewed water upward and provided a soothing sound not unlike a rain shower. Everywhere there were hedges, flowers and tropical plants. It felt like a touch of rain forest within an old world courtyard.

She followed slowly behind James as he ambled across the veranda, their every step creaking the gray-painted boards beneath their feet. They came to the stairway leading down to the courtyard and the lower level rooms.

"These used to be the slave quarters," he pointed toward the rooms in the L-shaped building that bordered the courtyard.

He continued slowly across the paved ground and placed the bottle and two glasses on a small wrought-iron table. He removed the cap from the bottle of whiskey, then gently poured them each a drink.

Neither of them said anything at first, and it was a bit uncomfortable for both. James was uneasy because he felt that Noelle was likely under the impression that he was upset at her. He wasn't; he was simply unnerved by someone opening a room that he had himself only opened a few times in the past year. It was the equivalent of an acquaintance at work making a boyish and lewd joke about one's mother only a short time after that person's mother had died. The coworker doesn't know and doesn't mean anything by what he said, but it still hurts the person to whom it was said.

James took a sip of his whiskey and watched Noelle do the same, wincing slightly as if to silently admit that she had not drunk straight bourbon in quite a while. He looked deep into her warm, golden eyes, which were silently begging him for forgiveness, and then he spoke.

"It was about a year ago . . ." he paused a moment. He knew this was going to be difficult for him as he fought back the tears that his emotions were summoning. "I was in California giving a lecture at Stanford. I had taken the summer off from teaching to promote a new book at some of the more prominent universities in the country. I always hated leaving Abigail and Max behind. It felt like I was abandoning them to do my thing, but Abigail was always supportive of my success and career. Sometimes they would even fly out to where I was, and we'd spend a week there as sort of a vacation."

"They didn't come out to see me this time, though. Abigail had taken Max to Baton Rouge to her cousin's wedding. They were there pretty late, so even though she didn't have anything to drink, it was late and she was tired. She called me a couple of times on her drive down I-10 because she was getting drowsy. We got into an argument the last time she called because I told her that she should have stayed at her mother's house in Baton Rouge, but she kept insisting that she needed to get Max back to the comfort of his own bed."

James became more distressed as he fought harder to conceal the obvious tears welling in his eyes and his quivering lip. Noelle gazed attentively, watching every word formed upon his lips as if to watch the speech materialize and flow from his mouth in print.

"That was the last time I ever spoke to her," James wiped his eyes. "The next phone call that I got was from NOPD telling me that my wife and little boy had been in an accident. So I rushed in on the first flight I could get, and tore ass over to the police station, and they directed me to the morgue."

He wasn't sobbing, but the tears were now rolling down his face in a way that Noelle had never seen on a man. They were passionate and unapologetic. They were sensitive, yet retained masculinity. They coursed in rivers around the hairs in his stubble, flooding the thickening forest on his cheeks.

"They said the college kid that hit Abigail's car had a blood alcohol content of .303. He should have been comatose somewhere, but instead he decided to drive to his friend's house. He left the parking lot by the river in the French Quarter, took Canal Street north, and hopped over the street-car median into oncoming traffic. He hit Abigail head-on at about fifty miles per hour, they said. Abigail died instantly, and Max went into a coma, dying about two hours later."

Noelle was speechless as she watched James's demeanor change sharply. His expression went from sorrowful and reflective to enraged and malicious in an unnerving amount of time.

"They were less than two miles from home!" he pounded his tightly-clenched fist in the wrought-iron table. "They did nothing wrong! She hadn't been drinking! And the motherfucker that hit them stumbled away with minor cuts and bruises! That fucking murderer is doing seven years for vehicular manslaughter!"

Noelle saw a release of emotions that she knew he had been yearning for, for a long time. It seemed that he had rage and remorse bottled up for a year, with no one to talk to. His eyes softened and the tears rolled as Noelle placed her hand atop his and gave him a look of condolence; needing not to be expressed verbally.

James was thankful for that. He looked down at her hand now clutching his, then back to her sympathetic eyes. His bitter frown turned to a slight smile of relief and peace in an instant. Perhaps that was all he needed. Was it that simple? Release?

He closed his eyes and nodded in completion, then stood up, releasing Noelle's soft hand. "We have a long day tomorrow. We could both use some rest."

Noelle stood up as they picked up their glasses, still nearly full of the toxic brown liquid James loved so much. He lifted the glass to his lips to empty the contents into his mouth, but stopped short, looking downward into the eighty-proof abyss. He lifted his eyes in Noelle's direction, lowered his glass to chest level, smiled and flung the liquid out to his left onto the courtyard's brick floor. Walking toward the steps leading up to the veranda, Noelle followed, smiling.

Chapter 13

Noelle emerged from her cozy guest room fully dressed in a casual white shirt and khaki shorts, her hair still wet and naturally shiny and curly. Water beaded on her neck still and she was surrounded by the smell of her specialty salon-grade shampoo and conditioner. She meandered through the house, following the aroma of coffee being brewed, finding James in the kitchen having a cup and reading the *Times-Picayune* newspaper.

She was taken aback by the appearance of the man standing before her. His red and black plaid pajama pants stopped just above his bare feet, which she thought were badly in need of a pedicure. She had to restrain herself from gasping at the well-toned physique of his bare torso. His shoulders were broad with lean muscles atop, connecting to his neck. His arms were not huge, but were defined, as were his perfectly round pectorals cresting over his tightly-rippled abs.

He was slightly startled by the popping sound that the old hardwood floor made as she continued her steps. He looked up from his paper sharply to see a spectacle of radiance before him. Her tiny feet were comfortably nestled inside a pair of multi-strapped leather sandals. They led upward into a petite pair of silky, tanned legs, bathed lovingly in the morning sun pouring in through the windows. Her shorts and t-shirt met perfectly in the center of the concave section of her hourglass figure and the shirt was just tight enough to accentuate her pert, round breasts.

She did not get offended. Actually, she was highly flattered by his admiration of her body. She worked very hard on keeping up with her diet and went to the gym nearly every day. She thought about how much time she spent in the lab doing research and in the field, and how few opportunities she actually got to show off her body to attractive men. All of the men she worked with tended to be bookworms and potheads.

Finally, he was able to regain his composure and take his eyes away from her. "Coffee?" he offered quite simply, lifting his eyes to her beautiful smiling face.

"Please," she nodded graciously as he turned to open the cabinet and retrieve an oversized coffee mug. "So, you seem chipper. No hangover?"

"I don't get hangovers," he said, his back still to the young geologist. "Milk or cream?" He turned his head to the side and his eyes to his periphery.

"Cream," she said as she watched him walk toward the refrigerator and pull out the paper carton. "What do you mean you don't get hangovers?" she puzzled over the statement. "I saw what you drank yesterday and how much you drank."

"Well, that's just the thing, isn't it? Sugar?" His back was still to his new companion.

"Two, please—and what the hell are you talking about?" she smiled.

"I was raised around an alcoholic father who let me drink from my mid-teens, I was in a fraternity at one of the most profound party schools in the country and my wife and child died violently," he said with no negative emotion. "I'm well-tempered in my alcohol consumption abilities."

"That's healthy," she smirked sarcastically, carefully taking the steaming mug of coffee from James.

"Yeah, I know," he slightly hung his head. "My liver and I haven't been on speaking terms in years," he began to smile.

James imbibed a healthy gulp of his coffee, never losing eye contact with the striking woman seated at the barstool across from him. Their eyes once again were communicating with one another. She grinned, leaning over the countertop, the corners of her mouth peaking upward sharply, yet softly. He took another gulp, finishing his all too important breakfast drink, set the mug down on the counter and smiled.

"I'll get dressed, then we'll be on our way," he said, strutting his well-kept male physique past his admiring friend.

"Take your time," Noelle said as she followed him with her eyes.

Chapter 14

Trolley car number 935 bumped and rattled slowly up St. Charles Avenue toward Audubon Park and Tulane University. The car was filled mostly with tourists with fanny packs and digital cameras around their necks, snapping photos of the majestic old nineteenth-century homes on either side of the neutral ground. These homes were, like elderly people of any neighborhood, quick with stories of eras past and the wisdom of the experienced. They had withstood the ages—hurricanes, floods, race riots and the Depression. But they were also eerie old gravestones—monuments to the long dead former inhabitants. Once, rich merchants and doctors and their high-born wives sat in the parlors sipping tea and mint juleps with their equally wealthy guests. Female nanny slaves tended the children, loving them as their own. Servants worked in the kitchen, preparing lavish Creole delicacies for dinner.

But those days were gone, and so were the people. The homes were updated with the latest in modern technologies. They were wired with electricity and had plumbing. They had televisions in each room, refrigerators and wi-fi internet connections. Yet one could sit in silence in one of the old parlors and still imagine, or even hear the footsteps of the slaves carrying dinner to the wealthy masters and the children playing upstairs.

The car continued to grind down the tracks, passing a mixture of old antebellum mansions and more poorly-maintained houses rented to college students. It seemed as though the car was traveling through a tunnel. Along the sides of the street stood centuries-old live oak trees that reached high toward the heavens and then laterally across the neutral ground to arc above the trolley tracks to form a biological tunnel around the street. James had always thought it was funny to watch people attempting to stroll down the sidewalks and trip over the broken and uneven chunks of concrete fragmented by the tree roots.

He watched Noelle, smiling and glued to the window of the trolley car. He had the feeling that she had never ridden the trolley, and perhaps had never made many trips into the Garden District. That had always been something that bothered him about visitors to New Orleans, even friends and fraternity brothers visiting for Mardi Gras or a party weekend. Everyone always insisted upon sticking close to the French Quarter. Even then, they always wanted to see Bourbon Street only.

James frequently tried to convince friends that there were more interesting bars in various off-Bourbon locations, even uptown near Tulane. No one wanted to see St. Louis Cemetery No.1, the French Market, or the Garden District. People forgot about the D-day Museum and Audubon Park. No one ever wanted to go with him to see Chalmette Battlefield, where the all too important Battle of New Orleans was fought. Everyone wanted to get drunk and get laid, and they thought that the only place to do that in New Orleans was an overcrowded club on the urine and vomit-flooded Bourbon Street.

After a particularly long and slow ride up the beautiful St. Charles Avenue, the trolley came to a screeching halt outside of Gibson Hall on Tulane campus. James and Noelle emerged from the car, dodging tourists and children. They leapt from the car, scanning their environments for a moment as the trolley departed again.

They waited a few moments for passing vehicles, then darted across the street toward the massive old building before them. Passing the structure, they admired the wonderful old trees and colorful flowering bushes all across the eye-pleasing campus.

Their pleasant stroll was only a few minutes, and finally they approached a medium-sized structure built in a modern fashion, probably dating from the 1960s. As they climbed the ten concrete steps leading up to the building, Noelle noticed the banner hanging from the top, and read it aloud: "Wonders of Ancient Technology."

"Prepare to be amazed," James smiled as they kept walking in the direction of the entrance.

He had never been to this exhibit, but he had an idea of what was inside, having seen and researched it all before. But one thing was inside, colleagues had told him, that he had never seen in person. And now it was perhaps even more important than ever that he see it.

Pushing the door open, they felt that rush of cooled air escape into the heat around them like a vacuum had just been released. Stepping into the expansive atrium, their footsteps echoed from the marble floors across the high walls and ceiling. Their footsteps repeated the sound as it mingled with the dull drone of museum patrons talking amongst themselves and waiting in the short line for tickets. They waited in line for only a few minutes until they approached the young female student worker behind the ticketing counter.

"Two faculty, please," he said. "Noelle, do you have your Yale ID?"

"What?" she was awakened from a sort of trance, looking around at her surroundings.

"Your Yale ID," he repeated, pointing at the ticket prices printed on thick paper and propped up by an easel on the ticket counter.

Adults $20
Children $15
Seniors $13
Students and Faculty $10

"A little expensive, huh?" Noelle commented, digging in her bag for her ID and presenting it to the girl behind the counter.

"This isn't just any exhibit." He produced a twenty-dollar bill and handed it to the girl in exchange for two tickets. "They don't just show you models of the ancient technology. They actually have people demonstrating how they work."

The duo began walking to the right toward the entrance to the exhibit. James could feel his heart racing, and Noelle could see the excitement in his manner. She grinned as she watched his fingers move and gyrate in anticipation. There was an increase in his step and an uncontrollable smile on his face. He reminded her of a little boy who was about to enter the zoo.

They walked into a narrow passageway and turned a corner into an expansive room full of elaborate exhibits and machines. In the back somewhere there was a flash of fire that startled Noelle, causing her to stop walking for an instant.

James's chin hung in a gaping, awe-stricken smile. It was a carnival of history and science. The gears and pulleys turned around in a symphony of innovation and progress. He tried to imagine what it was like for a common man in days long past to witness such spectacles. He guessed that the reaction would have been just as intended—the gods have smiled upon us.

The two of them strode past one of the exhibits, and watched as a man poured a bucket of water into a large brass container. Connected to a rod, which was attached to a larger structure, the container lowered to the floor as the other end of the rod turned upward. The end of the rod was pointed and was fixed in front of a series of notches extending vertically on a brass plate affixed to the structure. Slowly, the container began leaking water from a hole into a reservoir. As the container of water became lighter, it began to rise, and the pointed end of the rod fell to lower notches extending downward.

"What is this thing?" Noelle puzzled at the strange contraption.

"Water clock," he replied in simplicity.

"Clock?" she became confused. "They had clocks in ancient times?"

"Kind of," he explained, "but not like today, where everyone's got a clock on the wall. I mean, wasn't like Fred Flintstone with a sundial watch. But people figured out thousands of years ago that if you can leak water from a container at a fixed rate, you can measure the amount of time that it takes for it to empty. They even figured out a way to make the water recycle back into the clock continuously."

"Sounds like a pain in the ass to fit into a microwave screen," she smirked.

James smiled giddily as they moved past the ancient machine and on to the next piece. It looked like a miniature Greek temple, approximately thirty-six inches tall and complete with columns and a pitched, triangular façade.

"Ah," James marveled, "the mechanized theatre."

"Greek, right?" she guessed, trying hard to impress the well-learned history professor.

"Yeah, they invented drama, so it's only fitting that they invented the mechanized version."

"How does it work?"

"Similarly to the Roman odometer over there," he pointed to the man pushing a two-wheeled machine that resembled a wheelbarrow with a box instead of a hauling container. The two of them briefly watched the invention being pushed along a replica of a Roman highway.

"It's a series of gears and ball bearings," he continued. "Pretty complicated, actually. You wind it up, and a series of things happen with just the right timing. It actually looks kind of like a puppet show. Walt Disney would have been proud," he smiled. "Weights and ball bearings work the changing of the scenery, motion of the characters and even sound effects. They had boxes of sand that would empty creating the sound of rain, or balls dropping onto a small drum for thunder."

The two of them continued to walk through a seemingly endless maze of technology that Noelle had no idea ever existed. She absorbed with the wide eyes of a child the wonders around them.

"Correct me if I'm wrong, but shouldn't these inventions have gotten better and better over the years?" she puzzled. "I mean, by the present day, we should have been way more technologically advanced if this is where it started."

"I was waiting for that question," James smiled. "In the heyday of these inventions, most high learning and innovation was shared. The library at Alexandria, Egypt, held thousands of scrolls filled with this learning, and scholars from all areas of the ancient world flocked to it. Unfortunately, the library was destroyed, and much of the knowledge was lost. However, people in China and the Middle East continued to learn. It was just Europe that fell into the dark ages. They didn't begin learning again until after the crusades and the Renaissance. Our culture is based primarily on that of Europe's, so we've begun where they've begun."

"Yes, but why did Europe stop learning and innovating?" she was still confused. "Weren't they exposed to Greek and Roman culture? Shouldn't they have built on this technology?" she motioned to the exhibits around her.

"Now that, I've always been confused with," he smiled. "I've researched and studied that very question for years. Most historians think that when the Roman Empire split up, Europe reverted back to its backward ways. But I don't buy that. The Middle East was part of Rome, too, but that didn't stop the learning there."

"Did you ever find any answers?"

"The only thing I ever made a connection with has to do with natural disasters."

"You mean storms? Droughts?"

"More like earthquakes, tsunamis and volcanoes. It seems that Europe's fall into the dark ages coincided with a couple of hundred years' worth of wicked natural disasters. And it seems that the seismic activity happened every twenty to forty years in some sort of strange pattern."

"Weird," Noelle silently analyzed the geological implications. She drew on years of study and research to attempt to help James with his theory. Then came the grin of an epiphany. He could see her forehead muscles relax and her eyes soften. James half expected her to slap her forehead with her palm.

"I've seen something like this before," she said with a heavy breath.

"You have?" he said with a great level of surprise.

"Yes," she smiled. "Seismologists call it an earthquake storm."

"Earthquake storm?" he puzzled.

"Yeah," she continued with enthusiasm. "You can enter all of the seismic information for an area over time into a computer model, and track patterns from event to event. Stress is put on the bedrock below, and when it gives, there's an earthquake. But when the bedrock moves, the stress is transferred somewhere else, creating another potential earthquake situation. It's the law of conservation of energy. You can't create or destroy energy; only transfer it. Based on the information entered into the model, they've actually been able to predict where the next earthquake can occur. And they're working on trying to predict when."

"Wow, I don't know what to say," James smiled in amazement.

"Well," she smiled back, "you can start by telling me what this thing over here is."

James turned his head as far to the right as he could without moving his body, then his shoulders followed. He scanned the room in the direction in which she was pointing until his eyes became affixed upon a small display at the other end of the room. At first, his mouth dropped open slightly, then he began to smile in excitement.

"I don't believe it," he gawked. "I was hoping it would be here, but I really didn't expect . . ."

"What? What?!" she exclaimed.

"It's . . ." he paused a moment, "the Antikythera Mechanism."

Chapter 15

The few clouds in the flawlessly blue sky passed slowly overhead as the breeze swept over the vast plains below and gently kissed the ancient stone remains of a once grand city wall. The two men walked slowly and carefully over the broken, white-gray paths between the low-standing remains of long destroyed buildings. Their white robes flowed in the refreshing breeze as they spoke intently to one another in their native Farsi.

"I am honored that you asked to see me," young Khalim said reverently to his master.

"You have been a good and faithful follower," he smiled at the young prodigy. "Your father would have been proud."

"Thank you."

They walked silently for a few moments, passively studying the grim beauty of a once great settlement, now in ruins. Khalim kept his head low, watching himself step on the cracks in the stones and kicking small pebbles out of his way.

"Master," the young man lifted his gaze in the direction of the Shaoshant. His eyes were stressed and troubled.

"Are you all right, child?" There was a kindness in his voice.

"I have always done my best to be devout and faithful. But all of these people . . ." he motioned toward the tourists roaming the site and snapping photos of each other. "Are you sure this is the only way?"

"Khalim," the Shaoshant responded with kindness and understanding, placing his hand on the young man's shoulder, "do not question your faith. Stay true to the Avesta—it will provide the answers to all of your questions."

"But Master," he was still troubled, "is this what the Avesta's meaning is? Is this really the intention of Ahura Mazda?"

"All of these people you speak of," the aging man motioned to the tourists with an outstretched hand, "are evildoers. You know that. The

Avesta says that they must be purified in fire before they meet God. It was not I that prepared this holy place for what is to happen. Blood has been shed on these plains for thousands of years—since the time of the Egyptian pharaohs; since the time of King David. It was our ancestors who placed beneath us our means to bring the end."

"I understand, Master," young Khalim hung his head in reassurance.

"Good," the Shaoshant smiled and placed his arm around the young man's shoulders, benevolently embracing him. "The reason I asked you to meet me is that I have chosen you for a special duty."

"I would be honored to do my duty for God."

"The time is drawing near. Today, we begin our countdown to Ahura Mazda's revenge," he led the young follower down the steps and toward the tunnel beneath the mount. "You are to be the guardian of our holy place while I perform our sacred ritual."

"Thank you, my lord," the young man bowed his head. "I will not fail you."

Chapter 16

"What is the Antikythera Mechanism?" Noelle was totally confused. She motioned toward a very small object, about the size of a man's fist, behind a glass case. It was an odd, seeming to be a small, green wheel surrounded by some other corroded, green material.

"Well, first of all," there was still excitement in his voice, "Antikythera is a small island in the Aegean Sea, off the coast of Greece."

"Okay, I follow you so far. I got the name, and I assume it's some sort of mechanism?" she smirked.

"Yes," James smiled, "but not just any mechanism. It was discovered around 1904, by local divers harvesting sponges."

"You mean the divers were able to notice this little thing just lying on the sea floor?"

"No, actually, what caught their eye was a rather large statue. It was part of a wreck of a Roman ship, laden with looted Greek treasures. Most historians believe that it came from the island of Rhoades, and date it to at least 100 BC. Excavators a couple of years after the discovery of the wreck picked up what was thought to be a rock with a wheel embedded in it. As they examined it over the next few decades, they found many smaller gears within, and realized that the rock was actually a very corroded bronze encasing. They also found Greek inscriptions throughout the mechanism, indicating things like planets and signs of the zodiac."

"You mean this is some sort of clock?"

"Noelle, what you're looking at could very well be history's first computer."

Her expression indicated that she was dumbfounded. She stared at the object in blank wonder, but there was curiosity in her eyes and she looked at James, hungry for greater explanation.

"The original mechanism was larger than this, maybe the height of a filing cabinet and the width of the CPU of your computer, and consisted of anywhere between thirty and seventy gears. On the inside, there were markers indicating the positions of the five planets that the Greeks knew about. On the outside there were two dials on one side of the vertical rectangular frame, and one on the other. The main dial showed the Sothic calendar—the Egyptian calendar. Inside that, on the same dial was the zodiac, which could be adjusted to the Egyptian calendar. It even compensated for leap years. The other dials showed positions of the sun, moon, planets, and stars. So you could use a crank to program in a future date and tell what the position of the moon, sun, and stars was going to be."

"James, this is amazing," Noelle uttered in disbelief. "I had no idea that such a thing existed."

"I know. Pretty wild, huh?" he smiled, staring at the mechanism. "This thing has always fascinated me. Historians speculate that more of these existed, even larger ones that an entire city or town could use for any number of purposes." James paused for a moment, deep in thought. His mind sorted through countless ideas and information. She could see his eyes darting from side to side as he stared into the floor like it were an endless universe of thought. His narrowed eyes widened suddenly. They were both thinking the same thing, and when their eyes met, the notion was solidified.

"James, what if . . ." she stopped short.

"I know," he nodded.

Chapter 17

James and Noelle sat quietly inside a Creole restaurant on Conti Street in the French Quarter. The place was small, with red brick floors and rustic, faded scenes of antebellum New Orleans life painted on the taupe walls. Various plants and ivies adorned the perimeter. The bright noontime sun shown in from atop the surrounding rooftops and into the courtyard beyond the glass doors. It was classic New Orleans old-world homage; a colonial gem dripping with history and Creole flair.

Noelle savored the last few morsels of her seafood gumbo. The okra and filé exploded in her mouth along with the gulf flavors of the oysters, crabmeat and shrimp in the heavenly Creole stew. Yet James had barely touched his. He simply sipped his usual lunchtime beer, his thoughts lingering heavily on something else, far from the amazing food growing cold before him.

"James," Noelle broke the silence in a concerned tone, "are you okay?"

He delayed his response for a moment, meticulously picking up the beer bottle, touching it to his lips, imbibing a bit of the contents, and carefully placing it back on the glass-top table. His head was propped up against his fist as his elbow remained planted firmly on the table. The look on his face was of pure and intense wonder. He focused sharply on his bowl of gumbo as he searched his brain for answers to his many questions.

"Could it be that you stumbled upon one of these giant timekeeping machines?" he suddenly looked up and asked.

"In Italy?" the idea confused her.

"Well . . . yeah." He continued to half-stare into the glass table. "We know that the Anikythera Mechanism was found amongst a Roman shipwreck, so why wouldn't they have that technology? Besides, your cavern was found near the ruins of a Roman city, and not somewhere near a remote countryside volcano. I mean, it was found at Vesuvius.

The whole city could have used the device."

"Okay, so maybe it was one of these machines," she conceded. "But it was inside a cavern. Wouldn't it have been easier to get to if it were placed somewhere on the surface?"

"It makes no sense," James placed his forehead in hands in frustration. "The cavern, gears, bronze pieces, and tablet with Greek text—all found at the base of one of the most famous volcanoes in history. The Greeks were known to quarry and dig caverns in the area, but why would there be a machine down there?"

"And the stuff that the tablet read—the Zoro . . ." she stopped, trying to remember the correct name of the odd religion.

"Zoroastrianism," he smiled.

"Yeah, that," she returned the smile with a slight bit of embarrassment. "All of that fire and brimstone—it reminds me of Revelations!" she laughed.

James choked a little on his beer, wiped a small bit of it off of his lips with his hand, and heavily set the bottle down. He tried to regain his composure, coughing a little more.

"What did you just say?" he leered at his companion. After his question, he began to wonder why he asked it. He heard what she said, but he simply wanted to hear it again. *Why do people do that?*, he wondered.

"I said all of the fire and brimstone stuff on the tablet reminded me of Revelations in the Bible," she repeated herself.

James didn't know whether to laugh, cry or scream, but made no noise. His eyes widened and his jaw dropped as he put the pieces together. His eyes shot back and forth rapidly as his mind raced and his thoughts expanded.

"Oh my God!" he suddenly blurted.

"What?! What?!" she was startled. What had she said that could invoke such a reaction from him? She grabbed at his every gesture and expression, starving for more information. She couldn't dream of what it was like to take one of his classes. She found herself thinking that if she had a professor like him when she was an undergrad, especially one as good looking, she may have gone to class more often, and probably even learned something.

"Revelations!" he was becoming more excited. Half the people in the room were beginning to stare, making Noelle a little nervous and embarrassed.

"Okay, what about it?" she said, looking around at the staring restaurant patrons and twirling her brilliant dark brown hair.

"Dr. Broussard," he feigned formality, "you'd be surprised how many similarities there are between Christianity and most other older Middle Eastern religions. You have to remember that Christianity is the new kid on the block. It came from Judaism, which came from any number of earlier religions in the area. And it seems that Zoroastrianism may have had a direct influence on Christianity. Saviors, end of days, destruction of evil on earth—it's all there!"

"What do you mean?" she seemed confused. "Revelations is based on a dream that St. John the Divine had about what Judgment Day would be like."

There was an expression on her face and a doubt in her voice that unmistakably hinted that she was still quite firm in her traditionalist views on Christianity. She reminded James of an older child discovering from a kid in the school yard that there was no Easter Bunny or Santa Claus. It was a little heartbreaking for him to have to do, but he enjoyed it in a way.

"Noelle," his voice took on a softer tone, "John was exiled on an island by the Romans for his Christian beliefs. In those times, most Christians in the Roman Empire were persecuted—even fed to the lions in the Flavian Amphitheater for the entertainment of the people."

"Flavian Amphitheater?" she had never heard of this place.

"The Roman Colosseum," he simplified.

"Oh," she paused a moment to think. "James, I know all of this. I grew up Catholic."

"The point is that according to theory, many of the prophecies regarding the savior and the end of days has to do with Roman oppression. The Jewish prophecy of the Messiah may have been that someone would deliver the Hebrews not from evil in general, but from the Romans. Similarly, at the time that St. John wrote his Apocalyptic book, there were dozens more being written all over the Roman Empire. One was even written by Peter himself."

"Apocalyptic books?" she was beginning to loosen and take interest.

"They were writings—sort of prophecies about the end of days. They all said different things would happen, but one idea stayed the same. The days of evil would end, or really I should say oppression would end, and everyone who believed in Christ would be happy. Basically, it kept hope alive that they wouldn't be persecuted forever and added credibility to the growing religion."

"So what gives? Why have I never heard of these other books before?"

"Simple. Control. It's the same as the rest of Christian history. The less you know, the better the church can control people. The Council of Nicea decided in the fourth century which books out of hundreds to include in the Bible, and the rest were either destroyed or remain in a vault in the Vatican. I mean, there's a reason that the Bible remained in Latin text until the sixteenth century. The less you know about what it actually says, the better."

Noelle didn't know what to say. These ideas were radical to her. But what scared her most was that they made perfect sense. She said nothing, but her thoughts were traveling at the speed of light, and James sensed that, so he began to make his point.

"What if a lot more of the first Christians were more closely connected to Zoroastrianism?"

"Are you insinuating that some of the early Christians weren't Christians?" she seemed appalled.

"No, not really. But if you went back in time and visited a Christian congregation within decades after the crucifixion, you probably wouldn't recognize it. They were Christians, but what if they had a stronger relationship with Zoroastrians than anyone originally thought? What if St. John's writings reflect this?"

"Alright, I suppose it's possible. No one will ever be able to go back in time and ask them. But what does this all have to do with our discovery in Italy? What does it have to do with the Antikythera Mechanism?"

"Most cultures in the world are in some way connected somewhere down the line. Technology was shared throughout the Mediterranean. The Antikythera Mechanism had signs of the Greek Zodiac and the Sothic Calendar. The Roman alphabet was borrowed from the Greek, and that in turn has a strong connection to the Phoenicians and the Hebrews."

"So how did a Persian religion show up in ancient Greece? Apocalyptic Zoroastrian beliefs in Greek text in a cavern with some sort of machine near the base of Mount Vesuvius?" she still had no idea how it all fit together.

"Conquest? Religious missionaries? Who knows?"

James began staring once again, seemingly into oblivion. He was deep in thought about an impossible theory. He was churning inside, never having been this vexed about any historical theory in his life. He was about to ask what he deemed a very stupid question. He hesitated at even the thought of asking it.

"Noelle," he squinted slightly as he lifted his gaze to the beautiful woman across the table, "is it possible . . . ?"

"What?" she was intrigued.

"Is it possible that man can cause an earthquake?"

If his expression had not been so sincere and inquisitive, she would have given not a second thought to the notion that he was joking. Yet, he was not joking, and she somehow saw where he was going with this question. Therefore, she ushered out any temptation to smile, and tried to give as serious an answer as she could.

"I . . ." she paused, shrugging her shoulders slightly. "I don't know . . . I suppose it's possible."

She didn't know quite what to say, and could tell that was not the response James was looking for. She knew that his hypothesis was nearly an impossible one, and he was looking for the easy response to validate what he was thinking. Then she thought of something, "Have you ever seen the original Christopher Reeve Superman movie?"

"What?" he wasn't quite sure what she was getting at. "Yeah, I've seen it," he gave her the benefit of the doubt.

"Do you remember how Lex Luthor shot a nuclear missile into the San Andreas Fault and created a major earthquake?"

"Yeah, I remember," he smiled a little. "That's not quite what I meant. There were no ballistic missiles in ancient times. Do you think a machine could be crafted that could create a seismic event?"

The question fell and exploded like the atomic bomb described in the conversation. It was ludicrous. It was so far-fetched that she didn't know how to answer and didn't want to insult his intelligence, so she played along.

"Um, to create an earthquake, the stress put upon the bedrock has to be released or plates have to grind past each other," she chose her words carefully. "And in the case of a volcano, somehow, the pressure built up by the rising magma has to be released. So the rock plug inside the volcano has to give in some way. I'm not sure that an ancient machine could do such a thing."

"What if it was a very large machine," he pressed, "and it was holding the bedrock in place. If it were to fall apart or self-destruct in some way, could it release the pressure and create a seismic event?"

She was beginning to see exactly where he was going with this. Actually, it was beginning to make sense. The more she thought about it, the more it seemed possible. James could tell she was thinking long and hard about this idea. He was curious to see if she gave any validation to it.

"James, I don't think any geologist has ever given any thought to the idea. But I think it may be possible," she said with honest sincerity.

He began smiling excitedly again. He took another drink from his beer bottle and went right back to smiling. He couldn't begin to explain to her the implications of this discovery.

"Let's say that someone put an eruption-causing machine in that cavern over two thousand years ago, and it caused Mount Vesuvius to blow its top, decimating the city of Pompeii," she half-smiled. "Who would have done it and why?"

"Well, we know the text was in Greek, and we know it referred to Zoroastrian beliefs," he smiled. "It could have been some radical sect of that religion. And don't forget that the tablet said it was a warning. What if there were more of these? Can you imagine if the colossal disasters like the eruption of Thera, the earthquake at Rhoades or even the destruction of Atlantis were caused by the same kind of machine? This is huge! The tablet speaks of the end of days. What if there is one giant machine that would cause the destruction of civilization as we know it?"

"What, some sort of Apocalypse machine? Put there by an ancient radical sect of Zoroastrians?" she didn't seem convinced.

"Why not?" he continued. "You've seen today how advanced the ancients were. We've found the evidence in that cavern. So many different religions speak of an end of days scenario. No matter how differing they tend to be, they all seem to agree that it will happen. Revelations even speaks of a machine in the last days—a winepress killing thousands of people. Could that be a metaphor for some destructive machine—an ancient weapon of mass destruction? Instead of waiting around for God to destroy the earth with a bolt of lightning and fire and brimstone, what if some religious group decided that they were the instruments of God, and put into place a means to help the process along? There could be some machine out there that will destroy us still."

"But how?" Noelle was flabbergasted.

James smiled cunningly, then spoke: "Earthquake storm."

Chapter 18

Noelle twisted and violently pulled at her dark brown locks with a towel, drying as her bare feet creaked and popped the old hardwood beneath her. *Best shower ever,* she thought.

She had almost forgotten the steamy, sweltering summers in south Louisiana. That day had been particularly bad at ninety-seven degrees and the humidity of the Caribbean. It was like living inside someone's mouth. By the time they had gotten back to the old Beauregard Mansion, she had been drenched and re-drenched in her own sweat, compounded by the vapor in the air and the stench of the mud hole New Orleans was positioned upon.

She smiled to see James sitting at his large desk, silently and intently fingering through seemingly endless pages of historical works piled high in front him. She smiled as she caught sight of him, pausing for a moment to watch, and then pushed into the room. Once he had his mind set on something, he did not waver. Yet, she had also seen this trait as a negative thing. James now seemed to teeter on the edge of obsession.

James sat, still turning through pages in multiple books at a time as Noelle continued into the room, admiring her surroundings. She looked around in appreciation of the vast quantities of books, accented by numerous objects of antiquity. However, she was perplexed by the odd spectacle of the stereo at the far end of the room. She wondered why there was a small hole in the front paneling of one of the components, but she did not dare ask the question. She chose a different one.

"Have you found anything?" she broke the silence and his concentration.

"Not really," he looked up at her for a brief moment, and went back to turning pages and reading. "I found exactly what I thought I'd find. There's a lot about Roman and Greek culture . . . technology . . . Zoroastrianism and its influences on later religions . . ."

"Things you already know and have already thought of," she interrupted.

"Exactly," he looked up, now directing his full attention to Noelle. "This is uncharted territory. We're going to have to rely on our own knowledge and make our own theories."

"Rewrite history."

"Precisely."

They both sat in silence for several minutes, searching their minds for new input. They had been going over this constantly, and it was clearly tiring them both. James had barely slept since leaving Dr. Husser's office, despite drinking heavily. He was finding it harder to think critically in the face of near delirium.

"Well, you've made most of the connections for your theory, as radical as they may come off. You've almost got enough for a best-selling book in the academic world," she paused. "The only things that you lack are where the *big machine* may be, what it actually is and that stuff about the *son of God*," Noelle spouted.

"Yeah, that and the number," he continued to ponder.

"What number? I don't remember any number," she puzzled.

"Yeah, the tablet that you discovered included a number. I'd almost forgotten about it, too. I really didn't even pay attention to it when I read the translation." He searched through his pockets, looking for a copy of the translation. He had kept it near him since leaving Yale so that he could recant it when he needed.

He produced a piece of paper, and began reading. "DCLXVI," he read aloud from the sheet. In an instant, his mouth widened in shock, then it transformed into a smile as he placed his hand over his mouth.

"What? What is it?" Noelle was frantic.

"Another piece to the puzzle," he smiled. "DCLXVI is the Roman numeral for six hundred and sixty-six."

"Oh my God!" she was shocked. "All of that stuff that we said sounded like Revelations! James, that's a direct reference to it!"

"On the contrary, I think Revelations is a direct reference to the tablet," he smiled widely, almost beaming. "Remember that the eruption of Vesuvius predates the book of Revelations. Vesuvius erupted in AD 79, and most believe the Book of Revelations to have been written in about AD 96."

"But what does it mean?" she said, confused. "Six-six-six is the mark of the beast. Those who have the mark will feel God's wrath. Is the machine going to only affect those with the mark? That's an impossible notion. An earthquake can't select who it's going to harm."

"That's why I don't think it's a mark at all." The words echoed through Noelle's mind, toppling anything she had ever believed about her faith.

"What do you mean?" Her voice became meek, and perhaps disappointed.

"I think it's some kind of code," his tone was reassuring and warm. "The number appears in Revelations as the mark of the beast, and it appears in an earlier Greek text of Zoroastrian prophecy. That can't be coincidence. We've already gone over the possibility of a connection between St. John and Zoroastrians. It fits perfectly, but how?" They both continued to think.

"A deadline?" Noelle hesitated in saying it. She was in the presence of the most brilliant historian she had ever met. What if he thought she sounded stupid?

James did not respond for several moments. The wheels turned, his face stern and studious. He scratched his head. His eye twitched, and then he looked up.

"I think you may have something," he said to her as she smiled in relief. "Think about it. All this time, people have been trying to figure out what six-six-six actually means. The most popular theory is that it is the numerical value of a name. In the time of Christ, a popular game amongst the Hebrews was to use the number at which each of the letters of someone's name appears in the alphabet to obtain a numerical value for that name."

"Meaning?"

"For instance, *J* comes tenth, *A* comes first, *M* is thirteenth, *E* is fifth and *S* is nineteenth. Add them together and you get the number thirty-eight," he explained.

"Oh, I get it," she understood. "So where's the connection?"

"Most historians believe that six-six-six is the numerical value for Emperor Nero's full name, since Revelations was probably written in his lifetime. But a lot of historians and religious scholars have been trying for years to attach the number to some other ruthless world dictator in search for the foretold antichrist. Some people even thought Ronald Reagan was the Antichrist because each of his three names had six letters."

"Well, it kind of makes sense," she shrugged.

"Does it?" he looked at her inquisitively. "We've stumbled upon something big here. We've found a real-life Apocalypse scenario, and with some intriguing evidence to support it. We're talking about science instead of the hand of God."

Noelle thought about it for a long while, trying to reconcile her religious beliefs with her training in science. It was a difficult notion to swallow. Many people did the same every day. It was the most trying question that faced the religiously devout in this world—faith or science? And Noelle was, in fact, a scientist.

"You're right," she conceded. "But if the number gives a date, what is the date? AD 666?"

"No, that can't be it. This thing would have happened long ago," he began to concentrate again.

"It couldn't be six hundred and sixty-six years after Vesuvius erupted. That would be AD 745," Noelle calculated.

"Actually, it may be more like AD 728. There was a major earthquake at the base of Vesuvius in February of the year 62. That may be when our machine in that cavern went off, and it just took several more years for the eruption to follow."

"The earthquake may have loosened the volcano's plug, and it erupted later. That makes sense," she nodded. "But that still doesn't help us." She paused a moment, and spoke again. "What about the date, June sixth of oh-six?"

James's eyes lit up, as the statement clearly struck a nerve. It was a more feasible explanation. His thoughts began churning as he opened the file cabinets in his brain, searching for the knowledge to validate the idea.

"No," he shook his head, "the event would have happened years ago based on the Roman pre-Julian calendar. That calendar only had three hundred and fifty-five days. Ten days less per year for one thousand, nine hundred and forty-four years gives us a date somewhere in the 1950s. We would have seen the destruction of civilization by now, and we wouldn't be having this conversation."

He continued to think more on the June sixth scenario. It made sense, but he could not figure out how to get it to make better sense. It was the most possible of all of the ideas dealing with six-six-six as a date.

"Wait a minute," the epiphany overtook his emotions and expressions. "So this sect of Zoroastrians would have to know that six-six-six is a date, right? So, throughout history they could pick any date on any calendar they would want."

"You mean use any of the June sixth of oh-six dates throughout the future eons?"

"Precisely," he spoke with confidence. "What if the machine hasn't been running for over two-thousand years? What if it can be started whenever they want? Maybe they just spent centuries looking for the signs that never all seemed to come," he smiled. "Or maybe the sect doesn't exist anymore."

"Signs? What signs?" She had no idea what he was talking about.

"You know, the seven signs in Revelations that the end times are coming," he obviously thought she would have known about them. "Have you never seen one of those stupid *end of the world* movies? They're always about the seven signs and all that crap."

"Sorry," she lifted her hands, shrugging and shaking her head.

"Okay," he prepared to explain, standing up, and scanning his bookshelf. He waved his outstretched right middle and index fingers continuously from left to right and back to the left. He finally rested his eyes and his fingers on one book in particular. He reached for a King James Version of the Holy Bible that had beautiful bindings, but looked as if it were covered in the dust of neglect.

"In Revelations, there are seven seals, seven trumpets, and seven vials poured upon the earth that cause seven plagues," he explained as he opened the Bible and turned to Revelations.

"I'm detecting a nursery rhyme here," she grinned.

"Now, the seven seals are opened, and this sets everything in motion. This is where the natural disasters, famine, and war start. Some claim these are the signs. I guess you can interpret it this way, but I think this is just the beginning."

"Either way, these things are happening every day," Noelle made an important point. "And the trumpets?"

"I say the trumpets are the signs," he turned to chapter eight. "The first is a hail of fire. I see that as a meteor shower."

"There was a meteor shower last month!"

"The second trumpet calls for a burning mountain and sea life dying. Just recently, there have been forest fires in the Sierra Nevadas and there was an oil spill off the coast of Yemen. Apparently, thousands of fish and sea life washed up on the coast, covered with oil." He looked up briefly, then back down

"The third has to do with poisoned waters and a falling star. The falling star seems kind of like the first trumpet, but the poisoned waters . . . . Noelle, there is water pollution all over the world, and it's the worst in history. The fourth trumpet hails the blackening out of the sun, moon and stars."

"Kind of sounds like air pollution to me," she said.

"The fifth trumpet is a falling star—I could go on, but I don't need to. All of this is happening. John of Patmos even predicts wars in the Middle East with self-propelled, fire-breathing chariots like tanks and flying creatures with stringy hair that make the noise of a thousand horses—helicopters," he closed the Bible, and looked directly into her eyes. "War in Iraq."

"So what does all this mean?" she asked, frustrated. "Why didn't this thing happen on June 6, 1406? Why didn't it happen on June 6, 1806?"

"God only knows. Look, people have been interpreting the Bible and all of the other religious books and prophecies differently for centuries. The Mayans, the Chinese *I Ching*, Merlin and the Bible all have their end of the world scenarios, which are surprisingly alike and accurate so far. Maybe no one in the past has seen all of the signs come together at the same time, and around the right date. Maybe no one in the past ever came forward to announce that he was the Shaoshant. Maybe the sect doesn't exist anymore.

"So where does this leave us?" she was about to give up. "What do you make of it? Mystery solved?" She smiled. "That's it?"

"Noelle . . ." James turned his head to the left, toward a Hurricane Katrina relief fundraising calendar on the wall. He studied the picture printed there, noting the horror of the natural disaster that killed and displaced so many people. His mind drifted to the carnage of God's wrath and the apocalyptic measures of similar disasters world-wide. Then his eyes fell to the dates below the picture and spoke again.

"Noelle, June 6, 2006, is four days away." He took on a look of concern. "Let's say this thing exists. What if the sect does, too? What if they have seen the signs? What if they can still start the mechanism?"

Chapter 19

Khalim followed his Shaoshant deep into the tunnel beneath the sacred place. As his eyes became more transfixed upon the luminous glow stick his leader was carrying, he began to think. *How far does devotion go? Is our way the right way?* Khalim had always thought that the Shaoshant would come someday and Ahura Mazda himself would rain fire upon the wicked. He thought it would be a supernatural occurrence; something more literal. He never thought that the Shaoshant would come in his lifetime, and he certainly did not think that the end of the world would come by this means.

He tried to sweep the blasphemous thoughts from his mind as he navigated the narrow passageway, his knuckles often scraping against the quasi-jagged stone surrounding him. He clung to the words of the Shaoshant as they were walking on the mount. He knew he had to keep to his faith. That was the most important thing to do in any religion. The Avesta foretold of this, and he had to have faith that this man was indeed the Shaoshant who would usher in the last days and the wrath of God.

The passageway got slightly wider, and just as before, they suddenly felt the open space that was the sacred cavern. It was darker and colder than the last time. There were no fires burning. The quiet was eerie with no faithful followers chanting praises to the almighty. It all felt different. Their duties here seemed to Khalim to be so much colder and crueler. He winced momentarily as he looked around, shuttering in his gut.

The Shaoshant lit a torch fixed onto the wall on both sides of him as he entered. Beyond him, the cavern was only slightly more illuminated, but it did not matter. He knew this place well, and his feet and memory alone would guide him to his destination.

He began to traverse the dark, empty room with ease as Khalim trailed only a few steps behind, following the Shaoshant's freshly-lit torch, which came to seem a beacon of truth. The blessed savior came to a sudden halt, as did the torch. Khalim saw the fire from the torch slowly fall and become a falling meteor. The flames moved like they did before, first laterally, and then back around many a corner to surround completely the large object that became the focal point of the room.

Khalim was again mesmerized by it. He still had difficulty imagining how his ancient predecessors had managed to build such a thing. The only conclusion that he could come to was that this was truly God's work. He smiled with reverence. His wavering faith was returned to that of the devotion that had been instilled in him by his father and grandfather.

His eyes and his head turned upward as would a tourist visiting a large city for the first time. He carefully studied the contraption to the finest detail. He noticed that the main components were bronze, which surprisingly showed little corrosion. There was an enormous container made of bronze that was fixed upon a bronze beam. The other end of the beam rested diagonally at the base of the mechanism, directly above a wooden beam, but not touching. The container at the other end was high at the top of the machine, just below another large container that did not seem to be a part of the contraption itself.

That part of the mechanism hinged on a large bolt fixed in the center of a huge, square plate with notches carved horizontally and extending vertically from the top to the bottom. All of the metallic components were attached to a larger frame consisting of very large, but simple wooden beams.

It was a simple, cube-shaped main frame that rose from the floor of the cavern to the badly cracked and unstable ceiling above. Khalim noticed that the wooden frame seemed to even support the stone ceiling, as if it would fall should the frame be removed. The main box-shaped frame was supported by numerous cross beams, joined to the frame by iron spikes.

"Amazing, isn't it," the Shaoshant spoke in Persian, as he placed his left hand on Khalim's right shoulder.

"It is, Master," he spoke in awe, his eyes still fixed upon the mechanism of doom.

"It took many centuries for the wooden frame of this glorious device to rot enough," the Shaoshant began walking toward the machine.

He walked to the right, and picked up an axe hidden away by the mass of one of the lower wooden beams. The Shaoshant stood next to a thick rope that Khalim had not noticed before, but now traced upward with his eyes. The end of the rope was attached to the bottom of the bronze container that loomed above the machine. He noticed that the container sat upon another metal pole that was fixed horizontally to the rock on either side of it.

The aging Shaoshant said a barely audible prayer as he held the axe high above his head. Khalim squinted his eyes as he leaned his right ear in his leader's direction, trying his hardest to hear what the man was saying, but it was no use. As unexpectedly as the axe had appeared from behind the frame of the machine, it fell with speed and accuracy in the hands of the priest, cutting easily through the thick rope.

The now severed rope traveled quickly with a brief whistling sound upward in the direction of the container, as the bronze vat toppled, pivoting on its supporting rod. With a deafening roar, the torrent of water that was contained inside went crashing down into the empty container affixed to the beam. The other end of the beam immediately and swiftly shot to the top notch on the plate as the bolt that it hinged on groaned with the sound of ages of rust and neglect. The now full container of water was simultaneously rocketed to the bottom, and immediately began leaking a relatively small amount of the water inside.

"You see, by the time this container is empty, it will be back at the top, and the other end," he pointed to the lower part of the frame, "will come crashing against the wood. It will snap easily," he said in admiration. "The machine will consume itself and the world will come crumbling down with the top of this cavern."

"Ahura Mazda be praised," Khalim choked quietly, fear in his eyes and doubt in this voice.

"Do not worry," the Shaoshant consoled his young follower with a warm and sympathetic glance. "God's warriors who die in His service will be rewarded greatly. You have but to perform your honorable duty."

He handed Khalim a Chinese-made AK-47 assault rifle that had previously been leaning against the machine. He then handed him an extra magazine for the weapon, already loaded with bullets. Khalim stared at the rifle in his hands, which were trembling with a combination of fear and overwhelming honor. He then brought his troubled gaze back to the warm smile on his master's face.

"This is a dangerous and wicked time, Khalim," he again placed his hand on the young man's shoulder. "There may arise a betrayer of prophecy who you will need to confront. You must be aware that there is a way to permanently shut down the machine. You see, there are those who would prevent the will of Ahura Mazda from being carried out. Think of your own father. Think of the end he met at the hands of the vile oppressors at home in Iran. Those people are evil and misguided by myth and legend, as are most people in the world. They do not revere or respect Ahura Mazda. You must harness your fear into faith, and guard this place with your life."

Khalim drifted to thoughts of his father, his face bloody and broken and surrounded by heavy stones in the dust. He grew even more afraid than before at the thought of being alone in this cavern as he watched the Shaoshant pick up his still-lit torch, and begin walking toward the exit.

"Fear not," he said, without turning back toward Khalim, "I will be back before the end comes. Remember, part of my duty is martyrdom, too."

Chapter 20

The hour was growing late at the Beauregard house; James and Noelle were still in the study discussing the issue at hand. They were both growing tired. James had still not showered. He felt nasty. Until that point, he had been too focused on research to care. The grime of dry sweat mixed with dead skin cells coated his body in an invisible film that was undetectable except for the feeling and occasional mild odor.

One piece of the puzzle still lingered just beyond grasp, and it was becoming a nuisance. Both of the scholars were trying to understand a bit of information that would bring everything together, but it was unattainable.

"Okay, what does Jesus have to do with all this?" Noelle wondered. "I mean, I can see why Jesus may be involved because of the Bible. But I thought all this was Zoroastrianism. Why would the tablet have read *only the key that lies with God's son* will save everyone?"

"I know, I know," he replied, frustrated as well. "It doesn't make a damned bit of sense. It makes sense that the tomb may be in the Holy Land, but the key can't be in the tomb of Jesus Christ."

"Why not? It read that the key lies with the son of God. Jesus is the only son of God I know."

"Noelle," he switched to teacher mode, "first of all, both of the tombs in Jerusalem that people believe are Christ's tomb are empty. Even the Bible says that Jesus rose from the dead, so how can the key lie with him anyway?"

"That's true," she admitted. "Maybe that's why it seems so lofty and unattainable."

"Furthermore," he continued, "even though the eruption of Vesuvius was after the crucifixion, the text on the tablet was in Greek, telling me that it predates Christ by centuries."

"I'm still stuck on the *son of God* thing, though."

"You have to remember that in those days, there were a lot of religions being practiced in the Mediterranean area and the Middle East other than mighty Christianity, and certainly before Christianity," he said. "So in fact, there were a lot of *sons of God*. Hercules was a son of Zeus. Perseus was son of Poseidon. Demigods. Pharaohs were seen to be gods on earth, and they had sons and the same goes for emperors of Rome.

He began thinking further on all of the offspring of deities throughout the ancient religions. He was searching for one that may have significance in their puzzle. He began mouthing their names silently, and shaking his head after each one, eliminating their possibility.

"Hell, Alexander the Great was even proclaimed the son of a god!" he threw his hands into the air, about to give up.

"Alexander? Really?" Noelle admitted her ignorance.

"Well, yeah," he nodded. "He had been told from childhood that Zeus had knocked up his mortal mother. I always thought of it as just a story his mother told to keep her from looking so adulterous. But after Alexander became king of Macedonia at the age of twenty, he set his sights on conquering the east, particularly the Persian Empire. It was thought at the time that one of the possible assassins of his father, Phillip II, was sent by the king of Persia, Darius III. But before he went about conquering the bulk of Persia, he conquered Egypt, which didn't put up much of a fight. He traveled to the desert oracle of Siwa, where it was revealed to him that he was, indeed, the son of Zeus-Amen."

"Zeus-Amen?"

"Sort of a corporate merger of the chief gods of Greece and Egypt," he explained. "Anyway, this emboldened him even more, because he now equated himself with the greatest of all demi-gods, Heracles."

"Don't you mean Hercules?" she tried to correct him.

"No, Hercules was the Roman equivalent of the Greek Heracles."

"Okay, okay. Go on."

"Right, so," he continued, "after being proclaimed a demi-god by the priests in Egypt and also proclaimed Pharaoh, he began conquering Persia, and soon took Babylon."

"Babylon?" she was confused. "I thought you said he was conquering Persia, not Babylonia."

"Today, the only remaining part of Persia is Iran—this much is true. But in those days, Persia conquered the Tigris and Euphrates valley, including Babylon, which became the Persian capitol, and then pushed west toward Judea and into Asia Minor, or present-day Turkey."

"Oh," she said. "I got it," she smiled. "See why I'm a geologist? Not a right-brained person at all."

"So Alexander took Babylon," he continued, "and almost immediately took on the role of Persian Emperor. He even proclaimed that Babylon was his new capitol, began wearing Persian clothing, and took up Persian customs before moving out on his invasion of India."

"You said he took up Persian customs?" she inquired.

"Yes."

"Would that include religions?"

"How do you mean?"

"Didn't you say that Zoroastrianism was a Persian religion?" she explained her question.

James's eyes widened as he stared downward. He began running his hand through his hair, thinking about the implications that arose with that simple question. He went over every possible historical fact that he knew about the subject, and looked at them from every conceivable point of view.

"Oh my God!" he suddenly uttered. "Why didn't I see this before? Noelle, that's brilliant!"

"Why thank you," she smiled, and mocked a curtsy. "But now you have to explain to me why I'm so brilliant."

"All this that I've been talking about is evidence to prove that Alexander was notorious for picking up local customs wherever he conquered," he said breathily. "Why should religion be any different?"

"You mean you think Alexander the Great became a Zoroastrian?" she seemed to doubt it a bit.

"Not only that," he continued. "What if he became a prominent figure in the religion? He was perceived by so many of his men and the people of Egypt to be descended from divinity because of the speed and ease in which he conquered the known world. Look how much he accomplished by the time he died in Babylon at only the age of thirty-three!"

He paused a moment in Noelle's silence to solidify his thoughts before making his point. As always, he had to be precise, punctuating his speech with his fingers and hand gestures.

"If the Persians, particularly the Zoroastrians, perceived him the same way the Macedonians and Egyptians did," he said slowly and carefully, first looking downward, and then toward Noelle, "he could have convinced them that he was one of the foretold saviors that would visit earth. So he could be the *son of God* the tablet mentioned!"

Noelle was silent, looking over James's shoulder, lost in her own thoughts. She was trying her best to understand these new ideas and reconcile them with all of the religious beliefs she had been taught. It was frightening to her to think this way. Was she going to Hell for even entertaining the ideas that she had been hearing? She began to panic and speak swiftly and irrationally.

"So what now, James?" she stood up, all previous wonder exiting her expression. "Go off in search of the tomb of Alexander?"

"Why not? People have been looking for it for two thousand years. Wouldn't you want that discovery on your resume?"

"James!" she raised her voice slightly. "Do you realize that on the ruins of Babylon stands the city of Baghdad? If you want to go and get your ass shot off, be my guest! I'm going back to New Haven first thing in the morning!"

"Noelle," he said calmly and patiently, "we wouldn't be going to Baghdad."

"I thought you said Alexander died in Babylon," she calmed a bit.

"He died in Babylon, yes. But his best general, Ptolemy brought his body back to Memphis for burial upon taking up his rule of Egypt."

"So if this is a known fact, don't they know where the tomb is already?"

"No, not many have seen Alexander's body since sometime in the late Roman period. Some notable Arabs claimed to have seen it as late as the sixteenth century, but there is no mention of the location. You see, his body, most historians agree, was removed from its original resting place in the third century BC and placed in a tomb in Alexandria called the *sema*, or *body*. Some say it was brought there by some sort of Alexander cult. There, it remained on public display until the fourth century. It is, in fact, in Alexandria, I think. We just have to find it."

"This doesn't change anything," she became flustered again. "If you want to go off on some stupid adventure, go right ahead! I'm going home."

With that, Noelle turned briskly to exit the room. She had every intention of marching straight into her room, locking the door and packing her things to leave first thing the next morning. But before she could get more than three steps away from him, James rushed behind her, grabbing her left arm softly, but firmly. He spun her around in Humphrey Bogart fashion, and held her close to him, a shoulder in each hand. He looked deep into her eyes.

"Noelle, I need you," he said quite sincerely. "I need you to come with me. I can't do this alone."

"What if you're wrong? What if there's nothing out there? What if this mechanism doesn't exist?"

"Then at least it will be a fun adventure," he smiled. "But what if it does exist? If we do nothing . . ."

"Then let's tell the authorities," she reached for another argument.

"Tell them what?" he reasoned. "That there's some secret, ancient cult out there threatening mankind with an ancient earthquake machine?" It sounded more ridiculous than he thought. "You tell me, what would happen if a series of earthquakes were triggered in a wave worldwide?"

"Chaos," she shook her head tiredly. "Infrastructure would be gone. People would riot over supplies. Governments would be powerless . . ."

"We rely on technology and telecommunications and supermarkets," he finished. "No access to bank accounts. Markets would run out of food. I don't know how to hunt or farm . . . , do you? Power grids and utilities. Fires and crumbled cities. Primitive behavior . . ." he paused. "*Chaos* doesn't even begin to say it."

James released her shoulders slowly, imploring from his eyes to hers that she accept his plea and not continue to march off to her room. He waited eagerly hanging on to her every gesture and expression, until she sighed.

"Okay," she looked into his eyes, and then pointed her finger into his face, "but you pay for everything."

"Alright," he nodded, and smiled into her smile, "I wouldn't have it any other way."

Chapter 21

"God, this is going to be a long flight," James swallowed another healthy gulp of his bourbon and Coke.

Noelle watched him in entertainment as he repeated the flight ritual that he had before on the way from New Haven to New Orleans and on their connecting flight to Miami, before heading to Alexandria. He was clinging to his drink as if it would save him from death in an emergency, and drinking it without restriction to boost his courage. He was opening and shutting the window shade repeatedly, trying to decide whether or not he wanted to see his demise coming. She attempted to console him, or at least distract him, by conversation.

"So where do we look for the tomb in Alexandria?"

"Well, most accounts give the location of the Sema at the intersection of the main north-south and east-west routes through the old city," he replied shakily. "Last night, I looked at a modern map of the city. Many excavations were made at the intersection of Horreya Street and Nebi-Daniel Street, which are the streets believed to be the ancient routes mentioned in the accounts."

"Did they ever find anything?"

"Yes and no," he said, drinking more of his bourbon and Coke. "They found a lot of old Roman ruins, but nothing indicating a tomb. You see, most believe the very public tomb of Alexander was hidden because of vandalism and looting during some turbulent times. So, obviously the authorities didn't want anyone knowing where it was, and it was lost."

"So, how are we supposed to find it? What if these authorities were Zoroastrians who hid it for their own purposes?" she asked pessimistically.

"Some of the most credible accounts of Arab authorities through the centuries claim that the tomb is directly beneath the Nebi-Daniel Mosque at that intersection."

"So, if so many people think it is there, then why haven't they gone in and found the tomb?"

"There have been some concerns about the integrity of the foundations of the mosque being compromised by excavations, so not much has been done to dig around in the chambers beneath, which are much older than the mosque itself, I might add."

"So what makes you think that the authorities are going to let you dig around?" she said with a slight sneer.

"I don't plan on asking the authorities," he smiled.

Immediately, the plane shook with unexpected turbulence. The rest of the passengers did not react, but James could not help but shudder. Noelle merely smiled at his terror, sure that they were quite safe.

"It's okay, dear," she patted his leg, "only ten more hours to go."

Chapter 22

James propped his head up on his fist, grinning out the window of the cab hurdling down the streets of Alexandria. He loved being in new places; seeing new combinations of culture. Alexandria was an interesting cultural melting pot. Its history extended far into the fourth century BC. It was a city founded by Greece's greatest conqueror and one of its most revered national heroes. Its grandeur was surpassed by few in the ancient world and the modern eras alike.

James admired all aspects of the exotic Mediterranean city he was in. He marveled in silent awe from his taxi window, as did Noelle, who had been outside of the United States only a few times.

Most features in the more common areas of Alexandria were not unlike those of most desert-located and Muslim-ruled states in the world. Many of the homes and shops in the city were made of mud brick and even sandstone if the builders were wealthier. Mosques dotted the scenery, almost literally on every corner. There were, of course, very old mosques that were eighth century stone mega-structures complete with towering minarets and pointed dome rotundas. There were also modern mosques that dated to only a few years before and featured sheetrock walls and central air conditioning.

The Nile delta's jewel of a port, however, was built by the Greeks, so it possessed very few features that were distinctively ancient Egyptian. Instead, old and new structures tended to display a Greco-Roman flair, some subtle and some very obvious. Greek and Roman buildings that were still in good condition included various former temples and monuments, and most were used today only as tourist attractions. Furthermore, every year, archaeologists unearthed buried and long-forgotten ruins of Roman administrative buildings and Greek theatres. In its heyday, the city must have been a spectacle, crowned with its famous library and lighthouse, both long ago destroyed by fires and earthquakes.

The city that James and Noelle observed took on even further levels of diversity as the sun began to fall and Arabic songs calling for the final prayer of the day echoed through the streets. All over, native Egyptians unrolled their prayer mats and fell to their knees in worship. Near them, western tourists snapped photos of the ancient structures and Muslims practicing one of their most sacred rituals. James sneered a little, shaking his head as they passed.

At the same time, he was amazed at how western the ancient city had become. Because Egypt as a government had no real hostility towards westerners, and was part of the British Empire at one time, Alexandria had become an Islamic version of cities like New York and London. Pizza Huts appeared where once-majestic Greek buildings once stood. Roman roads were paved over with asphalt. There were coffee shops with free wi-fi next to thousand-year-old mosques and a McDonald's in every district and neighborhood.

One of the most profound features of the city was the coastal areas that lined the Mediterranean. One visits Egypt expecting to see pyramids and mummies. In visiting Alexandria, few would envision a part of the city that reminded them of the French Riviera. Refreshing breezes whistled over the deep blue waters to soothe sweating inhabitants. With resort hotels towering above the numerous palm trees and extremely old buildings intermingled, the coastal section of Alexandria was Marseilles, Barcelona, Rome and Panama City Beach all rolled into one.

At last, with a beautiful view of the sun setting over the Mediterranean just behind them, the taxi carried the pair of scholars to the façade of the El-Salamlek Palace Hotel, and parked at the curb outside the main entrance.

The hotel wasn't quite what James had imagined. He half expected some Greek or Egyptian temple replica—something to go along with the history and culture of the city. Instead, the structure was more like a Parisian art-deco building. It was beautiful, though not very large, and only two stories. It had been originally built by a former king as a hunting lodge. Today, its few but enormous rooms accommodated the wealthiest of visitors to Alexandria.

Outside, the hotel was constructed of the finest stone, with rectangular recesses adorning the lower sections of the façade. The expansive windows on the lower level were all to the lobby, and the ones on the second floor were to the rooms. They were arched with lavish balconies, complete with wrought-iron furniture so that patrons could enjoy breakfast and coffee on a mild Mediterranean morning.

James and Noelle entered the lobby and approached the front desk; a bellhop following close behind with their limited luggage cases. They admired the luxury of the construction and furnishings in the lobby, with its perfectly polished marble floors, high ceilings, beautiful chandeliers and top-of-the-line, hand-crafted furniture.

They quickly made their way to the desk and signed the appropriate paperwork before leading their bellhop across the expansive lobby to the elevator. After the short ride to the floor above, they walked to suite two, their luxury room, inserted the key and turned it, clicking the door open with ease.

They stepped in, James first and then Noelle, their eyes immediately widening as they soaked in all of the radiance of the room. The fine, crimson carpeting was impeccably well-maintained and accented by slightly darker square designs and flecks of gold. Covering the walls were old-world paintings dating as far back as two hundred years. The room was decorated with small antique tables, vases full of fresh flowers and fine drapes framing the towering windows. The furnishings could not have been chosen better. The television was placed inside a nineteenth-century armoire, which was positioned directly across from the four-post bed. In the next room was a seating area with antique coffee tables and exquisitely upholstered mahogany chairs and sofas. The room was covered with gold, from the crystal chandelier to the flooring.

As James handed the bellhop a hefty tip, he caught a glimpse of Noelle briskly walking toward the balcony, a dazzling smile on her pretty face. She opened the glass doors to catch the last rays of sunlight tracing across the sea and illuminating the skyline. Her view of the beachfront was as breathtaking as the room was.

"James," she said breathily as the bellhop exited and closed the door, "this place is beautiful. This is the nicest hotel I've ever been in."

"Yeah," he looked around smiling, "pretty nice. Beats the hell out of the Howard Johnson."

Their eyes met briefly, then their gazes diverted elsewhere before meeting again for a prolonged period of time. Their attraction to one another was unmistakable at this point. They slowly moved closer to one another, but not to the point of intimacy. There they stood before each other in silence, each willing the other to say the first word.

"So," James broke the silence, "we know what tomorrow holds. What about tonight? Wanna go out? See the town?"

"No," she smiled and moved closer to him. "I have a better idea," she said softly, and leaned in to kiss him gently.

Chapter 23

James sat at the small, but beautifully crafted white iron table perched upon his balcony overlooking the Mediterranean morning. It always seemed that humans could never quite replicate that particular shade of blue. It was early, and though it was Egypt in the summertime, the winds from across the sea kept the city cool. He pulled the fine Egyptian cotton robe, compliments of the hotel, together across his chest as the wind blew across his balcony. With his other hand, he lifted a fine bone China coffee cup from the table and brought it to his lips.

He savored the aroma and the taste of the sweetened liquid. Ethiopian coffee was a bit oily for his taste, but nevertheless much better than any of the conventional freeze-dried brands that he could purchase in supermarkets back home.

He lowered the cup back to the table, placing it near the other breakfast paraphernalia. There were China plates stacked with Danishes and muffins, shadowed by taller silver vessels containing fresh brewed coffee, cream, and tea. The sunlight was shimmering from the surfaces of these well-polished items, creating a fine ballet of luxury on his table.

He peered into the room through the panes of glass at Noelle, still sleeping in the four-post, king-sized bed. He admired her radiance and tranquility as she lay there beneath the fine linen sheets. He smiled sweetly, silently sipping his coffee. She made him feel warm and needed, something he had not felt in some time.

After Abigail had passed, any woman James had encountered eventually soured his emotions; a feeling like he had been unfaithful. Strangely, he didn't feel that way about Noelle. His thoughts began to fall into the realm of fantasy, wondering what it would be like to marry her. He tried to imagine if he would continue to see her after they parted. Or would she feel uncomfortable upon waking. He silently prayed that she would feel as he did, or at least have no remorse. She did, after all, seduce him. It would be a shame to have the remainder of their excursion into the ancient world marred by the discomfort of a regrettable fling.

Noelle's eyes were opening, and the first thing they focused on was a piece of nineteenth-century art on the opposite wall from the balcony. She did not move, her body mostly covered, except her head and her back, which was turned to James. As her consciousness caught up to her eyes, she began to finally remember where she was and what had happened the previous night.

Immediately, as with most women, these first thoughts conjured a feeling of regret. It was the instinctive reaction. They were not married, and with her proper upbringing, the first feelings were negative.

These feelings passed, however, and the regret faded into a warm feeling of slight emotional attachment. The thought of James's smiling face and strong arms around her caused her to grin uncontrollably and pull the sheets up to her chin in happiness.

As she began to move, she knew that to James, she was unmistakably awake, so she sat up, choosing not to cover herself with the sheets. She stepped out of bed, completely nude, as she observed his inability to divert his eyes. He was as a young boy on Christmas morning, amazed and ecstatic with the gifts before his eyes. She stepped, one foot in front of the other in perfect posture, toward the glass doors. Her eyes still carried the look of sensuality, golden in the morning sun, and mystified by the dark brown locks around them. She looked as a goddess with the sunlight glowing from her tanned body, as she opened the glass door and stood silently, gazing at James.

He was unable to stop smiling, sending her a message with his eyes that he reciprocated affection toward her. He couldn't imagine what he would tell her. He searched his thoughts for witty, affectionate, and even sarcastic comments that she would appreciate.

"I'd offer you a muffin and some coffee," he motioned to the breakfast on the small table, "but it seems you have other things on your mind," he grinned coyly.

"James," she smiled devilishly, summoning him with the bending of her right index finger, "you have work to do, and then . . . we have work to do."

"Then by all means," he set his coffee cup down and stood, "I've never been one to disappoint the boss," he began moving in her direction.

Chapter 24

The streets were already bustling with people as James and Noelle's taxi roared through the streets of Alexandria. The driver was silent, slightly bobbing his head to the rhythm of modern Arabic music from the radio as it filled the cab. The people on the streets, some tourist, some locals on their way to work, blurred by as James was sure the driver was traveling at a far higher speed than the law permitted.

From his window, he could see the remnants of eras past. The archaeological sites by the street displayed Egyptian sphinxes alongside Roman columns and theaters; a testament to the long and diverse history of the ancient city.

The cab turned onto Horreya Street and began heading toward its major intersection with Nebi-Daniel Street in the near distance. They could see the minarets and pitched dome of the Mosque of Nebi-Daniel looming in the distance above the increasingly heavy traffic below. This meant very little to Noelle except a chance to see a historic structure and participate in the culture of a land far different from her own.

James, however, had a quite different reaction to the mosque ahead. His heart dropped into the pit of his stomach, and he began to feel a little queasy as his thoughts ran amuck. There had been few instances in his life where he had felt the same sensation. He felt a combination of nervousness and excitement. There was hope and doubt. He had experienced this feeling on his wedding day and when his son was born. It was as if he were anticipating getting into trouble for something, though there was really nothing of the sort involved.

The car crossed the intersection and pulled up to the curb just in the shadow of the façade of the mosque. The two scholars exited the cab, and James reached into his back pocket to retrieve his wallet. He promptly paid the driver, who shot him a peculiar look. He knew exactly what the man was thinking, shifting his eyes from James to Noelle, and then back to James. He was first wondering what these Americans, who were almost certainly not Muslims, were doing entering one of the more famous mosques in Alexandria. More importantly, though the woman was wearing jeans instead of shorts, she, in her white tank top, was dressed way too liberally to enter such a holy place. Religious clerics inside would never allow her to enter the premises dressed in that manner.

It was not his concern, however, so he took the money from James's hand, and sped away without a word, leaving the two travelers staring up at the impressive and imposing complex with their hands shading their eyes from the blinding Egyptian sun.

The two beautiful pointed domes reached toward the heavens with splendid stone craftsmanship. They were framed all around by lower, off-white walls with raised decorative notches that were reminiscent of the battlements of a European medieval fortress. Though this was a newer mosque than many in the Muslim world, perhaps these archers' notches were a bit of a tradition, considering the experience Muslims had gained through the ages in defending their important buildings from Christian invaders.

"Moment of truth," Noelle turned her head, smiling at her counterpart.

"Yeah, well first we have to find a way in," he said without returning the smile.

"What do you mean?" she motioned toward the main entrance of the mosque. "The front door is right there."

"We have to be a little stealthier than that," he explained as he led her in the direction of the side of the mosque complex. "We're about to go snooping around where we're not wanted. Besides, you're not exactly dressed for church."

"So what would happen if they caught us *snooping around?*" she used the middle and index fingers on both hands to mimic quotation marks.

"I don't know," he shrugged, "but according to the stories from over the last couple of centuries, it seems that someone knows that something is down there, but they don't want anyone to find it."

"Who doesn't want anyone to find it? The government? The mosque officials?"

"Don't know. I don't think so. I mean, if the government knew there was an important find down there, I would think that they would be overjoyed to discover it," he puzzled.

"What happened in these stories you're talking about?"

"Well, the one that sticks in my mind," he began, "is a story about a city engineer in the mid-1800s. Apparently, he was assigned the task of trying to make a map of what the city would have looked like in antiquity. He claimed that while looking around in the crypt below the mosque, he found a passageway that no one had previously known about."

"What happened? Where did it lead?"

"No one knows. He never went down it. He was forbidden to go back into the crypt and his project was shut down."

"Wow, sounds suspicious," she smiled jokingly. "Sounds like we have a conspiracy theory on our hands."

He smiled as the two of them walked one of the side walls of the mosque's exterior until they suddenly came to a stop at a side door. It seemed as though the door was new, painted gray and with a modern deadbolt. There was a small, metal handle, but no doorknob. He analyzed the situation before extracting his wallet and reaching into one of its pockets. When he pulled his fingers from the depths of the slot in his wallet, two black metal objects appeared.

"What's that?" Noelle tried to lean in for a closer look.

"Lock picks," he held the objects up. He revealed to her two simple tools for picking locks. The first of the objects was a small L-shaped bar, and the other was a long, thin, wavy bar that somewhat resembled a serpent.

"History professor by day, and cat burglar by night," she smirked. "Why in the hell do you carry a set of lock picks on you?"

"I was a boy scout—*always be prepared*," he smiled. "Besides," he began working on the deadbolt, "when you come home drunk as much as I do, you tend to misplace your keys."

He placed the short end of the L-shaped bar into the bottom of the vertical slot in the deadbolt with the long end pointing to the right. With his left index finger, he applied clockwise pressure in the bar as he inserted the serpent tool into the top of the keyhole. He began raking the bar across the pins in the locking cylinder in an attempt to mimic the action of a proper key and cause the pins to align correctly, turning the mechanism. He repeated the raking action, glancing occasionally at Noelle, who was giving him a look that seemed to say, *I thought you were going to be an expert at this.*

"Yes!" James celebrated as the cylinder turned over and the deadbolt retracted from the hole in the door frame.

"It's about time," she heckled him. "I could have tunneled under the place in that amount of time."

"Smartass," he shot back as he carefully and quietly pulled the heavy metal door open.

He suddenly became a little more nervous as he poked his head into the slightly open door. He wasn't sure who, if anyone, would be on the other side. The thought of breaking and entering in a foreign country became less appealing of an idea. But there was no turning back.

Nervously, he turned his head from right to left, and then back again. His eyes scanned what seemed to be the main worship area of the mosque. He could tell that by the typical setup of the room. The floor plan was wide open, and quite large enough to accommodate a vast crowd of Friday worshippers. It was not an ancient mosque, yet being built in the eighteenth century, it wasn't new either. It wasn't carpeted like some of the modern mosques he had been to in the United States. Its floor was of a simple, polished gray marble, which was crowned by many traditional arches, pillars, mihrab niches that show the direction of Mecca, and Minbar pulpits that reminded him of the staircases and pulpits of American-colonial Episcopalian churches.

There were no pews in a mosque. It was not like Christian places of worship or Jewish temples and synagogues. Muslims were much more participatory in their weekly mass worship. They knelt and bowed. They chanted and meditated.

After a very long moment, James became more comfortable that no one was around to see them. It was not a Friday, and though there were surely clerics in the complex, they must have been in their respective offices or sanctuaries. He quickly moved the rest of his body through the slightly ajar doorway, and pulled Noelle in behind him. He wanted to make sure no one would see the bright sunlight beaming in through the open door. He did not need anything to draw attention to their presence. He promptly and quietly closed the door behind him, and turned the deadbolt back into its previous locked position.

"Okay," Noelle whispered, "what now? Where do we start looking?"

"I'm not sure," he answered, his eyes darting from one end of the expansive room to the other. "But wherever it is, we had better get to it quickly. There's not a lot in here to hide behind."

"I hope no one's watching," she began to seem worried as she scanned the area for signs of human life.

"I don't see anyone," he reassured her. "But I've got a weird feeling."

"Like what?"

"Like we're being watched."

Chapter 25

The mild Mediterranean breeze swept through the small Israeli town of Meggido, caressing the buildings and passersby while providing some relief from the brutal summer heat. It was not desert country like one would find further east, but the plains region in northern Israel could get a bit hot during the summer months. This day, however, was blessed by an uncommonly mild temperature provided by that westerly wind.

The long, wiry beard that the Shaoshant wore protruded far below his chin. The blend of white and gray strands shook and blew about along with the white robes and headdress that he adorned. He silently thanked Ahura Mazda for the cooling breeze, counting it a slight reprieve before his devastating will would be carried out.

The narrow streets were bustling with people for a small town. All manner of locals pushed on about their business, visiting the shops and living their lives completely oblivious to the sinister plot unfolding in the ruined fortress near them. The Shaoshant liked to watch them, wondering what was happening in their minds. Were they devout in their Jewish faith? Did they have great reverence for their god? Or had they been swept up in the secular and wicked world? It wasn't the technology and worldliness that made them wicked; it was the precedence that the secular took over God.

He turned his attention back to his own private table and the bowl of couscous he was having for lunch at the open-air café. The bowl of steamed grains created a medley of warm, natural flavors in his mouth with every bite.

His lunch was abruptly and rudely interrupted by the annoying ring tone chiming from his little black cellular phone. It was enough to startle him, then bring a scowl to his face. He hated cell phones; they represented everything that was wrong with this world. People were more concerned with being in touch with one another than being in touch with God. It did not matter to him which god, but just God in general. The cell phone represented a world that was preoccupied with career, rather than children. It represented a world that was addicted to money and material things. He hated his cell phone, yet it was unfortunately a necessary evil. He reluctantly picked up his phone.

"Yes," he opened the phone with a wince in his expression and verbally greeted the caller in Persian.

"There is a problem, Master," the man answered.

"The mosque?"

"Yes."

"And who is it?" he raised his eyebrows. "The Egyptian government? Treasure hunters?"

"They do not appear to be local government officials. I think they are Americans," the voice rang in the Shaoshant's ear.

"Ah, then they probably are treasure hunters or glory-seekers," he combed his beard in a downward motion with his fingers, as if in deep thought. "You know what to do."

"Yes, Master. I will take care of it."

The Shaoshant closed his mobile phone and set it down on the table. He closed his eyes for a brief moment as if to say a prayer. But upon opening his eyes, he did not look reassured. He was deeply troubled, tapping his fingers nervously on the table. *I must warn Khalim.*

Chapter 26

James and Noelle slowly walked through the common worship area of the Nebi-Daniel Mosque, their eyes wandering in all directions in search of any clue that might lead them to the vaults, and possibly the elusive tomb in question. However, the tomb of Alexander was not the only thing on their minds and was not the only thing they kept their eyes peeled for. There was a kind of paranoia that loomed about as they tried to remain alert to their surroundings and who may come stepping from behind one of the massive columns or from the side doorways.

They were not sure what would happen if they were to be caught snooping around in the mosque. Would they be simply shooed away for visiting without a tour group? Would they be ushered out because they were Americans who clearly were not Muslim? Would they be seen as tomb hunters, bandits or vandals? What would happen if someone discovered that they had broken in rather than walking through the front entrance?

They both tried to be mindful of the way that they stepped across the beautifully polished floor. Noelle felt confident in her step, as she was wearing very comfortable, new running shoes. James, however, cringed with each step he took forward, and so did Noelle. He often went long periods of time without buying new shoes. It did not matter that he had plenty of money. He simply was not interested in shopping for clothes or shoes. Nearly every day he wore the same brown leather, ankle-high boots. They were badly scuffed at the toes and the rubber treads on the bottom were beginning to become non-existent. The brown nylon laces had frayed at the ends and were wearing away at the eyelets that they were run through. More importantly, they squeaked each time he stepped down on the left heel, and Noelle was beginning to give him the look of a wife that implores her husband to just get rid of those damned things.

"So what are we looking for, Doctor?" Noelle grinned as she glanced briefly at James to her left.

"Not sure," he scanned the room. "Don't you kind of just wish there were a big neon sign above a passageway that read *Alexander's Tomb?*"

Up ahead to the left there was a well-lit passageway, framed by a doorway in the form of a pointed Arabic arch. The two colleagues advanced across the room carefully for fear that someone would be roaming down the hallway. They approached far enough to see that the path was empty. The rooms that lined the corridor looked to probably just be administrative offices and the passage to a different part of the mosque complex.

James turned his head back to the right to see yet another arched doorway that was much more dimly lit, and frankly seemed ominous. Noelle smiled at her counterpart in acknowledgement that this was the way they should go. She was stopped short by James's gentle, yet firm grip on her left arm. She looked sharply at James, confusion in her expression.

"This way," he motioned down the first corridor.

"Toward the offices?" she searched for an explanation.

"Just a hunch," he began moving with Noelle following closely.

Reluctantly, she complied, following James into the danger of being discovered by someone, all the while looking over her shoulder at the darkened passageway that she believed might be the right way into the crypt.

"James, what are we doing?" she stumbled behind him. "We're gonna get caught!" she whispered with force.

The white marble corridor gleamed in the artificial light provided by the halogen bulbs above. James turned his head upward in wonderment at the way that an eighteenth-century mosque can feature modern recessed lighting. They moved stealthily down the hallway unsure of what they might find.

From around a shaded corner at the far end of the corridor came the figure of a person. James was abruptly interrupted from his gazing at the ceiling by Noelle's frantic shaking of his arm. He looked down at her unwavering stare toward the other end of the hall. She looked terrified and panicked. He quickly turned his head in the same direction, then jumped back, startled by what he saw.

The man at the end of the hall, clad in black robes, had not yet looked up to notice the two Americans in the distance. A cleric, he was looking down at a copy of the Qur'an, studying for a coming worship service. He finally lifted his head from his book, but saw nothing. James, as quickly as he could, pushed Noelle into the nearest doorway to the right, and shut the heavy wooden door tightly behind them.

They crouched behind the door with their ears turned in a way as to hear the footsteps in the hallway. They listened anxiously as the footsteps came, closed in, and passed. Both of them released a sigh of relief as they realized they were momentarily safe, turned the lock and began to look around at their surroundings.

"Shit, that was close," James whispered, somewhat winded.

"Yeah," she sighed, "and I guess you didn't give thought to the possibility that someone could have been in here." She raised an eyebrow at James.

He acknowledged her with a grin and slight nod. The office was very small, more like a broom closet than the working space of an Islamic cleric. Of course, with a very old structure, innovation and remodeling could only go so far.

There was a small desk in the room, meticulously organized and with very little clutter. At the center of the plain, lightly-stained desk sat a notebook computer, which lit the wall behind it with some sort of moving graphic screensaver.

"I don't think it's been long since the owner of this office was here," Noelle pointed to the computer.

"You're probably right," he agreed with a concerned look on his face. "I think we need to wait a few more minutes, though," he said.

The rest of the office, they noted, seemed a bit cluttered. There is only so much that will comfortably fit inside a room this size. There were bookcases to the left of the desk laden with dozens of books about God-knows-what. James tried to make out a few titles, but he didn't know much about reading Arabic text. The rest of the office was full of things gathering dust in the corners—walking canes, umbrellas and even a Turkish scimitar, obviously a conversation piece rather than for fighting. The walls were adorned with various pictures of ancient Egyptian tomb art, photos of the Ka'aba in Mecca and group pictures of the cleric who occupied the office with other people that were indiscernible as to who they were.

Then James noticed something that he had not before. It was subtle, yet should have been obvious, he thought, in retrospect. His eyes squinted as he turned his head slightly sideways to the left, then the right. *What the hell is that?*

"James, I think it's clear. We should—" she began to stand up so they could exit, but was stopped short by his hand on her arm. Neither his head, nor his eyes left from what he was staring at. He said nothing at first, his eyes trained on the far wall behind the desk. Curious, Noelle followed suit, cast her gaze in the same direction and initially failed to see what he saw.

"What is it?" she looked around, and then looked at James.

"You see that?" he pointed across the room.

This wall was clearly not added over time. It was part of the original eighteenth-century construction of the mosque, but there was something not quite right about the sandstone blocks that the walls consisted of. There were new blocks, possibly not even sandstone, that were of a darker color than the rest. They formed the shape, on the far wall, of an arch doorway. James and Noelle caught each other's eyes, and then smiled.

Chapter 27

Khalim sat quietly in a darkened corner of the cavern to the left of the crevasse entrance, his shadow dwarfing his slender frame perched upon a red nylon folding chair. The empty American-made MRE packet lay on the floor, the beef macaroni and crackers gone, but the condiments still intact. Surely, in the very near future, one of these MREs would be his last meal.

His thoughts were laden with images of pain and sorrow, destruction and fire. His eyes drifted upward to the massive death machine across the cavern. It was lit by two halogen flood lights on the floor before it, angled in such a way as to illuminate it from the ground up.

The floods were powered by an ultra-quiet generator that ran on ordinary gasoline. It had been running for hours, and to Khalim's surprise, the spaciousness of the cavern had prevented any major build-up of carbon monoxide fumes. He silently, in the recesses of his mind, worried about that issue. He was to guard the instrument of Ahura Mazda's will, yet what if the Shaoshant or an intruder were to come, only to find the lifeless body of the young Zoroastrian lying on the floor? *At least it would be somewhat more of a peaceful death*, he thought, comparing that end to the prospect of being crushed beneath countless tons of rock, and possibly lying there for hours, mangled, trapped, and alive.

He wondered where his family was and what they were doing. He thought of his nieces and nephews kicking a soccer ball in the rocky, desert terrain just on the other side of the chain-link fence from their oil company-provided apartments. He lingered on family gatherings and the smells of the kitchen while laughter filled the tiny rooms full of uncles and aunts. The sounds of small children shrieked across the building as they chased one another in glee, weaving between the adults setting the tables for dinner.

He thought of the life-long friends he had gone so long without making contact with over the years. Like his family, they were all secretly Zoroastrians, but they, no doubt, had no idea what kind of plot was unfolding in that cavern. They were devout in their faith, but went about their daily lives believing the prophecies would someday come true, but not this week. This was common, he thought, in most religions worldwide. A Buddhist wishes to reach enlightenment, but does not necessarily pray for death. A Christian believes in the second coming of the Messiah, yet does not hope for the end of days to come tomorrow. People all over the world obsess over the Apocalypse, interested, yet hoping that it does not happen. Certainly, none of his friends would have guessed that their prophecies would come to fruition in the form of a machine. Without even realizing it, surely they stored away images of the hand of Ahura Mazda reaching down from the skies, touching the ground, and shaking the earth in such a way as to bring about the destruction of mankind by way of the supernatural.

His thoughts were suddenly broken by a new sound. It was a sound outside of the monotone hum of the generator that had become equated with silence to Khalim after all these countless hours. He tried to make out the sound and place where it was coming from, his head and eyes darting from side to side as a deer that hears the crackle of leaves nearby in the forest. At the instant that he realized what the sound was, he had already seen what was making it. There was an arm and a foot emerging from the narrow cavern entrance, though it was too dark to tell who it was.

He sprang from his nylon seat, simultaneously latching on to the shoulder strap of his AK-47, and bracing the butt of the weapon to his shoulder as he steadied, aimed and prepared to fire. His left eye was squinted as sweat poured into his right eye. He brought his right cheek closer to the stock of the rifle, aligning the sights on top and firmly applying pressure to the trigger.

The figure completely emerged from the shadowy entrance and Khalim could make out the image of a man in white, his head turning from left to right, looking for something other than the massive machine.

"Khalim," the voice gently echoed from wall to wall.

Khalim exhaled a sigh of relief as he dropped the weapon to his side, loosened his muscles, and hung his head. He recognized the voice as he should have recognized the white robes.

"Khalim," the Shaoshant turned and began walking in the direction of the rustling to his right. "You might have killed me," he uttered as he drew close.

"Master," he stuttered a bit in shame and embarrassment, "I beg your forgiveness. I-I thought you might be an intruder. I didn't mean to . . ."

"It's alright Khalim," he smiled warmly. "You are doing your duty to me and our Father," he placed his hand on the young man's shoulder. "I'm proud that you take your charge so seriously. I'm proud. I know you will defend this place to the death. You may have to do so."

"Master?" he questioned with a perplexed look. He didn't say so, but he was under the impression that only a chosen few Zoroastrians knew about this cavern and this machine.

"Khalim," the Shaoshant said sternly, his tone hardening into contempt. "Someone may discover the secret to our divine plan. Someone may come to stop the machine."

"But how?" he still looked confused. "This is a heavily-guarded secret." He didn't know much about the safety measures to insure that the plan was not interrupted, but he did know that it wasn't easy to unlock the secret.

"There," the Shaoshant paused for a moment, "are some people who may have stumbled or will stumble upon our plan. And if this happens, they may be led here. It's unlikely, yet possible."

Khalim looked as frightened as he was puzzled. He feared that he might have to really pull the trigger and personally take a human life. Yet he was boggled by the thought that someone would know *anything* about this plan or his religion. He prayed that no one interfere. It would be the ultimate sin for some glory-seekers to defile everything that Ahura Mazda had devised. "Do not worry, young one," the Shaoshant reassured. "We are currently working to remedy the problem. I have others helping to make sure that you never even have to see these intruders." He smiled. "They won't get very far."

Chapter 28

James and Noelle stood from their position leaning against the heavy wooden door in the cleric's office. Silently and stealthily, with the exception of James's squeaky left heel, they slowly made their way across the room, each taking a path around the desk in the center. Their eyes were trained on nothing but the far wall, each of them trying to make sense of it. James ran through every possibility of what this could mean. Was this some secret passage to the crypt below? Was it simply a walled-over old window? *No,* he thought to himself, *it couldn't be. Beyond this wall, there is more structure—not the exterior of the mosque.*

"James," Noelle spoke first, "is this a doorway?" She knew the answer.

"It appears so," he responded, never taking his eyes off of the wall and running his hands over the stones.

"This is granite. Gray granite," she began feeling the stones as well. "The rest are sandstone."

"Sandstone is what most of the older and ancient structures were built with in Egypt," he added.

"Yeah. You use what's in abundance, I guess. But to my knowledge, there aren't any major granite deposits in this area," she puzzled.

"What do you suppose that means?" he looked to her for geological expertise.

"I don't know," she paused for a moment to collect her thoughts. "It seems like a lot of trouble for someone to go possibly hundreds of miles away for a material when they could have used local stone."

"Especially before the twentieth century, with no modern forms of transportation," he caressed his hairy chin in thought. "It seems they walled this doorway, but maybe wanted to be able to find it again."

"That doesn't make any sense," she grimaced. "If you're going to wall up a doorway, it's usually permanent. Why make it potentially accessible?"

"That means whatever is beyond this wall is important. They didn't want anyone in here but them."

He continued to run his fingers across the grey, granite blocks, pondering over the possibility that this could be the crypt they were looking for. Was this it? All of the theorizing and speculation that sent them on this impromptu trip half-way around the world, in a way, seemed ludicrous in hindsight. Did they really think they would find some secret crypt containing a tomb that archaeologists have been attempting to locate for eons? Did they really think that they would find it from piecing together abstract sections of seemingly accepted history and theology?

Tracing his fingers in rectangular motions over the mortar and around the blocks, he looked over at Noelle still studying the stone. James was beginning to wonder if she was growing tired of the redundancy of looking at a wall for a lengthy period of time.

He looked back toward the granite, his right middle finger still tracing the mortar, and then he noticed something. He turned his palm back toward his face and took a closer look at his middle finger. He studied the powder and grit trapped in the oils of his skin, rubbing his finger and thumb together. With a puzzled look, he began clawing at the mortar with what little bit of fingernail he had growing from his index finger.

By this time, Noelle had turned her attention to his actions in bewilderment. She watched as he clawed away at a bit of the crumbling, brittle substance, and then almost frantically searched all around him for something. Finally, he reached behind him to the left, grasping a cheap, brass letter opener from the surface of the desk. Without hesitation, he violently stabbed at the mortar as if he were murdering the wall for sleeping with his wife, flinging substantial chips of grit in all directions.

Noelle was speechless as she watched the powder and chunks of mortar fall to the floor and collect like dust in a house badly in need of cleaning. In a surprisingly short amount of time, most of the mortar had been eaten away from around the granite block, and James was pushing at it without a second thought.

Astonished, James felt the masonry give way, and the block pushed through the hole it created, clanging upon the stone floor behind the wall with a thud that they both prayed was not heard by anyone. It was lighter and thinner than he had imagined, each perhaps only about four to six inches in thickness.

James backed away from the wall as if afraid of it, and then lifted his head with a gaze toward Noelle. She returned the gaze with an expression that said *what have you done?* He smiled at her, his face reflecting giddiness, rather than fear now.

"I guess whoever walled up this doorway really didn't want any trouble getting back in," he said with a smile.

Chapter 29

It had taken about ten minutes for James to chisel away the mortar from around the thin granite blocks, pushing them through, pulling them away, and laying them aside. He had done only enough to peek inside and leave enough room for them to crouch through. Luckily, the bricks had been laid in a staggered fashion so that not every block had to be removed.

The two of them stood there silently staring at the hole in the walled doorway as if it were going to begin talking to them. James had taken the trouble to create a hole, but now they were wondering if they had done the right thing. It was like spending hours preparing a gourmet dinner, but being unsure whether you wanted to eat it when it was finished.

"James," Noelle broke the silence, "what if we get caught?" She began to grow frantic. "Breaking in through the side door to do some sight-seeing is one thing, but this is vandalism!"

"Um," he wasn't quite sure what to say. He did not want to scare her by telling the truth that the Egyptian government takes tomb robbing very seriously. "I don't know what they will do. With any luck, we could outrun the old man who uses this office," he smiled.

"I'm serious, James!" she snapped back, and then realized that the occupant of the office likely had a key to unlock the door. All this time, they could have been caught. She rushed to the other side of the office, and turned the latch, unlocking the door so that she could peek out. Her eyes darted from one end of the hallway to the other, searching for possible invaders, but it was clear. She then closed the door, locked it and turned back to James, still worried about getting caught.

"Look," he tried to calm and reassure her, "we came all this way for a reason. Remember all of that talk at my house? Remember what all that apocalyptic shit means? It means that in a couple of days, we could see the end of the world—or at least the beginning of the end. Once it starts, there's no fucking stopping it."

Noelle simply hung her head, unable to fathom what would happen if they were to get caught. Here she was half a world away with a man she had so recently met and already had sex with, and now she was committing a felony in a country whose police carried automatic assault rifles.

"Okay, James," she began to stomp back in his direction, and then stopped, pointing her finger at him in reprimand. "But if we go to jail, I'm going to kick you in the balls and then you're going to tell the police that I was your hostage."

The scene looked more like a home improvement project than an excavation. Gray granite stones lay stacked somewhat neatly to the side, surrounded by dust and small chunks of mortar. She squatted down and began peering into the black abyss beyond the demolished section of wall before looking back up at James, begging him with her eyes to not make her enter.

"It's dark in there," she complained. "And no one has gone in there in how long?"

"Probably one hundred and fifty years," he replied.

"Yeah, did you ever see *Raiders of the Lost Ark*? Who knows what kind of creepy, crawly things are in there!" she looked at and pointed into the hole. "Snakes, bugs, demons! That's scary shit!"

She looked back up at James who had his arms crossed and a smiling look of disdain on his face. She tried to continue her point with her eyes, hoping his carnal knowledge of her would prompt him to take pity and not force her to follow him on his boyish adventure. His body language, however, was as solid a stone as the walls of the mosque around them.

"Okay, I'll shut up," she conceded. "But you're gonna need a flashlight. I don't suppose you have one?" she rolled her eyes.

"Always be prepared," he smiled, retrieving a small, plastic flashlight from his pocket.

He squatted down to Noelle's level, and shined the light into the murky shadows beyond the hole in an attempt to gather reconnaissance before they stooped into the unknown. The stream of light emanating from the plastic flashlight revealed a passageway not much wider than the doorway itself. Beyond the threshold was a level floor that was about twenty feet long and covered with dust and crumbled mortar. Just beyond, there was the beginning of a staircase that led downward.

"This is it," he smiled. "This has to be it! It leads down. It's got to be the crypt!"

Noelle smiled at his joy and excitement. Not being able to resist, she grabbed the back of his head with her right hand, pulled him in and kissed him firmly, catching him off guard. He succumbed, however, touching her left cheek before she retracted her lips and looked deeply and lovingly into his eyes.

"After you, Dr. Beauregard," she motioned toward the hole.

He said not a word, but smiled as he turned his head and looked into the blackness. He ducked his head and climbed into the hole, careful not to trip or bump his head on the bricks above.

Once on the other side, he remained crouched down as he pivoted on the balls of his feet, echoing the grinding sound of the grit beneath his shoes. He reached back over to take Noelle's hand, guiding her into the darkness as any gentleman would.

Both inside the recesses, they stood straight up, only to feel the slight tickling of a few spider webs around their heads. James began frantically swatting, trying to wipe off the silk as shivers of dread ran down his spine. He danced around as Noelle watched in amusement. She gently and calmly wiped away the cobwebs surrounding her. She internally laughed at James while he continued to swat at his back and shoulders as if there were a thousand spiders crawling on him.

"What?" he looked at her, finally calming himself. "I fucking hate spiders!" he shivered once more before shining the light around them and down the stone staircase.

James moved first onto the dusty step before him. The stairs were not made of brick, but cut into the bedrock at the mosque's foundation. He continued downward, Noelle now holding the flashlight and illuminating the steps in front of them both.

"These have been here much longer than the mosque," he spoke up as they sunk further below the foundations.

"How can you tell?" her voice echoed.

"The steps are cut into the rock—they're not brick," he pointed out.

"That doesn't mean anything," she rebutted. "The builders of the mosque could have done this out of convenience."

"Understood," he said. "But do you see how crude and rounded they are? If they had been carved in the eighteenth century, they would be flatter and have more sharply squared corners. Besides, thousands of years of foot traffic have made them smooth and rounded, as well."

"Thousands of years?" she asked. "What was here before the mosque?"

"Another mosque," he replied. "But before that, this was supposedly the site of a Greek temple built not long after Alexander had laid claim to Egypt."

"And the Greeks would have built a crypt under the temple?"

"Sure. They didn't always do that, but it wasn't uncommon. It may not have even been a crypt at the time. Depending on the size and structure of the temple, it may have been a place for rituals and sacrifices."

"Sacrifices," she looked disgusted. "How fitting it became a crypt!"

"No, not human sacrifices," he said. "They usually sacrificed sheep, goats, bulls, though I don't see how they could have gotten bulls down here."

He then stepped hard with his left foot, expecting another step, but quickly realized that the stairs were done. He almost fell off balance, but steadied himself, reaching out to his sides to aid his stability.

"We're here," he alerted Noelle behind him. "Watch your step."

She stepped down beside him, shining the light around to get a feel for her surroundings before they pushed further down a stone corridor. She passed the cheap plastic flashlight to James, who eagerly took it and began excitedly pointing it in all directions in hopes of seeing something interesting.

Noelle began to take in the sights of what this strange place had to offer. She tailed closely behind James, who moved cautiously, but couldn't wait to proceed further. To each side of the narrow passageway, there were stone shelves cut into the rock, one above the other, seven tiers high. Within each shelf lay the skeletal remains of long-dead and forgotten people, still surrounded by the garments they were interred in.

She became spooked and nuzzled in closer to James, grabbing onto the back of his off-white button-down shirt. Suddenly she became slightly ashamed of herself. She had never been in such a macabre setting, yet she had always thought of herself as a strong woman. She had few fears; one of them being snakes. James, conversely, seemed to have many fears. As far as she could tell, he was afraid of spiders, flying, quitting alcohol and smoking, death and life itself. He did not seem, however, to be afraid of dead bodies or being arrested in a foreign country.

The air felt old. There was no movement or circulation in the bowels of the mosque, so the feeling was quite stuffy, and warm. It smelled of dust and eons of dryness, compounded with old and stale death.

"How long have these bodies been down here?" she asked.

"These are the newer ones. They're Muslim-era. Probably anywhere between two hundred and twelve hundred years, getting older as we move further in. Look at the garments they're wearing. They get older, earlier-fashioned, and more deteriorated."

Pushing on, Noelle noted that there was a surprising lack of insects, spiders, or any other kinds of vermin in the passageway. They had not run into a patch of cobwebs since they were at the top of the stairs. It would have been unmistakable if they had, judging by James's previous reaction.

They quickly reached the end of what seemed to be a finely-cut, squared corridor. Perhaps the vault had been there for much longer, but the Muslims obviously refined the space into the catacombs it had now become. As the shelving to the sides ran out, the passageway converted into more of a tunnel-like space. They watched the ninety-degree angles where the walls met the ceiling change into crudely and hastily-chiseled stone. It began to take the shape of a mine shaft more than a burial place.

The end of the line materialized before them. It was the wall of the stone confines, and upon seeing it, James could feel his blood pressure rising and his pulse increase. His face was turning red as expletives formed in his head, preparing for the tantrum to follow. However, saving her the experience, he saw the tunnel turn sharply to the left, opening into more of a spacious surrounding.

He stopped short and Noelle fumbled into him. Shining the light into the hollows, they remained cautious of any pitfalls or surprises. Inside the large cavern was a space full of short, waist-high objects or structures. They were hard to make out at first, but upon further study, James knew exactly what the room was.

"Wow," he moaned, smiling and finally moving further into the cavern. "Look at that!"

"What?" she blindly followed him inside. "What is this?"

"A necropolis," he took in the amazing sight.

"Dead . . . space?" she shrugged.

"You got the dead part right—*necro*," he commended her. "But *polis* is Greek for city."

"City of the dead?" she corrected herself. "As in another graveyard?"

"Precisely," he answered. "You see all these structures?" he shined the light around.

"Don't tell me, tombs?" she observed.

"Yep," he said, noting the rectangular cube shape of the small, white stone monuments.

"Holy shit!" she had an epiphany. "Like the mausoleums in New Orleans!"

"Exactly," he confirmed. "Just like in St. Louis Cemetery No.1, Lafayette Cemetery in the Garden District, and all over the city."

"I always found them creepy," she noted. "We'd drive around at night on the way to do some partying in the French Quarter, and we'd always have to cross over that really big one right after the interstate splits from I-610. I thought it looked like a city for the dead. I had no idea the Greeks actually called them that."

They moved slowly among the small tombs scattered around the room in no particular order. There was no organization to the layout. Even in most of the strange cemeteries of New Orleans, the graves were laid in a grid. These were haphazardly configured all around with only the center path that they walked to provide some sense of order.

Further along the pathway, James noticed something far in the recesses of the cavern. It was difficult to discern what it was. It was tall and vertically rectangular. It was ominous and imposing. Drawing closer, the beam from the flashlight was able to reach it. Then James realized what it was.

"Whoa."

Chapter 30

Overhead fluorescent lights flooded the cluttered office, drowning everything that was exposed in the most unnatural of artificial luminescence.

The concrete walls were painted gray and were bare, save a few certificates, honors and awards. The only thing to make the drab a little more bearable was the bookshelves that lined much of the wall space. Even then, however, the shelves were unorganized and jumbled with various books, magazines and junk papers; an obvious dumping ground for junk mail.

The desk in the center was not much better. It was a gray, metallic relic reminiscent of old teachers' desks in the 1970s and 1980s. Atop the desk stood a mountain of papers, stacks of files and various office supplies. One could tell that its owner had once tried organization from the small wire baskets at the front and center.

At the center of the mess was a small laptop computer, fitted with a mouse that was plugged in via a USB port. In front of that, near the front edge of the desk was the centerpiece of the jumble. It was a gold-plated name bar, etched in Arabic: Captain Amir Qadurra.

The phone rang on the right side of the cluttered desk, and the rather large man sitting behind it didn't acknowledge at first. He was fixated on the paperwork he was feverishly trying to complete. His long, white sleeves were rolled as far as they could go up his thick forearms and his red tie was loosened from around his unbuttoned collar. He was unkept, yet the gold badge on the left side of his chest made it somehow alright. His brown lips, fixed among day-old stubble, mouthed inaudible Arabic words as he sloppily filled in the blanks of some form he was filling out.

The phone continued to ring and finally he seemed to notice, looking up from his paperwork and running his thick fingers through his black, yet slightly graying hair. He seemed very tired with swelling beneath his brown eyes and an expression of fatigue that indicated he had not slept well in days.

"Qadurra," he sighed, picking up the phone, and bringing it to his face.

"Captain," the man on the other end said in Arabic, "we just got a call from the Nebi-Daniel Mosque reporting a break-in."

"This is the wrong department," he said in a tone that seemed like the beginnings of frustration. "I deal with antiquities, remember? Call me when someone has stolen a mummy or something."

"But sir, you don't understand . . ."

"I don't deal with routine break-ins," he interrupted, beginning to lose his temper. "Besides, how does someone break into a mosque that is open to the public? It's probably someone looking for the vaults again."

"Sir, I think that someone has *found* the vaults!"

"What?" his expression changed to that of confusion.

"The priest called and said that someone punched a hole in a wall in his office, beyond which was a small room and a staircase leading downward."

His amazement almost drew his attention completely away from the underling on the other end of the phone. His mind raced with what the find could be and who these people were. Treasure seekers? Scholars? Archaeologists?

"Sir?" the man checked to see if the captain was still there.

"Um," he paused, collecting his thoughts, "yes, I'll send my two best men," he assured him, and hung up the phone.

Chapter 31

James and Noelle moved closer to the far end of the room and tombs began to disappear into their periphery as they remained transfixed upon the sight ahead. James looked down at his feet to see that the nearly white powder and dust from the ground had totally covered both of their shoes just as it had covered all of the ancient tombs.

Reaching what seemed to be a flat, stone wall, they paused to study and moved their hands over the cool surface. They could feel eons of dust grinding between their skin and the stone. It was out of place, being that the rest of the cavern was either inexpertly carved out or naturally occurring. But this section, curiously, was flat, smooth and finely crafted from some distant Egyptian quarry. James moved to the left to study the edge of the massive façade. He ran his right middle and index fingers up and down the small gap between the smooth piece and the rougher wall that was more congruent to the rest of the walls in the room. He looked upward to estimate that the smooth piece reached about twenty-five or thirty feet up, sharply cut across about fifteen feet, and then cornered again back toward the ground. He crouched down, shining his flashlight at the bottom of the wall to see another small gap between the floor and the smooth section of the wall. Standing up, he silently stroked his goatee and inched his way in reverse. Standing for a moment in study of the object, he finally spoke.

"It's a door," the words echoed through the room and then vibrated into Noelle's eardrum.

She turned her head behind and to the left, glancing in his direction, then turned back to the wall, stepping in reverse and coming to a stop by his right side.

"A door?"

"Uh-huh,"

"A door to what?" she wondered aloud. "Is this our tomb? Is this the doorway to Alexander's tomb?" she looked at him inquisitively.

"I don't know," he shrugged. "Could be, that is, if we're in the right place. For all we know the tomb doesn't even exist. This could be one of the Ptolemaic kings or some rich asshole merchant or something."

"Well," James shrugged, "there's only one way to find out!" he began moving back in the direction of the strange, sealed doorway.

"Wait," Noelle followed, ready to offer her pessimism. "How do we do this? This wall is a hell of a lot thicker and sturdier than those blocks in the office. Are you going to bore a hole into this thing, too?"

"I don't know," he set back to studying the door. "We'll figure it out."

"Figure it out?" she stopped, stood straight, and placed her hands on her hips. "It's sealed. It's huge. It probably weighs several tons."

"It probably has a way in," he smiled at her. "No one builds a doorway that he can't go through." He continued to study.

He moved to the left of the structure, once again running his powder-covered fingers along the edge. Looking a bit further to the left of the doorway, he stopped and spotted something of interest.

"Aha!" he smiled, then began laughing. "I can't believe I missed it before!"

"What? What?" she trotted over to him.

Bathing in the beam from the flashlight were three large circles, perhaps four inches in diameter, vertically aligned and parallel to the doorway's edge. The top one contained the carving of a horse, the middle appeared to be an erupting volcano and the bottom was yet another horse.

"I don't know what the hell it is," he laughed excitedly, "but it's interesting! Hey, see if there are more on the other side!"

"They ran to the right, skidding to a stop at the other edge of the doorway to find three more circular engravings. The top circle contained the carving of what appeared to be bodies or dying people, the middle contained a horse, and the bottom showed the same.

"This is weird," Noelle laughed, getting a little excited as well. "Four of the six have horses on them."

"That is weird," the smile began to fade from his face as he pondered what all of it could mean. "Horses, horses . . ." he paced a bit with his right hand over his chin. "Horses. Horse whisperer . . ." he continued to think aloud. "Horse shit. Horseback riding. The four horsemen."

His eyes widened and his head shot up and turned to Noelle, whose expression of epiphany matched James's. "The four horsemen! That's it! The four horsemen of the Apocalypse!"

"Revelations," she added, nodding her head and smiling. "But what are these circular emblems? What does it mean? A way to open the door somehow?"

"I don't know," he studied them further. "The horses are part of the seven seals," he said, walking over to look more closely at the other emblems. "There was, if memory serves, a white horse, a black horse, a red horse, and a pale horse, each with a horseman."

"I don't see any indication of color on these horses," she carefully studied one of the carvings, rubbing the detail with her finger. As dust fell from the carved emblem, she noticed a change in the appearance. At first it was faint, but then she began to see a distinct color change within the detail of the horse. It was red.

"James!" she called out to her counterpart standing to the left of the stone doorway. "Rub the interior of one of the horses."

He did just that, revealing that the top horse was painted black. The bottom horse, having removed the dust, was painted white.

"Astounding!" he smiled in amazement. "Great work!" he commended her. "What color are yours?"

"One's red and the other has no color," she said, rubbing the final horse.

"Alright, we know that these definitely represent the seven seals in the book of Revelations," he began to think heavily.

"But . . ." she lost her smile for a moment, "what do we do with these?"

"I don't know," he puzzled. "What's the first seal in the Bible?"

"No clue. You're more of an expert on this than I am."

James thought deeply about the situation, closing his eyes in an attempt to draw information from his filing cabinet of a brain. He tried to visualize the passages, tuning in to his past memories of reading the book of Revelations dozens of times. He began to whisper, his eyes still closed and his head nodding until the words crossing his lips became audible.

"*Come and see. And I saw, and behold a white horse . . .*" he opened his eyes. "I've got it! Where's the white horse?"

He looked before him to see that the bottom emblem was that of the white horse. He ran his fingers over and around it, looking for a clue as to what they were supposed to do with this knowledge. He noticed that just to the interior of the edge of the outer circle there was a tiny gap running the entire circumference of the carving. Without hesitation, he glanced over at Noelle, and then back at his white horse, applying increasing pressure to it. The circular carving moved with his pushing hand into the recesses of the stone wall and stopped with a popping sound that echoed through the cavern. It was followed by sounds of crumbling stone within the wall, a slight shift of the stone doorway and a small plume of dust from the crack between the doorway and the wall.

"What the hell did you do?" Noelle seemed shaken. She didn't know if something was going to fall on top of them, the door was going to open, or if something else awful was going to happen.

"It's a locking mechanism!" he laughed a little. "They're all a bunch of goddamned buttons! I'm not sure, but I think the pushing of these buttons crumbles some sort of deadbolt system that keeps the door in place."

"So all we have to do is hit the buttons?" she began to push one of the emblems.

"Wait! Stop!" he shouted at the last moment, startling Noelle, who promptly retracted her hand. "I think we have to go in order."

"You mean the order in which the seals are opened in the Bible?"

"Yeah, it makes sense. In Revelations, they're opened in a certain order. It didn't say that they were all opened at the same time. I think these buttons are jumbled to confuse people. Look, the first seal—the white horse—is the third one in this column."

"So what happens if they're pushed in the wrong order?"

"I don't know. It probably just doesn't open."

"So we have one shot at getting this right," she nodded. "Which one's next?"

He closed his eyes again, visualizing the page in his mind, and began to mouth the words, reciting the scripture to himself. "*Come and see. And there went out another horse that was red . . .*"

"Red?" she confirmed. "I have that one," she placed her hand on the middle emblem. "I hope this is right," she shook her head, and then pushed the button, listening to a repeat of the sounds that the first button made. "Okay, two down."

"The next is . . ." he placed his hand on his temple, "black! I have that one," he exclaimed, and then pushed that button inward and listened to the sound of the crumbling stone.

"Next is pale?" Noelle inquired, ready to push in the final horse.

"Um . . . yeah!" he confirmed as he listened to the popping of the button and watched the shift of the door.

"Okay, what's next? I have the dying people over here."

"Yeah, and I have the volcano."

His eyes twitched from side to side as he pondered silently the final order of seals. They seemed to have gotten the first four correct and James hated to get it wrong in the end.

"*Behold a pale horse. And his name that sat on him was Death,*" he blurted calmly. "I think that the fifth seal spoke of people slain for the word of God."

"I have the button with the dying people, so here goes," she said pushing the button, and hoping that it was correct.

The emblem sunk into the recesses of the cavern wall, producing the increasingly familiar sound of crumbling stone. Then there was one left, and James promptly and confidently applied pressure, listening to the crumbling sound once more.

Stepping back, they felt as if their task was done and waited to see what would happen. Would the door swing open allowing them to gain access to the mysterious room or passageway? Should they begin pushing it inward? Or was there something that they forgot?

"I'm such an idiot!" James smiled and laughed at his absent-mindedness.

"What?"

"There are seven seals," he continued to laugh. "Here we are waiting for something magical to happen, and we forgot the last seal."

"Where is the seventh seal?" she looked around. "I only saw six on the walls."

"Yeah, that's a good question," he looked around on the walls and the door itself, brushing away ages of dust to see if there was yet another button caked beneath.

Neither of them found anything and became a little frantic and frustrated. James had to stop, take a deep breath, and clear his head. He stood before the massive stone doorway with his head dropped and his eyes closed, then stepped back to look at the larger view.

Moving backward and surveying the panorama, the ground beneath his right heel felt a bit strange. It was as if there was a hole, or that the ground was sinking, but only just beneath his right heel. He stopped immediately, not moving a muscle, and carefully picked up his right foot, bringing it forward, away from the previous spot.

"What is it?" Noelle seemed perplexed by James's strange movements.

"Don't know. Come and take a look," he responded.

Illuminating the ground they began brushing away dust, careful not to disturb what may lie beneath. It surprised them that what they were searching for was not just under the surface. It was deeper; covered, perhaps, by as much as an inch and a half of the fine powder. Beneath their dust-coated hands, something began to take shape. It was the edge of yet another circular emblem, but much larger.

"This has got to be it!" Noelle exclaimed as they started removing the powder and the carving became revealed.

The emblem dwarfed the size of the others on the wall, about eighteen inches in diameter, and much more beautifully carved. The two marveled at the scene depicted and what time and care that must have been taken in preparing such detail.

There was a mountain in the distance surrounded by clouds that shot down lightning amongst people standing in awe, each with one hand covering their mouth. The ground was broken and cracked from the mountain down to the forefront while skeletons lay strewn everywhere.

"Wow," James could think of nothing better to say.

"Yeah," she agreed. "Beautiful, but creepy, huh?"

"This is definitely the seventh seal. You see the storms, earthquakes, and death?" he pointed out.

"Earthquake storm," she looked into his slightly terrified eyes. "What about the people standing around with their mouths covered?"

"I seem to remember something else in that verse about half an hour of silence. That's probably it. But what's interesting is that there are obviously dead bodies here and those are victims, but the others don't seem to be frightened. It's more like reverence. I wonder if these people represent the Zoroastrian keepers of this secret machine."

"And the silence is about making sure not to reveal to others what's about to happen?"

"Maybe," he fell silent in thought for a moment before getting back to the task at hand. "Okay, you ready?" he asked.

With Noelle's nod, James began pushing the emblem with his hand, first with a minimal amount of force, but found that it would not move. He then applied more pressure, soon putting most of his upper body strength into it.

"Need help?" Noelle smiled mockingly.

He simply shot her a look of embarrassment, masked by sarcasm as he straightened his legs and stood up. He then stepped directly onto the large emblem, hoping that his full body weight would finish the last seal, yet it would not move.

"Did we do something wrong? Did we hit the other seals out of order," she looked around in disbelief.

"It's heavy. Come here," he said as he jerked her toward him by her hands, and pulled her into his arms for a little kiss.

There they stood on the seventh seal of the Apocalypse, kissing sweetly, when the button moved slightly, drawing their attention from each other's lips. Suddenly, the seal moved the rest of the way, sinking about a foot into the ground, creating a long, progressive sound of stones popping and crumbling. The ground visibly shook, unsettling the dust as it moved in a chain reaction fashion in the direction of the stone wall. The popping moved and vanished into the wall as one last popping sound was made, spewing debris from every inch of the gaps between the door and the cavern wall.

The large stone slab first began to slowly lean forward and toward them as they stared in disbelief. As it gained momentum, however, there was no stopping. It rapidly accelerated, falling directly towards them, sending James into a frantic scramble as he leaped to the left, and Noelle did the same to the right.

The several-ton stone slab fell toward the ground with every bit of the force of Isaac Newton, stirring life into the air as it neared its stopping point. It crushed several tombs as it came falling down with a loud thud, sending a cloud growing within the cavern as if there had been a meteorite to hurl the earth into nuclear winter.

James rolled over unable to see and barely able to breathe with such a heavy cloud of dust filling the room. He was covered in a thick layer of gray dust, coughing and struggling for breath. In light of what just happened, the only thing on his mind was the safety of Noelle. He did not hear her rustling around or calling his name. His fears that she had been crushed beneath the slab were growing. He would never forgive himself for dragging her off on some foolish adventure only to get her killed in one of the most horrible ways imaginable.

"James," a voice called out, echoing from wall to wall, and intermittently coughing. "James, are you all right?"

"Yeah," he sighed heavily in relief. "What about you? Are you okay?" he called out.

"I think so. I can't even see you!"

James picked up the flashlight to shine it in her direction, and at first it looked like a car's high beams trying to cut through a heavy fog.

It did not work. It simply reflected off of the particles of white-gray powder. After a few moments, the air began to somewhat clear and he could make out Noelle's dust-covered body.

He jumped to his feet, shining the light in her direction. He stepped up onto the slab that had once stood erect before them and walked over to take Noelle's hand.

Dazed and shaken, they both looked toward the wall that the slab had fallen so violently from. The beam from the flashlight revealed a darkened space beyond the slab's former home. *A passageway?* James thought. *A room?* He was not sure what they would find.

"Shall we?" Noelle gestured, smiling.

"We shall, indeed," he smiled back.

James felt like Howard Carter about to open the tomb of Tutankhamen; about to rewrite history, or, perhaps, become severely disappointed.

They stepped down from the stone slab and onto the cavern floor. They were not in a passageway or corridor to another room. Whatever they were to discover was right there before them.

The room cut into the recesses of the cavern wall and was about the size of the average family's living room, yet with a ceiling that reached about thirty feet up. Within the chamber, there was a raised rectangular pedestal of stone. It almost seemed to resemble an ancient stone altar, and upon it, they could finally see, was a thing of wonder and amazement.

Surprisingly, there was nothing particularly special about the interior of the tomb. There were no engravings or artwork as there were in the tombs of the pharaohs. It was as if the people who interred the man within this cavern spent more time on the elaborate locking system and less time on the reverence of the man.

James and Noelle stopped short, gasping at what they saw. They knew that whatever they had found was quite important. To Noelle, it was simply a thing of beauty, but to James, it was the discovery of a lifetime. He felt tears nearly well up in the corners of his eyes at the thought. Anyone who was truly interested in history often became overwhelmed at the sight of an important historical place or object. This was something that dwarfed all of those feelings.

Before them, perched upon the stone altar was a rectangular object that stretched to approximately eight feet in length, three feet in height, and four feet in width. It was a coffin made of exquisite panes of glass or crystal, and framed at the corners by the purest gold. The beauty of the coffin was muffled by the recently-fallen coat of dust.

"Oh my God! This is it!" he smiled uncontrollably. "This is the tomb of Alexander the Great!"

"Are you shitting me?" she was amazed. "How can you tell?"

"This is exactly the description of the coffin from when it was on display at the heart of Alexandria. This is how it was described by the Roman historians. Glass panes, framed in gold," he pointed out the details he was describing. "The coffin and Alexander were lost, but apparently, he was hidden. Someone didn't want him found!"

"Zoroastians?" she suggested.

They half-rushed to the coffin, excited to peer inside, yet wanting to remain respectful. They did not want to treat this as a couple of kids running into a candy store. With that, they slowly made their way onto the stone pedestal, and stood over the coffin. James's heart thumped like a bass drum as he smiled at Noelle, imploring her permission with his eyes. She simply smiled at his exhilaration, and gave him a nod of approval.

He nervously brushed off the dust as best he could from the top pane to reveal the gray and ancient skeleton of a long-dead king. But peering into the coffin through a dusty pane of glass was not enough for him. He needed to open it. He frantically searched for a way to open the coffin, and quickly spotted golden handles affixed the top and bottom of the glass pane. He motioned to Noelle to move to the bottom end of the coffin, and grab that handle, as he took hold of the top one. In unison, they looked at one another, lifted the surprisingly light cover, and carefully stepped down to lay it flat on the ground.

"Oh my God," he repeated. "I can't believe we're actually here! He's been down here for nearly two thousand years, and no one ever knew!

People walking around above us for eons, and here he was all this time!"

"It's hard to believe," she said.

"I mean, this is the man who conquered most of the known world and beyond by the age of thirty; he's the greatest conqueror of all time! Hero to even Julius Caesar!"

Darting back up to the top of the stone altar, they once again gazed down upon the long-decayed king. The skull faced toward the heavens with a golden crown of laurel leaves fixed around it. Even in his state, he looked majestic. He was wrapped in a once white, but now aged and dingy kingly robe with purple borders. Between his right arm and hip, there was a beautifully carved and white-plumed Macedonian helmet. It was made of iron, carved into the likeness of a lion, its fangs jutting down around where the king's eyes would be. Across his torso was his circular shield, a hoplon about two-and-a-half feet in diameter, and expertly etched with Greek engraving.

"Ooh, I hope I can remember enough to translate this," he remained fixed upon the shield.

"Alexander," he fumbled in excitement, "emperor of the world and son of divinity. The fate of the world hinges on his regal symbol of power."

"Symbol of power?" Noelle pondered. "What is a king's symbol of power? His crown? His sword?"

"His scepter!" James removed a long, golden rod from beneath the shield.

It was about five feet in length and topped with a deep purple jewel that was the size of a softball. It was elegant and beautiful—befitting an emperor of the known world. Then he noticed that at the bottom end, there was an irregularity. Cut into the two-inch-diameter rod of gold, there was a notch that extended about three or four inches up the shaft.

"Drop the key!" a deep voice echoed through the hollows of the room in an Arabic or Persian accent.

Startled, James dropped the scepter back into the coffin as they both looked through the opening of the chamber to see two men in flowing white robes holding AK-47s with their sights trained upon them.

"Oh my God!" Noelle gasped.

"God?" the man responded. "You have no respect for God! Your evil hands have tainted this holy place, and now you will die."

Suddenly, there were several loud pops of gunfire. The two men fell instantly, crimson blood seeping from the wounds in their backs.

Chapter 32

"Oh my God! Oh my God! Oh my God!" Noelle repeated frantically as her head darted around the interrogation room at the police station.

There wasn't much to see in this room that would draw a person's attention. She was simply taking in the whole picture and trying to make sense of what was happening to her at this moment. The plain, gray walls were not decorated, but seemed newly painted, casting a bit of a glare in their bright luster. The only things in this empty space were the gray metal chairs that felt cool on their bottoms, an eight-foot rectangular table before them and two more chairs on the other side of it.

"Holy shit! Holy shit! I can't believe this! I'm never going to see my family again!" she continued to rant as James remained silent.

There was nothing for him to say at that point. Noelle was already voicing every fear that he may have had. For the moment he was trying just to remain calm. There was no point in having both of them become frantic and panicked.

"Shit! I should have never listened to you!" she didn't even look at him. "We're going to jail in a foreign fucking country! A dark, dank jail where they don't feed you and you spend the rest of your life there and no one ever knows what happened to you!"

"Noelle," he finally spoke. "Calm down. We're not going to jail," he hoped he wasn't lying. "Look, we're not even cuffed," he lifted his wrists.

"What the fuck does that matter?"

"I don't know. Maybe they see us as victims, aside from being criminals. I'm sure the U.S. consulate will get involved. We'll be alright."

"This is Egypt, James! They don't fuck around when it comes to tomb robbers!"

He tried to think of a good response, but nothing came to mind. The truth was that she was correct. Things had come a long way since British dominance in the area lifted. This was not the Egypt of Howard

Carter, and the government did not take kindly to foreigners carting off loads of priceless treasures and artifacts.

"Hello," a surprisingly cheery voice echoed through the empty room as the door on the opposite side was flung open.

This was not at all what either of them had expected. This man, despite his unkept appearance, rolled up white sleeves, loosened tie and unshaven face, seemed quite polite and respectful. "How are you two doing on this fine afternoon?" he smiled as he sat across from them.

Neither of them answered. Perhaps it was out of shock, or even fear. Or maybe they had become used to the *right to remain silent* judicial system, and knew not to say a word.

"Please," he continued, "speak with me. We are all professionals." There still was no response as his gaze darted from each of the Americans to the other. "Allow me to introduce myself. I am Captain Amir Qadurra. And you must be . . ." he looked at his files. "Dr. Beauregard and Dr. Broussard," he spoke their names with surprising accuracy.

They all sat for a very long moment in complete silence. Noelle and James knew not what to say, if they should say anything at all. Captain Qadurra implored them with his eyes to say something, although he knew that they would be cautious in communicating with him.

"What kind of trouble are we in?" James finally spoke without an emotion in his expression.

"Well, that depends," the captain replied.

"On what?"

"On what your intentions were in the tomb," his eyes lowered to the file before him. "Tomb robbing is a very serious offense in Egypt. It says here that you both are scholars from very highly reputable universities in the United States, so I would hope that your professional ethics would prohibit the plundering of our national treasures," he looked back up at them.

"We're not tomb robbers!" Noelle finally spoke, very defensively.

"Okay, okay," he tried to calm her. "But you must then explain to me what you were doing in an unknown tomb beneath the Nebi-Daniel Mosque. If you had a theory that something was down there, why did you not contact our government ministry of antiquities? Why did you not bring one of our teams with you? Why keep it such a secret?"

There was a long pause. Noelle did not want to speak again, as she was edgy and anything that would come from her mouth would be abrasive and rude.

James thought for a moment in order to choose his words wisely. He could not very well tell Captain Qadurra this unbelievable story of an ancient machine set to destroy the world, could he? Who would believe that?

"Every story about the possible discovery of Alexander's tomb has ended with what seems to be a cover-up," James finally spoke. "I didn't want our efforts silenced."

"You do not think that our government would love to hear of such a find?" he looked perplexed. "As we speak, archaeologists are heading for the site. We already have some of the items within the coffin here at our office. Evidence. You understand," he smiled.

"*You* do?" James perked up, showing excitement without thinking of the consequences.

The captain looked strangely at him. His expression became slightly more stern and suspicious.

"Dr. Beauregard," he said, "what were you doing there? What were you looking for?"

"I was looking for the tomb of Alexander the Great," he replied calmly. "No more. No less."

The captain's smile returned, although he still suspected something else beneath the surface. His face brightened once again, his expression reverting back to its original warmth, and his tone regained a level of patience and friendliness.

"Very well," he smiled, "and it seems you may have found it. Congratulations and thank you."

Both James and Noelle's faces turned a shade of bewilderment, unable to believe that they may get off that easily. They gave each other a quick glance from the corners of their eyes, yet did not move a muscle in their necks.

"That's it, then?" Noelle said calmly, sounding a bit relieved.

"Well," Captain Qadurra sighed, "we may not charge you with tomb robbing, but you are guilty of vandalism and trespassing, both of which carry a hefty penalty. In light of such a great discovery that we would have never known of before, this may be reduced to a very large fine."

"Do you take checks?" James spoke swiftly.

"Of course," the captain smiled softly.

"Then we're free to go?" he began to extend his legs and stand, but he was cut short by a simple lifting of the captain's hand. James then began to lower himself into the seat once again in slow motion.

"Unfortunately," Qadurra spoke a little more sternly as he peered downward at his files, "there is another issue that we must discuss."

The two Americans were blank in expression, but teeming with thoughts and emotions. They knew exactly what that issue was, yet still had not made sense of it. There had been no time, really. They watched two men get shot right in front of them, then they were whisked away to the police station. James had not stopped shaking. He had watched two men die, something that, despite his attempts at erasing it by way of clenching eyelids, would not be done away with.

"Who were the men that my officers shot in the tomb?" Captain Qadurra said frankly.

"To be honest with you, I don't have a fucking clue," James was quick with a response.

"Please do not use that type of language, Dr. Beauregard," he sharpened. "Very few times have I known of a case where two men attempted to kill another with automatic weapons and the two men were unknown to the victims. Only in war does that happen."

"Sir," James tried to be very respectful in light of Qadurra's despise of foul language, "we don't know anyone in Egypt. I have no idea why anyone would want to kill us or how anyone knew we were in those vaults."

"Hmm," he stroked his chin while looking down, "this troubles me. My officers heard one of the men tell you to drop the key before dispatching them. What key? What are you hiding Dr. Beauregard?"

"Tell him," Noelle nudged, giving him a nod that signified it was okay to come clean, even if the captain did not believe them.

"Okay," he closed his eyes, and then opened them just as fast. "Dr. Broussard's geological team made a discovery in Italy that suggested the possibility of an ancient machine that if placed in the right location, could bring about the end of days."

"Really?" Qadurra nodded, a bit shocked. He did not know how to respond, but he intended to listen respectfully. "And you believe this right location was beneath the streets of downtown Alexandria?"

"No, I'm not yet sure where the location of the machine could be, but there was a reference that the tomb of the *son of a god* held the key to shutting it down. Naturally we thought of Alexander, and here we are," he could not believe he was telling this to the cops. The more he spoke it, the less even he believed it. "The key, I think, is the scepter within the tomb that we opened. It has a strange notch cut into the end of it, perhaps for shutting the machine down. I don't know," he shrugged.

"Dr. Beauregard," he tried to process this information and to not insult the scholar with his skepticism, "who would build such a destructive machine?"

"Perhaps the same kind of men who would build a nuclear weapon, gas an urban population with nerve agent or fly an airliner into a highrise office building."

Captain Qadurra was taken aback. The statement was bold and cutting, but he had to admit that it made perfect sense. All of these things were true. Humankind is capable of some terrible things. Why would it be hard to comprehend that an ancient society would build a weapon of mass destruction?

"Perhaps the same kind of person that would follow a historian and a geologist into a lost tomb and kill them?" James added.

"Did your discovery in Italy mention a name to these ancient people?" Qadurra pressed.

"Zoroastrians," James said without emotion. "A Zoroastrian cult that may very well exist today."

"And did the information you have indicate a time frame as to when the machine will destroy the world?" Qadurra could not believe what he was asking.

"June sixth. That's in two days."

A mobile phone rang, filling the room with the piercing tone and giving them a bit of a start as they had seemed to fall into some sort of solemn trance. James's heart pounded ferociously. He shivered and sweated. Captain Qadurra, reached down to remove his phone from his belt clip, flipped it open and greeted the caller in his native tongue.

The two American scholars sat in silent suspense as they listened to tones in the policeman's voice to try and understand what could be going on. Neither of them spoke or understood his language, but were desperate to know what was being said.

After a few minutes of conversation with the caller, the captain closed the phone with the familiar clicking of plastic on plastic, and laid it down on the table before him.

"That was one of my detectives calling from the medical examiner's laboratory," he peered at the two of them. "There was nothing out of the ordinary about the two men who tried to kill you except . . ."

"What?" James was riveted.

"They both had the same tattoo on the inside of their right wrists."

"Of what?"

"He said it looked like a vase or urn with flames rising from inside it, does this mean anything to you?"

James's jaw lowered, a smile forming at the corners of his gaping mouth. It was as if this smile covered his whole face, disbelief and joy intertwined and slathered across his dingy face.

"Captain Qadurra," he leaned in, "that symbol is the Living Flame. It symbolizes the manifested presence of Ahura Mazda. It's a Zoroastrian emblem of the faith."

The captain could not believe what he was hearing. All he could do was rise to his feet and respectfully nod to the two detainees.

"Please stay here for the moment," he backed out of the room. "I must confer with my colleagues. I will return."

Chapter 33

James and Noelle began to grow impatient as they both fidgeted with the buttons on their clothes, their hair and any other normally insignificant items on their person. Noelle frequently looked at her watch to confirm that it had indeed been nearly half an hour since the kindly captain had left the room with a promise of return.

"Where the hell is he, James? It's been forever!"

"Something doesn't seem right, I know," he looked worried. But his mind drifted to the tattoos on the wrists of the men that were about to kill them. "Isn't that amazing?" he suddenly seemed chipper.

"What?" she looked slightly agitated.

"About the tattoos. Those were Zoroastrian tattoos. This is huge!"

"James, I'm more worried about getting out of this police station. We'll worry about the Apocalypse later."

She had more to add to her frustrated sentiment, but she was interrupted by the turning of the doorknob. They both perked up expecting Captain Qadurra to walk in with papers to sign and a warm farewell. But they noticed that the man that entered the room and closed the door was not the goodly captain they had grown to like. This was a younger, well-kept man wearing a very nice navy-blue suit. He had all of the indications of a police detective, including the badge and the sidearm.

"Who are you?" Noelle blurted. "Did Captain Qadurra send you to release us?"

"No," the man spoke as he drew his weapon, "I'm here to dispatch you."

He lifted his right arm and pointed the handgun directly at her in a moment that seemed to be in slow motion. His finger was on the trigger and his slow pace of walking toward her was as sinister as the slightly crazed expression on his face.

The door opened once again, and an oblivious Captain Qadurra stepped into the drab room carrying a long, thin canvas bag. He was about to say something to the two Americans, but quickly realized what was happening.

The unidentified man holding the gun spun around to see who was intruding on his assassination, but the captain was quick to draw his weapon. Qadurra very precisely took aim at the intruder, squeezed the trigger of his sidearm and discharged a single round. The force of the forty-five caliber bullet piercing the man's chest knocked him back a couple of feet, throwing his arms out to the side and spattering his essence of life forward. He fell onto his right at the feet of the scholars, who were horrified to see yet another man lose his life that day.

They could both tell that Qadurra's adrenaline was coursing through his body at full speed. His every breath was short, as if he were fighting to absorb enough oxygen into his blood to calm him against the idea that he had just killed a man. He had never been responsible for the loss of another's life, and for that reason, it took several moments for him to become calm.

Once he regained his composure he slowly and shakily stepped in the direction of the corpse lying on the floor. Returning his pistol to the holster on his belt, he stooped down, adjusting the canvas bag over his shoulder. He reached for the right-hand cuff of the dead man's sleeve and pulled it back with a jerk to reveal just what he had suspected. There, emblazoned on the inside of the wrist, was a tattoo of the Living Flame.

He lifted his gaze to the shocked Americans before him. It seemed to take several moments to break the silence.

"You must go," he grabbed James by the bicep of his right arm and began leading them out of the room. "Surely someone must have heard the shot, and they will come to investigate."

They hastily made their way to the door, and the captain flung it open, looking in every direction down the hallways to check for any signs of officers or further intruders.

"You should have no problem getting a cab outside," he led them down the hallway toward the back exit. "Have the driver take you to the nearest train station. I will take care of the intruder and how the artifact became missing. You will not be pursued," he handed the canvas bag to James, staring directly and piercingly into his eyes.

James unzipped the bag slightly only to see the jeweled head of Alexander's scepter glimmering in the fluorescent lights. He looked sharply back into Qadurra's gaze in shock and amazement.

"Why are you helping us?" he couldn't resist asking.

"Dr. Beauregard," he placed his massive hand on James's shoulder, "originally, I had no intention of giving you what is in this bag. But it seems that your situation is dire. There have been two attempts on your lives today, and that must mean there is truth to your claims," he smiled. "I will pray that Allah looks over you on your task. Now go!" he pushed them out through the exit doors.

The sunlight was blinding after spending so much time indoors. They both instinctively raised their hands to their brows in an attempt to shade their eyes from the harmful rays. Almost immediately, Noelle raised her other hand to hail a taxi, and one promptly pulled up to the curb. The two hastily climbed inside, scepter and all.

"The nearest train station," James quickly ordered to the driver, who nodded in acknowledgement.

"No, wait!" Noelle stopped him. "The El-Salamlek Palace Hotel first!"

James looked at her as though she had lost her mind.

"What? We have to get the fuck out of Dodge!" he chastised her. "That's clear on the other side of town!"

"Twenty miles," the driver announced uninvited.

"I'm not leaving without my bags," she growled at him, and then turned back to the driver. "The hotel!"

Chapter 34

The taxi roared into the driveway directly in front of James and Noelle's hotel, coming to an abrupt halt. Noelle did not even wait for the car to come to a complete stop before throwing the door ajar and leaping to the cobblestones below.

After exiting the cab, James walked briskly up to the rolled-down driver's side window, appealing to the driver to look up at him. He seemed a kind enough man with a nice, honest expression. There was wisdom and experience in the gray hairs that riddled his thick mustache.

"You see this?" James produced a one hundred dollar bill from his wallet. "It's yours when we get back," he put it into the front right pocket of his pants. "Wait for us," he reiterated as he ran off after Noelle.

"Yes, but the meter is still running," he half shouted in his thick Egyptian accent.

"Fine," James waved, not even turning around and still proceeding through the front door. "I'll make it worth your while!"

He raced across the lavish lobby, his shoes clacking against the polished marble floors and the one shoe squeaking intermittently. He nearly collided with several people on the way to the elevator.

They both stood silently and only looking at one another briefly a few times. The elevator stopped and the doors opened. They both prayed that there wasn't a couple of men on the other side with machine guns, ready to blast them onto a course to meet their maker. And as the doors slid apart, there was nothing; only the hallway.

Reaching their room, they inserted the key and opened the door. They seemed to be in the clear with no sign of anyone following them on the road, nor were there any suspicious gentlemen in the lobby of the hotel. But their room was a different story.

There seemed to be nothing left untouched in their room. Most of the furniture had been turned over, the bed was stripped of linens, and their suitcases had been emptied out. Each and every drawer in the dresser was pulled completely out and the closet was wide open. The both of them just stood there in awe and amazement. He shook his head at the thought as he watched Noelle, who was almost in tears going through all of her belongings.

"What could they have been looking for?" she turned to him. "How did they know we were here?"

"Who knows?" he shrugged. "Maybe they were looking for passports, personal info—anything about us to give them an edge." Then, of course, he remembered the bag on his shoulder. "And maybe they thought we already had this."

Her face turned from the expression of being violated to that of worry. She started to cry as she was overloaded with emotions. James rushed over and held her tightly without saying a word, then took her by the shoulders, looked into her eyes and spoke. "We've got to get the fuck out of here."

She dried her eyes and nodded, trying her best to regain the composure of a strong and independent woman, and then set about looking around for anything that she may need from the room. There was no time to pack up all of their things. The intruder could, for all they knew, be in the restroom, unknowing that they were even there. Noelle quickly darted across the room gathering a few noteworthy items. She snatched from the floor a clean red tank top, khaki shorts, and a change of panties. She grimaced at the thought that a complete stranger had touched her underwear. They found their passports still lying on the dresser, and threw them into her purse.

"Okay," she shook the thought and darted for the door.

They both exited and headed back down the corridor toward the elevator, but before they could touch the *down* button, the elevator, already moving, chimed as it stopped at their floor. As the door began to open, they could see a man standing just on the other side of it. They both spun around the corner, terrified.

Stunned and silent, they watched the man pass the corner, walking down the hallway, praying that he did not turn his head in the direction of their little alcove. He could have been anybody, but they did not want to chance it.

James turned his head to the left to discover that at the other end of the alcove was a door that led to the service stairwell. He quietly tapped Noelle and motioned in the door's direction.

The interior of the stairwell was typical. There were taupe-painted metal stairs and railings that clanked and vibrated with every step that they took down toward the lobby floor. It did not matter if they were soft-stepped, the bare concrete walls and floor allowed for no absorbance of the noises that happened within the confines. Every step, rubbing of the metal railings, and every breath echoed from wall to wall. They could only hope that none of their enemies were present in the stairwell.

Soon, they were pushing the aluminum release bar of the lobby-level door, and exited the stairwell, heading for the front entrance. The only thing on Noelle's mind was reaching that door and heading for the train station. With every step, James's eyes and head were moving from one end of the luxurious lobby to the other, scanning the room for anyone that eyed them with excessive interest.

They reached the front doors and exited the air-conditioned building into a slightly humid and increasingly hot climate to find that their loyal cab driver was still awaiting their return. The cabbie smiled, having spotted them, and even got out of the running car to open the rear passenger door for them.

"No luggage, sir?" he inquired as the cab sped forward, merging into traffic.

"Nope," he shortly spoke, simply handing the man the promised one-hundred-dollar bill, which the cabbie eagerly took. "Misr Station—quick."

"Yes sir," he replied, and began the nine-mile journey to the train station.

Chapter 35

The taxi sped down the street by the old familiar mixture of ruins that they had seen earlier in the morning. James did not realize they would be visiting this neighborhood again today. He had not noticed the train station then, but he could now once again see the minarets of the Nebi-Daniel Mosque just a couple of blocks away. How ironic that the day had led them through so much trouble and to all ends of Alexandria, when, provided that the conditions were right, they could have simply walked from the mosque to the train station without any trouble and exited Egypt without a stir.

The cab came to a screeching halt in front of the station as the two travelers climbed out from the back seat. James didn't even wait for the driver to present him with the total, as Noelle, as headstrong as she was, was already walking toward the entrance. He simply handed the driver another one-hundred-and-fifty dollars or so, fully aware that he was vastly overpaying.

He caught up with Noelle just as she was moving through the front entrance of the station, and they both began dodging people in the crowd in an attempt to traverse the distance to the ticket counter. He looked upward at the massive façade, a hold-over from British control of the nation. On either side of the three large arched doorways were towering sandstone replicas of Big Ben in London, without much of the gothic flair, and with a slight mixture of Islamic minaret architecture. Yet with the two clocks atop the ends of the façade, it paid homage to its inspiration. The rest of the structure, however, was directly inspired by the British—Victorian in its style, complete with contrasting sandstone and red brick, and spans of arched windows on each side of the entrance façade.

While waiting in line for their tickets, James frequently looked around at the hundreds of faces that passed through the station. He was aware that he was growing a bit paranoid, knowing that they were being hunted by an ancient and apparently violent sect of Zoroastrians. So far, they had shown the ability to track a perfect stranger, follow them into a secret crypt, and infiltrate the Alexandria Police Department, posing as a cop. Literally, any man in this station could be one of them.

After several minutes of waiting, and a near nervous breakdown on James's part, they made their way to the front of the line. Without a moment's delay, James began to negotiate the sale of two tickets.

"What do you have east of here?" he asked the suited man behind the counter.

"East?" Noelle wondered. "Why east? Why not west? Or south?"

"Look, my best guess is that this machine is in the vicinity of old Persia."

"Your best guess?" she was horrified. "You don't know where we're going next? What if this machine is in fucking Budapest or something?"

"Look," he eyed the uncomfortable ticket clerk, who was sure he was watching the common fight of a married couple, "I haven't thought this thing past this point. Right now I just want to get out of Alexandria, and my gut tells me that since the Zoroastrians came from Persia, that's where we're going."

"Okay," she threw her hands up in defeat, typical of a married couple.

"East?" James turned once again to the clerk.

"The furthest east we have is Suez, but there are connections from there to Damascus, Tel-Aviv, Jerusalem . . ." the clerk spoke in accented English while looking at his computer screen.

"We'll take two tickets," he stopped him short.

"You will have to hurry, sir," he handed James the two tickets in exchange for cash. "The train leaves in five minutes. Platform two!" he yelled across the growing distance between them at the man and woman briskly walking away. "Americans . . ." he rolled his eyes and then called for the next in line.

The two walked swiftly as they passed beneath the blue and white sign printed in many languages that said platform two was directly ahead. Even as fast as James could walk without actually trotting, he found difficulty in keeping pace with Noelle, who was several steps ahead of him.

He gripped the two train tickets extremely tightly, staring at them from time to time while adjusting the strap of the canvas bag over his shoulder. Upon reaching the correct platform, they saw that the train was preparing for departure. Very few people were roaming around the area as they must have already boarded. Fortunately, the doors had not yet closed and the railroad staff were still there taking the tickets of a few late comers.

They approached one of the doors with a man in typical blue uniform with brass buttons and a flat-topped hat that resembled an accessory of a World War II-era formal army uniform. He was a kindly-looking gentleman, probably in his sixties. Gray hair had all but taken over his once black mustache that sat perched upon his gentle smile and long, vertical dimples. *Finally, someone I'm pretty sure isn't going to try to kill us,* James thought.

He nodded to the travelers in welcome, extending his hand without a word in the universal gesture that calls for one's boarding pass. James handed them over, then nodded *good day* and followed Noelle into the inner body of the train car.

They moved down the narrow aisles taking in all of their surroundings. Its dark carpet had not been steam cleaned in some time, as it had numerous small stains discoloring the once deep red.

Hydraulics sounded with the releasing of pressure as the train began to creep forward. They had their pick of seats, so Noelle chose a random row that was completely vacant, and moved down to the window seat. James followed, sitting beside her and sighing in relaxation. This was the first time all day that he had been able to rest and release the tension that had been building in his muscles.

Noelle sensed this immediately, feeling the same way. She smiled at him as if to forgive him for all of the near-death experiences over the course of the previous few hours and took his hand in hers, gripping it firmly. She then turned her head back to the left to watch the covering of the station pass away into the scenery of downtown Alexandria.

Seemingly from nowhere, a man appeared to James's right. He was wearing a gray business suit with a white shirt and royal-blue tie. He was a younger man, perhaps in his late twenties, who fit the profile of a young business intern on his way to a business trip. He carried with him a black briefcase with gold hinges and fasteners, a newspaper, a blanket and a book.

The man seemed to scan the car as if to search for an empty seat, of which there were plenty, but despite the fact that there were only about thirty people scattered around in random seats, he chose to sit right next to James in the aisle seat. He was polite enough, imploring James with his eyes to allow him to sit there and nodding with a smile on his freshly-shaven face. Without a word, he placed his briefcase on his lap, which he had covered with the blanket, and opened the blue and yellow cover of some book that James could not read the subject of, as it was in Arabic. In order to preempt any small talk with the gentleman, James simply tilted his head back in his seat, and closed his eyes.

Chapter 36

James awoke to a message from the conductor over the intercom system. His eyes were glazed and he could barely make out that the sun was still up over the desert. Noelle was still peering through the tinted window at the marvels on the other side. She had never been to the desert, much less the outskirts of the Sahara. The rocks, the sand and the wadis were fascinating to her, and she had barely averted her eyes from the window the entire ride.

James had briefly woken up a few times during the course of the trip to see her staring out across the delta region. When most people think of Egypt, they think of desert, which is a fair assessment of the country. But many fail to realize how green the Nile River valley really is—especially near the delta. He had watched her for a few moments each time gazing out across the occasional delta branch and rich farmland.

He stretched his back and contorted within the small confines of his seat. His eyes began to clear as he rubbed them, clearing the crust that had formed in the corners. His buttocks were tingling from being seated for too long, and his neck sore.

"What did the conductor say?" he finally spoke to the young man beside him, having to clear his throat a little.

"He said we will be in Suez in a few moments," the business intern looked up from his book for a moment and spoke briefly and politely.

"Did you have a good nap?" Noelle smiled, finally realizing he was awake.

"Yeah," he stretched again, "I needed that. You should have slept, too."

"I know," she shrugged, "but it's so beautiful here."

"Maybe you could live here after you retire," he jested.

He felt something poking him in the side. It wasn't sharp or painful, but surprising. At first, he assumed it was the young man's elbow or the cell phone on his belt, but the look on Noelle's face told a different story.

He slowly turned his head to the right, first to see that the young man was staring directly at him. The dark brown eyes may as well have been glowing red. There was an anger in his look. Malice lives in such a stare, even hatred. Looking down at his side, he saw a pistol with a silencer that was increasing in pressure against his kidney. He brought his eyes back to level with the young gunman's, sending a message of confusion.

"When the train stops," he began to speak, "this bag that you have will come with me. Do not try to stop me or follow me. Neither of you will be harmed. I will simply walk away. You cannot have the key, and I assure you that I will kill both of you if you try to stop me."

James did not know what to do or say. Many things came to mind—pleads to rethink his affiliation with the religious sect and to think about all of the people who would suffer and die if the machine were to set off a deadly series of natural disasters, but the words could not manage to reach fruition in speech. Would the man listen anyway? Faith is a powerful thing. People in Varanasi, India, bathe in the Ganges River for its healing power, though the reality is that the sewage and pollution in the waters kill many people with diseases like cholera. There are Christians in the southern United States who handle rattlesnakes and drink poison out of faith that God will protect them from harm. Faith has fueled wars and cruel punishments for the crime of heresy. Perhaps the men of the Zoroastrian cult saw the destructive end of mankind as a welcome event in light of how *evil* the human race had become. Perhaps to them the end was a positive thing in comparison to the sadness and heartache of the human race.

The train slowed to the pace of a crawl as it moved through the city of Suez. James looked out beyond Noelle's horrified expression and through the window at the town surrounding them. It was not nearly as grand at Alexandria. It was much like what El Paso, Texas, is to Houston. The structures were smaller and cruder, unlike the grand buildings and charm of Alexandria. He could see the large ships and tankers a few miles away moving sluggishly along the canal, making their way into the Mediterranean to bring their goods to the markets of Europe. Overshadowing the simple dwellings and shops of the town were numerous refineries and warehouses that were characteristic of an industrial port.

As the train pulled into the small, covered depot, James contemplated his actions. It all seemed crazy. He should simply let the man walk away with the scepter and take Noelle back to the United States where they would be safe. But for how long would they be safe? Immediately after returning home they could be watching breaking news about some disastrous earthquake or volcanic eruption somewhere in the Middle East. A few weeks later, the same could be happening in India or Eastern Europe. When would it be America's turn? He had a unique opportunity to make a difference in the fate of a planet. He trembled at the thought; the responsibility. He did not know yet what he would do. He had lived his life as a professor and businessman. He was not a hero. He had no training or global purpose. He was a man. An alcoholic. Nobody.

The train halted and the young would-be killer looked into James's eyes with a smile as he grasped the shoulder strap of the canvas bag, preparing to exit the car with it once the doors opened. But he made a fatal error. He first moved his left wrist in front of his face to check the watch that was affixed to it, releasing the shoulder strap for a moment. He then tried to organize his belongings and went to open the briefcase to replace the pistol inside, thus removing it from the professor's side.

James made a split-second improvised decision, one that he could not believe even as it happened, and grabbed the man's right wrist, tilting the direction that the gun was pointing up and to the right. It was a motion that was all he could think of to avoid himself or Noelle being shot. This clearly surprised the gunman whose only instinct was to pull the trigger as he had promised, sending a single shot through the window, producing a single hole in the glass and the characteristic web of cracks beneath the thin film of tinting.

A silenced gun still makes a sound, but the few people in the car were far enough away from the blast that the sounds of the metal-on-metal screeching of the car's wheels on the track, and the sounds of the hydraulics, muffled the silenced blast enough that no one turned around.

The two men struggled for several moments over control of the weapon. In an act of desperation, James brought down a swift, powerful blow to the man's groin, repeating the motion, causing him to grimace and wince in overwhelming pain. He did not know how many times he bludgeoned the man's testicles, but with the force and frequency considered, he was almost sure that he was rupturing at least one of them.

This kind of pain was overwhelming enough for the young Zoroastrian to give it precedence and loosen his grip on the pistol. James capitalized on the opportunity, wrenching the gun away from the man's hand and taking it in his own.

Noelle could think of nothing more to do in this short struggle but to stand slightly, her back firmly pressed against the cracking window behind her. Her hands were enclosed around her mouth and nose as she was gasping in shock and terror, unable to make any other varying sounds.

James, however, was still acting purely on instinct. He had the gun in his hand and he was now standing as the train came to a stop completely. The highly evolved human brain was trying to enact his conscience, telling him to spare the man's life and that he had done enough. Perhaps he had a family who relied on him. But his more primitive instincts took over. He couldn't have this assassin following them. He had come to kill, and would likely stop at nothing. It had to be done, and with that, he reluctantly pressed the end of the silencer to the man's chest and spent a round into his body, creating a hole that spewed a few small droplets of blood first onto James's shirt and pants, and then to a swift pour soaking into the victim's white shirt.

He was in awe over what had just taken place. It was mortifying, weighing heavily upon his heart that he had just taken a human life. This man was someone's son and possibly someone's father. But self-preservation had won the moral battle. He and Noelle were obviously being targeted and this meant that they may have more encounters like this before the end of their journey. These were dangerous people, and they would stop at nothing. He did not want this man following or sending another into the correct direction. With that, he flipped the safety switch of the Sig Sauer forty-caliber pistol and tucked it into the waistband of his pants at the small of his back, and then concealed it with his shirttail.

Without wasting a moment after the doors to the train car were opened, James and Noelle leapt out onto the desolate, industrial platform of the train station. There was almost no one around, save a few passengers that were exiting the same train and depot employees doing their various jobs.

They both knew that they had to distance themselves from the train as quickly as possible, and began moving. At first, James started looking for the ticket office so that they could book another voyage to a different city, but he had no clue where to go from there. Deep in thought, he simply stood still, trying to work things out in his head.

"James?" Noelle tried to get his attention. "Are we going?" she began to grow a little frantic.

"We can't get on another train," he said to her. "It's too risky. They know we came to Suez, so someone else will either catch up with us on the train or kill us before we even get on."

"So what, a plane?" she offered another way.

"No. No more public transit. It's too risky. We need private transportation," he looked around for any clue as to what to do.

"What? You don't own a car here. And I know you're rich, but Jesus! You can't just buy a car for the day!" she didn't know what other options there were.

"Nope," he smiled. "Come on," he led Noelle quickly for the parking lot.

The two of them ran out through a doorless exit passage cut into the crude metal walls of the train depot. This led into a concrete-paved employee parking lot that contained about two dozen different cars, most of them old models of European or Asian manufacturing. As far as the eye could see, they were surrounded by the orange expanses of desert, as if they were in a parking lot on Mars. James walked from car to car lifting the cover to each one's fueling port and reaching inside. Noelle's brow tightened in bewilderment.

"We don't have time for games," she said in a patronizing tone. "If you're playing *duck, duck, goose*, I don't think you're going to get one of those to chase you."

"Aha!" he shouted excitedly as he found what he was looking for.

"What?" she rushed over to see what the product of his strange behavior was.

"Some people hide the spare key inside just in case they lock their keys in the car," he produced a small key covered on one side with duct tape. "Not a bad ride," he looked over the late-nineties Honda Civic, inserted the key into the locking mechanism, and opened the door.

"What, we're gonna steal the car?" she chastised.

"Borrow it," he corrected.

"Yeah, like the neighbor's hacksaw, and he never sees it again," she commented sarcastically as she climbed into the passenger seat next to him. "Although you did just kill a guy, so you might as well get into grand theft auto, too."

He smiled over at her with a sly demeanor as he put the key into the ignition and cranked the engine, which James could tell right away was in need of a tune-up and changing of the serpentine belt. But this car would do just fine for the moment.

"So where to, Professor?" Noelle crossed her arms and looked out across the desert.

"I don't know. I told you I haven't figured it out yet," he was getting frustrated. "And we don't have time to figure it out here so we may travel for hours in the wrong direction before we figure it out!"

"Sorry. I know it's stressful," she softened her tone. "It's not like anyone knows where Armageddon is going to happen."

James's eyes widened and his ears perked up as he listened and processed what she said. He laughed out loud at how unimaginative and blind he could be. He chuckled, unable to stop, and shaking his head in disbelief. *Why didn't I think of that?*

"Yes they do. They know exactly where Armageddon is, and we're going there!" he shifted the car into drive and sped out of the lot.

Chapter 37

The young boy crouched to the ground, running his small, tan fingers through the grass growing between the ancient paving stones, scrounging for pebbles. He took in the breeze and cast his gaze out across the vast valley below. In the distance he could see cars traveling down the highway and even military vehicles making their way down the road.

He began tossing the pebbles down the hill, seeing how far they would go beyond the ruined fortress that surrounded him. He had heard the adults say that this was a *har*, or mountain in the Hebrew tongue. It didn't seem like a mountain to him. It was very steep and towering for a hill, but he thought it was no more than that.

Sounds traveled a far distance across a valley and plain, such as the one he was standing on. He could not see the origin of the dreadful noises, but he knew that somewhere far from his location, there was death. He did not like the idea of death and destruction. The booming tank fire, mortars and rapid machine gun fire in the distance made him think of unpleasant things that he had known all his life in his own country. The Israelis and Muslims in the distance were undoubtedly killing one another, but for what?

He hurled more pebbles over the side of the hill, the sleeves of his white garments hindering his follow-through. He tried to push them back up his arm, but they were too loose and fell back down the length of his arm.

This is not where a boy of barely six years wanted to be at the moment. He wanted to be back home, running through the streets playing soccer with his friends. He wanted the comfort of his mother's loving arms whenever one of the Muslim kids teased him about his faith. He wanted his own bed in his own small room. He did not want to be on the summit of this distant *har*. But this is where his father said he must be. He said that it was important that he be there.

"Adimah," he heard his father calling his name. "Come this way. It is time," his father, clad in similar flowing white robes, motioned for him.

"Yes, father," he answered, dropping the remaining pebbles in his hand and running to his father's side.

"Today is a special day," his father said in Farsi, smiling as they walked along the ancient path.

They walked down the stone steps cutting into the mount. Adimah could tell they were descending below the fortress as he ceased to feel the cool Mediterranean breeze. After the last step, they turned sharply to the left, entering a dark tunnel carved out of stone. The boy gripped his father's hand with increasing firmness as they traveled further into the recesses of the hill fortress. It was frightening, as if they were descending into the underworld. His father patted his hand and smiled, assuring him it was okay.

Somewhere just past the midpoint of the tunnel, his father came to a stop and motioned to a crack in the wall. The young boy was horrified at what that meant. What if the stones fell in on top of him? What if there were biting insects or snakes? Yet his father nudged him in the direction of this crevasse, and followed behind him.

Adimah could smell something burning but continued on with not a clue what was on the other side. Oddly enough, the smell of smoke was comforting. He did not know why, but he felt a strange calm come over him. Perhaps the smell of burning oil and wood reminded him of home.

It seemed that he would never reach the end of the long pathway. He looked back at his father who, unlike himself, was larger and had to work his way between the narrow spaces sideways. Turning back to the front, Adimah could see glowing light reflecting from the cavern wall, and finally he could see the end.

As he stepped into the vast cavern, he could see the familiar sacred fire burning before him. The walls appeared orange in the glow of the flames. But most of all, he was shocked by the number of men standing inside. There were hundreds of followers dressed as he was, looking back at him in wonderment and silence. No one dared touch him, nor speak to him. They simply moved aside as he traversed the cavern floor, his father behind him clutching his shoulders.

Ahead, he could see the priest. His purple robes were always a dead giveaway, and he seemed to eye him in the same way as the rest, yet with a happy smile. Behind him stood a massive bronze and wooden structure. The boy stared up in wonder and awe, wide-eyed as he moved forward. He had never seen anything like this. It was amazing. He wondered what it was for.

Aside from the large structure in the background, Adimah had seen this scene before. Hundreds of followers gathered in praise of God, calling on Him to bring peace and do away with evil. But they were never this quiet, and he had never been the obvious center of attention.

He was guided by his father up to the altar where the priest stood smiling. Adimah could see the Avesta open before him. The priest then spoke to the masses, reading from what looked to be the book of Yasna.

"When, O Mazda, shall piety come with right, with dominion the happy dwelling rich with pasture? Who are they that will make peace with the bloodthirsty liars? To whom will the lore of good thought come? These shall be the deliverers of the provinces, who exert themselves, O good thought in their action, O Asha, to fulfill their duty, face to face with thy command, O Mazda. For these are the appointed smiters of violence," his voice boomed and echoed through the cavern. "And this is he! The smiter of violence!" he placed a hand on Adimah's shoulder. "I give you the one who will restore peace! I give you the Shaoshant!"

The crowd of men cheered in reverence as the young boy stood confused. He couldn't be the Shaoshant, yet everyone believed that he was.

"This must be kept secret from even your families, for his identity must remain unknown for his safety until the time that he brings the peace of Mazda back to the world."

The ringing of his cell phone interrupted the Shaoshant's thoughts as he looked out across the familiar valley, watching the afternoon pass. He shook off the memories of his childhood and that fateful day. He retrieved his phone and then opened it without saying a word.

"Master," the man on the other end said in Farsi, "Omir is dead on the train."

"This is disappointing," he said calmly. "And the key? The Americans?"

"They stole a car. They still have the key."

"Follow them. Surely they will never find the machine. Wait for them to stop for fuel, then get it."

"Yes Master. Of course," he paused, even hesitated. "But I must tell you that they are heading north from Suez."

"In this direction?" he stopped to ponder the possibilities of them finding the location of the machine. "They are clever. They did find the tomb after all," he began to look worried. "Just stop them. Kill them if you must—just get the key. I want the key!" he closed his phone in anger, then calmed again at the sight of the beautiful valley before him.

Chapter 38

"Israel?" Noelle gasped as the last rays of the sun began fading beyond the horizon behind them. "Great! I could stand to get shot at a few more times. It will be fun!"

"It will be fine," James reassured her. "We'll be far from any significant fighting. This place is largely forgotten by most people."

"Well that sounds reassuring. If it's so important, why have people forgotten about it? I'm not convinced."

"Misinterpretation," was his only response.

"Oh yeah? And what is that supposed to mean?" she was beginning to get angry.

"Look," he remained calm, "what is the place that the Bible says is the site where the end of days will begin?"

"Armageddon," she spouted as if it were effortless. "Everyone knows that."

"And that's where we're going."

"You mean that place exists?" she was surprised. "I thought that was some sort of ancient Hebrew metaphor that we could never understand."

"Oh, no. It's a very real place in northern Israel," he nodded his head in confirmation.

"Then why have I never seen it on a map?" she puzzled. "That's a pretty important place. Why have I never heard a priest mention it specifically?"

"As I said, it's a misinterpretation. The Bible is full of them. You have to remember that most of the original texts of the Bible were in various Hebrew dialects, and then they were translated into Greek, Latin, more modern European languages and then the good old seventeenth-century King James English that we all love."

"So the Bible is full of mistakes?" she looked troubled.

"Scary, huh?" he grinned. "I mean, *tengo hambre* is Spanish for *I'm hungry*, but literally, it actually means *I have hunger*. Sometimes we lose some of the meaning when we translate. What do you think happens when you translate a translation of a translation of a translation? And that's not taking into account the various double meanings, slangs, and metaphors that the Hebrews may have used that we know nothing about."

"So what was John trying to say in Revelations when he wrote *Armageddon*?" she hungered for more.

"Har Megiddo," he replied.

"What?"

"Har Megiddo," he repeated. "Har is Hebrew for *mountain* or *mount*. Megiddo is just the name of the place. Mount Megiddo is the place where the last battle will take place. Armageddon is just a perversion of the name."

"So the final battle will take place on a mountain? The Bible doesn't say anything about that."

"There's a lot the Bible doesn't say. But no, the actual battle will supposedly take place in the Jezreel Valley below," he began to explain. "This is the site of the first recorded battle in history—between the Egyptian forces of Thutmose III and the Hittites. It is the site of probably thousands of battles fought right up until about 1972. The armies of Egyptians, Hittites, Canaanites, Hebrews, Greeks, Romans, crusaders and Palestinians have all crossed through Megiddo Pass. Generals like Vespasian, Ptolemy, Joshua and Alexander the Great have been there."

Noelle raised an eyebrow at the name of Alexander. It was beginning to make a little more sense.

"Napoleon himself said it was the perfect place to hold a battle. And overlooking the valley is a little mountain, or really a large hill. It was the perfect place to build a fortress as it overlooks the pass and could easily guard against invading armies. So its importance was known long ago. There are about twenty-six levels of occupation on the site, meaning twenty-six different construction periods. The current fortress was abandoned in about 300 BC, but the structure dates to the time of

Solomon," he began chuckling a bit as he had a revelation.

"What?" she was hanging onto every word.

"I seem to remember that many of the fortresses atop the mountain have been destroyed by an earthquake."

"The earthquake storm," she gasped. "Where did you say Megiddo is?"

"Open the glove box and see if this guy has any maps," he motioned.

She opened the little hatch, and reached inside, finding a wad of folded paper wedged between the cheap plastic walls of the compartments and a badly damaged owner's manual. She pulled open the neatly folded maps, spreading them out across her lap and began to examine.

"There," he poined toward Israel. "About midway between the Mediterranean and Syria and between Nazareth and the West Bank dispute border."

She sat in the passenger seat trying to picture geological maps of the region. Her eyes were shut tightly, and even her fists were clenched as she tried to access the information in her head, overlaying the maps in her head onto the one in her lap.

"James," her eyes opened widely. "If I'm right, Megiddo sits on top of a major fault line!"

"God damn it!" he raised his voice. "I hate being right."

"Why do you have to curse like that? I mean the blasphemies," she asked calmly.

"I don't know. Does it bother you?"

"A little," she took a tone of compassion. "You're not very religious are you? I mean you seem a little jaded about religion. Is it because of the loss of your family?"

"No, I don't think so," he began. "It started long before that. Beaten by nuns in Catholic School for misspelling words from an early age was a start. But mainly it's because of education. I began to look at religion very differently."

"I'm highly educated," Noelle responded. "And I still have faith."

"Yeah, but the discipline of geology is different from history. I began to look at religion from more of a historical standpoint. I analyze and critique the Bible. I pit the Adam and Eve story against scientific facts of human evolution and migration. I use the reason of The Enlightenment and the Renaissance. I see Christian rip-offs of previous religions like Mithraism, Hinduism, and Zoroastrianism. I've studied the evil deeds of the Catholic Church during its existence. I began to wonder how much of the Bible is true. How much is simply myth—just like the Greeks and Egyptians explaining natural phenomenon with a supernatural story? Who decided what we are to believe—God or man? And what about all of the people around the world who are not brought up around Christianity? Are they just going to go to Hell? There are so many questions!" he lamented.

"But through all that, God still exists," she spoke softly. "Men will always take a good and pure religion and use it for their own controlling reasons. What if all of the religions in the world formed from the same god revealing himself to the world in different ways? What if the same god has just been interpreted differently by different cultures?"

"God revealing himself? Interesting point." He pulled his pack of cigarettes from his pocket and began to light one, rolling down the window a little. "You mind? I haven't had one since this morning."

"No, go ahead. Anything will smell better than this car. I think the car itself has B.O.," she laughed.

"What about you?" he mumbled, trying to light the cigarette which was moving up and down with the movement of his lips. "Hasn't your faith ever been tested?" he inhaled the first drag, blew it out, and began speaking normally. "Hurricane Katrina tested a lot of people's faith—mine included. I sat in my house all alone, braving it out over a bottle of whiskey. It wasn't long after my wife and son died, either."

"I haven't quite gone through the hell you have," she admitted, "but everyone gets those trials and tribulations. I was in New Haven during Katrina, but seeing it all unfold on CNN was heartbreaking. I couldn't talk to my family in Baton Rouge for three weeks, and yes, I did question why God would allow this to happen to people. But it passed. He has a plan."

"CNN pissed me off," he took another drag. "Bunch of northerners who have never been through a hurricane before commenting on shit they knew nothing about. *Why didn't people get out?*" he mocked. "Because they don't have the money! *Why hasn't the government made it in?* Because the place is flooded out! There's no fucking way in!" He paused. "Sorry. I'm still bitter. It's been less than a year," he smiled.

"Yeah, that seems to be a common theme with you," she smiled.

He just smiled in return. He knew he had become cynical and jaded about a great number of things. His value of life, particularly his own, had become skewed. He saw religion from the perspective of a historian, studying it as a sociological tool that man used to control the masses. Perhaps the idea of God and the afterlife were both a psychological coping mechanism to deal with the notion that everyone dies. He was fed up with the government and had lost faith in humanity. He believed that the youth of America was ruined and posed a threat to the future of its society.

"That reminds me," she had an afterthought. "Speaking of your harboring of grudges and bitterness, there's something I've been wondering since the meeting in Dr. Husser's office."

"Okay, go on," he smiled cautiously, clueless as to what this could be about.

"You seem to know Dr. Horn very well, but there seems to be tension between the two of you," she began. "I'll be blunt: Why do you hate him so much? What happened to your friendship?"

"Ooh," he sighed deeply, unsure of where to begin. "Okay, well, I've known him for a long time—since rush week our first semester at LSU. We were good friends, even best friends up until a couple of years ago." He paused for a moment.

"He was always kind of a dick," James then continued. "If you were to meet and spend time with Tim, you either loved him or you hated him. I just kind of accepted him for who he was. But there was always that potential for him to do something to piss me off. I even stood by him as he cheated on girlfriends, convinced he was telling the truth when he spun some crazy, off-the-wall explanation of what happened. But a couple of years ago, not long before Abigail and Max died, he had come into town to visit, and, as usual, I let him crash at my house. He's a notorious bachelor, you know—completely unfit for monogamy. One night, we were drinking and playing cards—me, Abigail, and Tim. We were having a blast talking, joking around and reminiscing about the college fraternity days. In fact, that's all he talked about; every time I saw him. I found out later that Tim had been reading books on card counting and other poker tricks to cheat the opposition. Well, I caught him dealing from the bottom of the deck. It pissed me off and I proceeded to call him a cheat and an asshole. He, of course, denied everything. So I got up and went to take a piss, maybe to calm down a little, and then I'd be over it. But when I came back, I walked right into the middle of Abby slapping him across the face. I saw his hand on my wife's breast. She immediately told me that Tim had propositioned her to come to his bedroom after I was asleep. So I jerked him up, cracked him across the jaw, kicked him out, and told him to never speak to me again. And he didn't until just the other day."

"Wow," Noelle looked stunned. "I don't know what to say. I'm sorry."

"Yeah, it's still a bit of a tender spot," his expression was one of pain masked by apathy. "It wouldn't have been so bad if Abby hadn't have died soon after and I lost her for real. I probably could have written it off as the alcohol's doing and forgiven him, but compounded with the loss of my family, that memory was just too vivid and painful."

"I'm sorry I brought it up," she once again regretted her stumbling into his painful past. Yet, it seemed impossible to avoid bad memories with the man.

"You couldn't have known," he reassured. "And on that note, I'm going to offer my own apology. I'm sorry I almost got you killed a few times today."

"It's okay. You're not perfect. Just perfectly human," she smiled.

He smiled without a word. He accepted the way he was. He knew he was flawed in many ways. But he was who he was—he needed not apologize for that.

"Get some sleep," he grinned. "I just saw a sign that we're about twenty miles from Bir Hassana. We'll fill up there. But get some sleep and we'll trade off later."

She smiled gently, then adjusted her seat as far back as it would go. She looked into his eyes with affection and then quickly dosed off.

Chapter 39

The young boy sat comfortably in his favorite leather chair, surrounded by scores of books that he had not yet read. There were books of all sorts—fictional novels by Ray Bradbury and Kurt Vonnegut, antiques by Dickens and Doyle, poetry, textbooks, science, philosophy, and his favorite, history.

At the age of six, though, he still preferred books with at least some illustration. Each month, he came home from school with an order form that was distributed by his teacher. It was an order form for books. So each month, the boy's mother sent him back to school with the completed form and a check for the total of the books that he wished to own.

They were usually history and adventure books. He now owned volumes of reading material on every imaginable subject including dinosaurs, mythology, ancient Egypt, ancient Greece, the Romans, knights, castles, wars and samurai. He spent hours in the library of his home, not in front of the television, but reading his books and some of his father's. So naturally, he could spout endless information to his teachers and family members with amazing accuracy. He was often the center of attention at his parents' dinner parties when he snuck from his room in his pajamas. All night, he would hear the laughter and chatter, longing to be a part of the fun that was being had. He would mingle amongst colleagues and family members, dwarfed by their size until guests, champagne in hand, would notice him, smile, and gawk at how cute this little boy was. From that point he would engage these often well-educated men and women in very intellectual conversation, much to their surprise. And then, like clockwork, his mother would discover that he had escaped from his bed, and lead him gently by the hand back to his room, his father cursing the situation angrily.

It was becoming late and the young man was already in his blue two-piece pajamas. He was growing drowsy as he rubbed his brown eyes and stroked his ear-length brown hair. Yet he could not put this book down, though he had probably read about Howard Carter and King Tut dozens of times.

"Son," his father's gruff voice echoed from behind the beautiful cherry desk across the room, causing the boy to turn his head in that direction. "Come over here," he smiled.

The boy closed his book, leapt from his seat, and began to traverse the red floorboards that separated the two of them. He watched his father poring over records and proposals, his eyes never leaving the pages before him. He approached in caution, never really sure why he was so intimidated by the man. Perhaps it was the deepness and insincerity in his voice. Maybe it was his size.

"Yes, Daddy?" he approached his father from his left.

"You want to come and see what your dad does for a living?" He briefly shot a glance at his son and then returned his gaze to his work.

The young man looked at the papers, records and books that lay spread across the desktop in front of his father. He was making notes in the margins of typewritten pages and studying over numbers. The boy didn't quite understand it. To him, it was all completely meaningless. But his dad began to explain.

"You see, we're looking into publishing this book," he pointed to some title. "We have to figure out how much money to put into the printing, artwork, marketing, and various overhead to make that happen," he used his pen to point to a set of numbers and simple math. "That will determine whether or not we will print it and how much to charge in the book stores for the book."

The young boy simply stared at the paper, the writing and the numbers. It did not make sense to him. He had not a clue what it took to publish a book. He only knew that they came from stores and order forms and that he enjoyed reading them. His look was blank and empty, as if he were focusing beyond the paperwork, trying to see through to the wood beneath it. His hands were clasped behind his back as he swayed side to side and front to back on the balls and heels of his feet.

He kept making odd expressions, contorting his lips and raising his eyebrows.

"You're not interested," his father recognized this in his boy's expression, and began to get frustrated. "You're going to have to learn this sooner or later if you're going to take over the company someday," his voice showed a hint of sternness. "When I was your age, I couldn't wait to find out what my dad did. I loved to go up to the office and watch him conduct business. And he taught me all I know about the publishing industry. That's what I'm trying to do with you!" the sternness turned almost to yelling.

"But Daddy, I don't understand it," he was truly frightened. He didn't want to disappoint his father. He was trying to seem interested, but he just wasn't. "It's boring," he pouted.

"Boring? Don't understand?" he was taken aback. "What's not to understand? It's simple economics!" he began to get angry. "God, you're so stupid sometimes! Go back to your stupid fuckin' book!" he pointed in the direction of the leather chair.

"But Daddy . . ." he tried to recover and get his father to continue teaching him.

"But nothing! You're not interested, so go away!"

The boy turned slowly, slouching his shoulders and hanging his head, and then walked away. His dad was a strong and stern man, so he tried not to show his emotions. He had never seen his father cry or be sad, even when Grandpa died. For that reason, the young boy tried to contain his urge to release the pain and rejection that was welling up inside him. It, however, was no use. First came the runny nose and subsequent sniffling, and then the convulsive jerk of his diaphragm and breathing. Finally, there were tears. They were the large fat type that would form in the corner of the eyes and, without effort, roll down one's cheek.

What added to the pain of the moment was the walk back to his chair. He did not look back at his dad for fear that his face would still bear the expression of anger. There was a great deal of shame that he had to be watched back to his seat by his disgusted father, and in an act that could take away from that feeling, he quickly moved from a sulking trudge to a full sprint toward the door, sobbing all the way past his mother who was standing in the doorway, arms folded.

"Dan," she began to chastise him, "you hurt his feelings! What are you thinking?"

"What?" he defended. "He's my only child, and someday he's got to carry on the company," he said sternly.

"He's six years old," she shot back, "and besides, what if he doesn't want to go into business? You've got to let him make his own choices; nurture his own interests."

"What's not interesting about being a publishing executive?" he threw his hands in the air. "He'll be rich. He'll be happy."

"You're rich, Dan," she cocked her head to the side. "Are you happy?"

"Sure I am!"

"Then why are you so angry all the time that you have to crush your only child's feelings?" she questioned.

That was the correct button for her to push. His face turned deep red, and his already bitter expression turned to one of near hatred. His blue eyes were piercing, simply complementing the redness of face and creating a terrifying and sinister look. He stood from his chair, poised for attack, but not in a physical way. He had an extreme amount of intelligence. This tended to make him arrogant, whether he was trying to be or not. Most people who knew him either loved him or hated him because he was very condescending in terms of academic knowledge and did not mind telling someone when they were wrong. Moreover, his intelligence often paired with his vicious temper to create an ability to wound even the closest family member personally and dreadfully.

"You know why I'm so unhappy sometimes?" he began yelling. "You! I don't know why I married such a stupid, ugly woman! And you passed the stupid gene on to your son!"

She could not say a word. She never could after he said things like that. If he were ever put into a situation where he did not know what to say or did not have intellectual reasoning to produce a comeback, he resorted to personal attacks, and it certainly worked against his wife.

The only thing she could do was try to pretend that it did not hurt her. If she showed the vulnerability, he knew that it could be exploited. This time, however, was different. Her husband had just attacked her and their son. Her arms remained folded as she stood propped with her shoulder against the door frame. Her eyes began to produce the tears of a thousand insults as her lips elongated, stretching them thin. She was trying her best not to allow her emotions to rise to the surface and sob uncontrollably. But it was in vain. So to hide the anguish and release, she turned immediately and walked out the door and down the hallway to her son's room.

She paused to wipe the tears from her eyes, and regain her composure before entering the room to console her baby boy. She gently pushed the door open, revealing the bright blue paint on the walls, Bugs Bunny posters and various toys strewn about, all veiled in a semi-darkness produced by the muted setting sunlight glowing through the beige curtains. He was laying face-down on his baseball-print sheets. He was still weeping into his pillow with muffled sobs and soaking the pillow case with tears.

His mother lightly stepped in his direction, and though he could hear that she was in the room, he did not reveal his face. He was afraid that it was his father, but knew it was his mother from her scent. She always carried the fragrance of lilac. He could feel his mattress shift as she sat on the bed next to him, and began rubbing his back.

He rolled over and looked into her eyes. They were still a bit bloodshot, and he well knew why. He heard the fighting night after night as he would try to fall asleep with his hands over his ears.

"Mom," he uttered that single word with nothing else that he really could say.

"Shhh, sweetie," she comforted, "you don't have to say anything. I know."

"I don't think I want to be like Daddy when I grow up," he sniffled.

"Honey, you can be anything you want to be," she reassured him, "and you will be great at it. Just make sure you love what you do. You're special and you're smart. You will do something great—I know it. Be that. Be extraordinary," she whispered and smiled.

James blinked a few times trying to clear the images from his head. The light and lack thereof were beginning to play tricks on him. He had been driving all night, and he had become accustomed to the dark, but now the sun was beginning to rise to the east across the desert. The first rays were trickling in though the passenger window. He kept feeling his eyes cross, so he would shake his head and blink rapidly.

Luckily, they were not far from the small city of Qiryat Gat. The sign that he had seen before said that they were only a few kilometers away. They had been within Israeli borders for quite some time, but it was going to take a little longer to get to Megiddo since he was trying to steer clear of Jerusalem and the West Bank. Finally, they could pull over and perhaps get some breakfast and rest for a moment.

Noelle awoke as the sunlight created a red glow through her eyelids. She yawned and stretched her arms high above her head as her legs curled up toward her chest. She wiped her eyes, turned her head to the left and smiled as she tried to focus her eyes on James.

"Wow, I slept all night," she grinned. "I normally don't sleep well in a car. Oh, I'm sorry I didn't relieve you—you should have woken me up!" she suddenly realized that James did not get a break from driving.

She then began removing her tank top, jeans and panties, wiggling around in the seat. She changed from her dingy, discarded clothing to the fresh garments that she had grabbed from the room.

"No, it's fine," he shrugged, smiling and unable to remove his eyes from her. "I got a nap on the train. Besides, you looked so peaceful and I enjoyed the alone time. Alone with my thoughts—I enjoy that sometimes," he finally returned his eyes to the road, correcting for a slight swerve produced by his distraction.

"Wow, are we stopping?" she suddenly changed the subject, seeing that they were at the outskirts of a town.

"Yeah," he said. "I might as well fill up the tank again, stretch my legs, and get some breakfast."

"Breakfast?" she puzzled.

"Yeah, breakfast," he grinned sarcastically. "You know, that meal that you're supposed to eat every morning with coffee? It's the most important one," he smiled with a certain level of mock cheesiness.

"Yeah, I know what breakfast is, smartass," she smiled, amused. "I mean, breakfast in Israel?"

"I'm sure they eat something in the morning here," he carried on.

"No, no, no," she shook her head. "I mean what kind of breakfast would they eat? I don't foresee hash browns, and definitely not a pork sausage patty or slab of ham!"

"I don't know. Let's pull over here and get gas," he motioned toward a station to the right.

He pulled the Honda into the filling station, trying to make out the name on the sign, but he did not know enough Hebrew to decipher it. Driving the car up to the right of the number three pump, he shifted into park and stepped out, stretching his back and legs.

"Breakfast?" he asked Noelle with a smile as he filled up the gas tank.

"Sure," she replied. "What do you suggest, professor?"

"Um," he looked around at his surroundings, "how about a falafel?" he spied a stand across the street.

"Yeah," she nodded, "I like those. Always get it once or twice from the street vendors when I visit friends in New York."

"Okay, cool," he secured the latch on the gas pump to keep it running. "Two falafels coming up!"

He winked at Noelle, which surprised him. It was one of those instances when he did something completely out of his character.

He turned and made his way for the street, looked both ways, although it was too early for any serious traffic, and began to trot across the dust-covered pavement to the falafel stand. As he approached, he could already smell the aroma of frying chickpeas and fava beans.

The people working the stand immediately showed exuberant attention for him, ready to make a sale that would help feed their family. They began preparing the pita bread and grabbing for the falafel balls, asking in their heavily accented English how many he wanted. James simply held up two fingers.

"How much?" he asked the old woman.

"American?" she did the calculations in her head. "Five," she finally replied after a moment of deep thought.

As he extracted the five dollar bill from his wallet, he wondered if that was an accurate conversion of currency. He handed over the money in exchange for the food. The people in the stand thanked him profusely, as they passed around the bill, a rare sight for inhabitants of this town.

A blood-curdling scream broke the normal sounds of the street-side as James turned sharply to see what it was. It was terrible. It dripped with fear, almost palpable and fleshy in nature. Noelle. James felt his heart drop into his stomach.

He dropped the food from his hand, and began to sprint across the street, this time not even checking to see if there was a vehicle coming. What he saw across the street was a man in very plain clothes entering the driver side of the Honda. Noelle had been pulled into the car and was struggling with the man from the passenger side. The stranger did not have much time before James made it to the car, and he had to subdue the woman, so in one swift motion, he back-fisted Noelle in the forehead, rendering her unconscious and slumped over the dashboard. He slammed the door shut, cranked the engine, put it into drive and sped off down the street.

James now had a choice. His first instinct was to run down the street after them, but he knew he would never catch them. The man had to have come from somewhere, so he scanned the gas station for a car, and saw that there was a 1980s model Toyota parked behind the spot where the Honda was. The driver side door was ajar, so he concluded that this was the man's vehicle. He quickly jumped into the car but found no key in the ignition. He sighed in terror as he watched the Honda grow further and further away. It contained Noelle and, of course, the scepter of Alexander the Great.

How could I let this happen? His thoughts were of remorse and self-chastisement. *I'm so fucking stupid!*

He began to look around the interior of the cab for any indication of who this man was. He opened the glove compartment, and rooted through various items and papers until he found what he was looking for. It was a small leather-bound book, severely worn, that resembled a bible. Yet it had that growingly familiar symbol emblazoned on the cover. It was of the Living Flame.

"The Avesta," he sighed. Then he knew where that Honda, Noelle and the scepter were heading.

Chapter 40

Noelle's head bounced with the movement of the car. Her eyes were closed in her unconscious state while a reddish knot was forming on her forehead from the car-jacker's vicious back-handed blow.

The driver was sweating profusely. He looked around the back seat briefly trying to find some sort of towel or cloth to dry his dingy face. All he saw on the back seat was the canvas bag, and he smiled. His mission had been accomplished. He was sad for his fellow worshippers that had fallen prey to fate in attempting to capture the key. Yet he knew that their service would be rewarded by Ahura Mazda.

He looked over at his captive, who was still not awake. He knew he would soon have to find a way to bind her hands and feet. She was quite a fighter—much less submissive than the women in his home country of Iran. As insubordinate as she was, however, he did not wish to do what he was doing, although it had been necessary. Surely the man that was her accomplice understood that they would kill her if he tried to follow. If he were smart, he would stay away and hope that she would be released in time.

He had to admit, though, that he understood what this man saw in her. He cast a long gaze at her well-rounded, tanned thighs. He admired her petite body. It was not often that he was able to see such revealing clothes on such a beautiful woman. Though he was not Muslim, nor was he of the same belief that women should be completely covered, it was not a common sight in Iran. He wondered if she would awaken if he caressed her thigh. He began to convince himself that he had struck her hard enough that she may not even wake up if he pulled the car over and enjoyed her body for a time. He would be gentle.

He shook the thought from his head. Earthly impulses should not take precedence here. He was doing the work of his master and his god. The prophecy was to come true soon, and the whole purpose of it was to destroy evil and the unclean, animal impulses like these.

He took his cell phone from his pocket, opened it, and pressed the *send* button twice, redialing the last number that he called. After a couple of seconds of ringing, a man answered.

"Master," the kidnapper said in reverence, "I have the key."

"Excellent," he replied with relief. "Ahura Mazda will reward you."

"There is more, my lord," he continued in Farsi.

"Yes?"

"I could not take the key without taking the American woman," he almost hesitated in telling the Shaoshant.

All the kidnapper could hear was a concerned, but not angry, sigh and breathing. This was not quite the news he was expecting. He paused for a few more seconds, and then spoke.

"It could not be helped, yes?" he began. "This will produce one of two results. The other American will either stay far away in fear that we will kill her if he shows up—and we will—or he will be valiant and try to come after her, and we will still kill her, and him as well. I am certain he knows where to go. We must keep a watchful eye. No one can be allowed to prevent what is to come."

"Yes, Shaoshant," he said, and then closed the phone.

Chapter 41

James was bewildered and exhausted. Thousands of thoughts ran through his head, his mind already weary from a long night of driving.

He feared for Noelle's safety as she was surely a liability to them. Would they let her go after the plan was completed? Would they complete the deed, and then kill her anyway, just for spite? Likely, she would die as the machine self-destructed.

Fairly sure that the Zoroastrian car-jacker took Noelle to dissuade him from following, he could not wait and see what the outcome would be. He was not going to wait to see if she eventually made her way back to the United States only to have to explain to her why he left her at the mercy of a fundamentalist cult. There was something greater at risk here.

James was tired, dirty and thirsty, and struggled to think straight. He had to find water. He found a local store and quickly made his way over to the refrigerated cases. He opened one of the doors and basked in the cool air that escaped. He reached out his left hand to remove the largest bottle of purified water that he could find, walked over to the cashier, handed him way too much cash, and walked out, opening the bottle frantically. He quivered with joy as the cool water rushed into his desert of a mouth and into his gullet. The shockwave of cold glowed from his belly in a circular ripple effect.

Somewhat refreshed and hydrated, he was finally able to calm himself and think straight. He stood outside the shop and tried to remember the map from the Honda's glove compartment. It had showed a railroad that ran through this part of the country, but he was not sure if it crossed through Qiryat Gat. No longer having a car, this seemed like the best option.

He ran toward the street, which was beginning to bustle with more traffic, and frantically tried to flag down someone who would give him a ride.

An old, white pickup truck stopped in the middle of traffic. It nearly caused a collision, but the drivers behind the truck seemed strangely used to the occurrence, and simply diverted around it.

The truck pulled up to James, the passenger-side window rolled down, revealing two average-looking laborers on their way to work. They were smiling and friendly-looking; eager to help.

"You need ride?" his heavy accent complimented his slightly less-than-perfect English.

"Yeah," James replied. "Is there a railroad station in this town?"

"Railroad," he thought aloud. "Railway," his smile perked up. "Yes. You want to go? Get in back! I take you! I take you!" he motioned to the truck bed.

James nodded appreciatively and climbed over the nearly unsecured tailgate and into the dingy, rusted bed of the truck. He sat down on the hot metal, always remembering what he was told from a young age never to sit on top of the sides of the bed. He braced himself with both hands and jerked a bit as the driver floored the accelerator, sending the pickup soaring down the street in the direction of the train depot.

Chapter 42

Noelle's eyes had not focused yet, but she was beginning to come to. She had no idea where she was and could remember little of what had happened. She did, however, recognize the odd smell of the Honda that they had *borrowed* from the parking lot in Suez. But there was a new smell that her nose was detecting. It was the smell of new sweat mingled with old sweat. She silently prayed that her eyes would focus, and that the odor was emanating from James.

There was a salty taste in her mouth that she could not quite identify. She started to panic as she realized that she was, for some reason, having trouble breathing and she could not move her legs or hands.

She was lying on her back and could feel her hands bound between her and the seat of the car. Her eyes focused and she saw a man hovering above her. She was now face to face with her captor. He was not pleasant to look at. His deeply acne-scarred face was filthy and dripping with sweat, which was falling to her lower torso and soaking into her tank top. Terror filled her very being as she continued to feel the man's hand probing between her inner thighs.

She noticed that the man was shirtless, bearing a tattoo of the *Living Flame* on the right side of his chest. *Why does this man have his shirt off?* She began mentally and emotionally preparing herself for what was to come, and then the man removed his hand from her legs. He stood tall outside of the car's back seat, looked around, closed the rear door and stepped into the driver's side, and cranked the engine.

Noelle was relieved, or as relieved as she could be as a captive, bound and tied in the back seat of a car. She looked down to see that her feet were bound by a strip of the cloth that once was a part of the man's shirt and that the gag in her mouth must have been flavored by his sweat.

Chapter 43

James felt a bit self-conscious as he walked down the central aisle of the train car. He drew looks of disgust directed mainly at his appearance. He had not had a shower or change of clothing since the morning of the tomb discovery. His hair was matted down, dingy from dirt, dust and sweat. His face, although he had washed it as best he could in the restroom of the train depot, was still shiny, pink from sun exposure, and shadowed from the inability to shave in the past couple of days. His off-white button-down was quickly beginning to resemble more of a deep khaki, or even tan color, while his jeans were brownish with sweat-mud. One could no longer even tell that there was blood spatter on his clothing. It had dried into a deep brown color, and blended in with the earthen grime that also covered his garments.

Facing exhaustion, he did not care what the people thought. He was on a mission.

He looked around at all of the people on this train, and thought about all of the people in the world who were, at this moment, just carrying out their daily lives, unaware of what was to happen soon. They had no idea that the end was near. It did not matter what their religious beliefs were. They would all die in the name of one religion.

Chapter 44

For hours the Honda had been roaring down the highways, passing scenery that Noelle could not see to enjoy. Hills and valleys of green, kissed by the sweet Mediterranean winds made for a breathtaking sight.

The kidnapper loved this place. He could understand how the Hebrews saw this as the *Promised Land* and why so many armies had fought over it. It was beautiful.

Noelle could not see the speedometer from her vantage point, nor could she see the odometer. This man must have been driving at speeds that were in excess of eighty miles per hour. He must have been attempting to get them there before the catastrophe began. He was focused, determined, and therefore dangerous.

The car finally slowed. The rose and gold of the evening sky with its contrasting purple clouds were no longer passing her by at such a swift rate. And then suddenly, they came to a halt.

A shockwave of panic came over Noelle as the man stepped out of the vehicle and once again approached the back door. He opened it with a jerk and a stern look on his face, proceeding to grip her ankles with his long, dingy fingers and pull her from the seat. She began her muffled screaming, flailing her head around and kicking violently in resistance to her captor. He struggled with her, trying to gain a firm grasp on her legs amidst the kicking until one powerful jerk of her legs found her tennis shoes landing firmly into his nose.

"Bitch!" he exclaimed in the Farsi equivalent and took a couple of steps backward, reeling from the blow.

Both of his hands were cupped over the center of his face and his eyes were welling up. He felt disoriented, as if the blow somehow affected his equilibrium. He was hunched over, his head hanging a bit as he removed his hands from his face slowly and looked into them to assess the damage. The blood was flowing slowly from his nostrils and over his top lip. He could taste it as it dripped into his mouth.

His face was turning red as his body shook in rage. Noelle braced herself for the pain that she knew was coming. The man, in a sharp, precise motion, removed from his waistband a pistol, pulled back the slide to chamber a round, and pointed it directly at Noelle's forehead. He removed yet another item from his pocket, touched a button and released a blade.

With the pistol trained sharply upon her, the man moved closer, the switchblade in his other hand. Noelle's eyes widened with fear as her mind raced with thoughts of what he would do. She knew that the gun was there to keep her from struggling, so she had no plan of doing so, although a gunshot wound to the head may have been preferable to what he was about to do with the knife.

The kidnapper came to a halt before Noelle's feet and stood there silent as the anger exited his expression. In fact, he was beginning to smile, even as the blood was coagulating on his face. He looked her over again and again, then slowly moved the blade lower, towards her legs. The shiny steel caught an occasional glimmer of sunlight as he moved it along the length of her thighs. He did not touch the blade to her skin as he brought it down past her knees. Noelle shivered with fear as she looked while groaning and crying for this to stop. The blade moved evenly toward her feet, and in a jerk of his hand that nearly made her faint in terror, he sliced through the cloth that bound her ankles together, releasing her feet.

"Get out of the car," he stepped back several steps, putting away his knife and pointing the gun in her direction.

She slowly sat up as best she could with her hands still tied and scooted closer to the edge of the seat. Letting her feet touch the ground for the first time in hours, she stood, tears still rolling from her eyes and her legs shaking uncontrollably. Her nerves were firing, causing her stomach to ache and her muscles to twitch.

"You go before me," he said. "If you try to run, I will kill you. You will lead us up those stairs," he motioned to his left where there were a set of stone steps carved into the mount. "Now go."

She moved away from the car slowly, keeping her distance from the stranger as he moved closer to where she was standing. He stepped in reverse, keeping his eyes fixed upon her, then briefly turned his gaze to reach down to the floorboard and retrieve the canvas bag containing the scepter.

She took advantage of the moment, and as quickly as she could ran in the opposite direction. He heard the rapid footsteps on the ground, and as soon as he picked up the bag and looked back at her, he raised his pistol in a trajectory high above her head, squeezing the trigger. The unmistakable sound that the gun made echoed throughout the area; an echo that the Jezreel Valley was certainly no stranger to. At first, Noelle thought she was shot, but she was in no pain, nor did she topple to the ground. She simply stopped and thanked God that the man had not completely fulfilled his promise.

"Try that again, and the next one will find its place in your head," he approached her. "Now move—up the stairs!"

Her feet slid a little as the carved steps were surprisingly smooth from thousands of years of foot traffic. She looked upward and could see the fortress atop the mount. It must have once been magnificent. The white-gray stones were eroding and wearing away, but surely the walls once stood tall, guarding all inhabitants from attacking armies from the far reaches of the ancient Middle East. She had been to ruins throughout the world, studying the geological features of the planet. She had seen Pompeii, Athens, and even Ur. But those places, as important and old as they were, were nothing in comparison to what she was about to enter.

To the untrained eye, it was just another ruined fortress that dotted the region. People who lived in the old world were surrounded by such a rich and far-reaching history, that they seemed to disregard and take for granted.

With each step upward, she rose higher above the valley and mountain pass below. James had said this was the site of the first battle of recorded history, where the Hebrew leader Joshua had been. This was to be where the final battle between good and evil would take place. At that moment, Noelle felt as though she might actually be there to see it.

"Now straight forward," the man said as they reached the top, entering a once magnificent gate and traversing the large stone pavers. "To the back of the fortress."

They walked back past the ruins of buildings that once stood on the site. The walls had been reduced to one-foot-tall areas of stone that framed rectangular spaces. They were mess halls, homes, kitchens, and armories. Noelle tried to imagine what it was like to live here. She pictured ancient people going about their daily lives. Women brought water and food into the homes, men performed various duties and stood guard over the gates and walls, and children played in the streets without a care. She could not imagine what it may have been like for these people when the fortress was under siege or when earthquakes shook these walls to the dirt.

Reaching the rear of the fortified mount, Noelle saw another staircase to her right, which led down a shaft, and instinctively she knew that this was the next direction to go. She hoped that this was the right way. She was growing tired of his orders. She began descending into the great hole or shaft dug into the mount. She felt like Alice, following a rabbit into his hole, uncertain of what kind of wonderland she would find at the bottom. Finally, after winding down the spiral-cut staircase, she reached the bottom, immediately recognizing the sound and feel of wooden planks beneath her feet.

The evening sun was setting in the west, its light diminishing in the shaft that surrounded them. She could make out the curvature of a rock tunnel and could tell that it was man-made. It was too smoothly bored into the hill for this to be naturally occurring. She was astounded that the ancients had the knowledge and patience to carve such tunnels and staircases into the rock. They were truly masters for their age.

They walked across the wooden planks as she caught the glow of the glow stick her captor had just cracked. She tried at some point to count how many steps they had taken, but in the face of exhaustion and growing fatigue, she gave up and lost count somewhere in the three-hundreds.

"Halt," the man finally said. "We go in here."

If she didn't have a sweaty cloth tied around her mouth, she would have asked him where. She could barely see anything. The sun had begun to drop past the horizon and the few remaining rays of light revealed no door or continuance of the tunnel, save for straight forward.

"To the right. Watch your step," he directed her to leave from the walkway onto the stone floor.

From behind her, an iridescent green glow cast her shadow on the stone wall, and revealed the large crevasse in the side of the tunnel.

She began moving sideways into the large crack. She struggled with edging her way through the passage, her hands still tied behind her. Her palms and wrists were scraping against the sharp stone as she grunted from the dull pain.

The orange glow upon the walls of the crevasse ahead of her, paired with the smell of burning fuel and wood, told her that she was nearing the end of the passage. Her heart raced as she moved closer to the brightening glow.

The crevasse passageway finally opened into an enormous cavern. The ceiling was high, orange with the glow of flames from a great fire positioned in the center of the room. The sacred flame and crude torches that hung in their metal holders on the walls formed a halo of fire around the cavern's centerpiece.

Noelle gasped as her head moved upward, tracing the height of the giant structure. Never in her life had she seen such a thing. The massive wooden beams with bronze gears and dials creaked and groaned as water poured from the bronze container hoisted in the air. It was slowly moving upward and seemed to be near the end of its journey to the top of the machine. She did not know what this meant, but the positioning of the bronze bars against the dial notches seemed to not be a good thing.

She finally took her eyes off of the mechanism, noticing a stirring from the corner of her eye. There were two men, one young and one old, standing from their chairs to the right of the structure. In her awe of the machine, she had almost missed them. For a moment, she even forgot that she was still bound and gagged.

"Ah, a visitor," the Shaoshant smiled as he slowly approached her. "You may remove her bindings and her muzzle," he put his hands together. "I do not believe she will cause us any problem."

Noelle heard the sharp clicking sound of her kidnapper's switchblade, and without turning around, she allowed the man to cut the strip of cloth that tied her wrists and remove her gag. With her hands and mouth free, all she could do was stare the old man down with contempt, while breathing heavily, relieved that she could fully intake a lungful of oxygen.

"Why are you doing this?" she scowled.

"It is written," the Shaoshant replied warmly with a smile. "It is the prophecy. We will cleanse the earth of all of its evils, as the Avesta foretells."

"*You* are evil!" she raised her tone. "Who are you to play God?"

"You will show respect for the Shaoshant!" The kidnapper shoved her firmly in her upper back, causing her head to snap back. "He is our savior!"

"You . . ." her eyes widened, remembering James's words. "You are the Shaoshant?"

"Remarkable," the old man was amused. "You are familiar with the Avesta," he smiled. "Yes, I am. And you must also know that I am God's representative. Therefore, what we are doing are in fact His wishes."

"You're wrong," she shook her head.

"Get her an MRE," he motioned to Khalim, who was watching from behind the Shaoshant. "And allow her to relieve herself in a dark corner," he smiled at her. "And remember to be respectful of her gender. We are not barbarians."

Chapter 45

James exited the train early on the morning of June sixth, refreshed with a cigarette in his mouth. He was surprised that they still allowed smoking on the trains in Israel. It was not demonized as it was in the U.S. Back home, it seemed the only place he could smoke anymore was beneath a blanket in his closet.

He had been smoking almost continuously for the past twenty-four hours, nervously fidgeting and restless. Although it was approximately only sixty miles between Qiryat Gat and Pardes Hanna where he now arrived, he had a several hour layover near Tel Aviv and many delays close to Netanya. It had been a full day trip. He would have been better off hitchhiking in the bed of a pickup truck full of sheep.

He had been able to rest, although it was broken sleep and interrupted often by his smoke breaks. He was still dingy, un-showered, unshaved and hadn't changed his clothes in days.

Exiting the slightly less-than-busy train station in Pardes Hanna, he faced another challenge. How would he get to Megiddo? There were no railways that ran directly there and he did not know where to begin to find a bus line.

James examined his surroundings. Aside from the occasional ruined site of an ancient building or crusader stronghold, the countryside was very much like home. In fact, the plains, hills and farmland set him to thinking that he may have well been in Nebraska. This was very quaint and a bit cosmopolitan for a smaller Israeli town. He had pictured things the way they would look in a busy Moroccan souk with all of the vendors, odd smells, livestock, and noise. But this place was like the suburbs. The buildings were nicely constructed and brand new Asian-made cars zipped up and down the streets carrying the passengers to work. He paused for a moment, took another drag of his cigarette and decided to go ahead and hitchhike the rest of the way.

He moved in closer to the street to analyze the traffic that was flowing through the town. He was attempting to pick out a vehicle that was more construction or agriculture-oriented. It was ultimately a farming town and he was completely surrounded by fields and livestock pastures.

He spotted an old Datsun pickup, circa 1980s, coming to a halt at the intersection, and tried to flag it down. But the driver sped off, though the passenger had seen and was staring back at him. Another small pickup truck drove by and this time the driver spotted his outstretched arm and upturned thumb, pulling up beside him.

"Need a ride?" the man said in Hebrew.

"I need a ride," he replied in English, not knowing that he was just asked that question.

"Oh, American," the driver said, hunched over the passenger in the single cab pickup. "Where you go?"

"Megiddo," James hoped the vehicle was going that way.

"No, sorry. We just go across town."

"Thanks anyway," he waved off the man.

He was beginning to lose hope when another truck pulled over to offer assistance. There were three men jammed into the small cab of the slightly newer Nissan.

"Ride?" the driver asked in English this time.

"Yes," he slouched, expecting yet another disappointment. "I'm trying to get to Megiddo."

"Yes, Megiddo!" the driver smiled widely. "Get in the back. I take you there!"

"Really? No shit?" he replied in an overwhelmed manner.

"Shit?" the driver asked with a confused look. "What does this mean—no shit?"

One of the other passengers leaned over towards the driver, mumbling something in Hebrew as the man's eyes opened widely in epiphany. He understood.

"Shit," he spoke to James. "Yes there is shit in the back. We are shepherds."

"That's wonderful," he said politely but facetiously as the driver smiled and nodded. "You're going in the direction of Megiddo? It's not out of the way?"

"Oh, no problem!" he smiled. "We go to Afula. Megiddo is near. Get in! Get in! Beside, you look like shepherd, too," he pointed to James's soiled and unpolished appearance.

He hung his head a little in the face of the comment, realizing that the joke was on him, though he wasn't sure if the driver knew that he was even making a joke. He walked around the back of the truck, and climbed over the secured tailgate, noticing that the man was not lying about the feces. There were little bits of dried sheep dung strewn about the bed, and it smelled of a livestock barn.

Before settling in, James realized he needed to know how long this trip would take. He rapped on the small sliding window to the rear of the cab, prompting one of the passengers to open it. "How far is Megiddo?" he asked.

"About thirty kilometers," the man replied.

James was certain it would be at least another couple of hours before they arrived at Har Megiddo.

"Thirty kilometers? No shit?" he almost shouted in delighted surprise.

The driver did a bit of a double take in James's direction, and with that, put the vehicle in gear, speeding off down the street, their new passenger in tow.

Chapter 46

Noelle sat in her small wooden chair to the right of the cavern entry-way, her back stiff and unable to get comfortable. She had become accustomed to her surroundings—the ever present flames, the glow and shadows cast onto the stone walls, the old man chanting relentlessly from behind his altar and even the ominous contraption that loomed in the near distance. Its beams creaked and the bronze groaned as the water poured from the container and bars continually changing position. The sound that the water made falling from the air into the stone pool below it was like a small never-ending waterfall.

The men had not bothered to tie her to her chair. She was in no way bound or restricted, except by the large assault rifle held by the young man seated to her left. She may have been afraid of the gun, but strangely she was not afraid of the man. Inadvertently, she had made eye contact with him several times while she had been seated there. Khalim, as she had heard the Shaoshant refer to him, gave her a gentle vibe. She could see it in his warm, brown eyes. He seemed scared and unsure.

"Where are you from?" she tried to strike up a conversation.

Khalim simply stared at her, his widening, round eyes tried to apologize for his silence.

"He will not speak to you," the Shaoshant briefly stopped his incessant chanting. "He has been instructed not to. He is to focus on the holy deed that is at hand. He needs no distractions."

"Holy?" she squinted her eyes and faced the old man. "You call this a holy deed? This is murder! This is genocide. Haven't you ever heard of *thou shalt not kill?*"

"Killing your fellow man is, indeed, against the laws of our supreme being," he never raised his voice. "But this is the fulfilling of a prophecy. This is the purifying of the world from evil—killing sanctioned by Ahura Mazda."

"You know, lots of men have said things like that," she gave him a look of despise.

"Oh?" he raised an eyebrow.

"Yeah," she continued, "the Inquisition, the witch hunters of Salem, the Crusaders, the men who waged the Thirty Years' War. They all killed in the name of God. I guess that's a loophole in God's law, huh? It doesn't apply when it's in God's name and against someone who doesn't believe the same thing you do."

The Shaoshant did not respond. She was unsure if this was because he felt he did not need to justify his actions, or if he was truly caught in a debate that he could not win. Nevertheless, he said not another word to her. Instead, he turned his eyes back to the holy book lying before him on the altar and resumed his chanting of verses and prayers to his almighty.

Noelle turned her head back to the left and lifted her eyes to meet Khalim's. He was now staring at her. Formerly, he would only hold eye contact for a brief moment, and then consciously avert his gaze. Now he could not seem to look away.

"Khalim," she whispered very softly as to not draw the attention of the Shaoshant, "you don't have to do this. You're younger than him. You're stronger. You have a gun. You can put an end to this and we can go safely back to our families. We don't need to purify the world of evil. God or Ahura Mazda will do that *himself*. Please. You are the only one that can stop this. Take your faith out of man and put it back into God!"

The whispers, as light and quiet as they were, did attract the attention of the Shaoshant. He could not, however, discern what words were being spoken, but he was sure they were directed at young Khalim. He did not stop his chanting. Instead, he quieted slightly in a futile attempt to hear what this woman was telling his protégé.

"I told you," he finally stopped his praises to his god, "he will not respond."

Noelle's heart froze. She said nothing for several moments, though her eyes never left Khalim's. She probed his unchanging expression for any fleck of comprehension or sympathy for her and what she had told him. "I wasn't talking to him," she turned her head toward the old man, "I was praying." She feigned a look of desperation and loss of hope. "I was praying to God for mercy."

"Good," he began to smile in a pleased, but almost sinister way, then stepped down from his altar. "That's good. You should make your peace with God." He then turned to the machine, raising his hands into the air. "For today is the day! Very soon, this instrument of Ahura Mazda will come crashing down and a great earthquake will ripple from this holy place! And it seems," he paused to look at her over his shoulder, "that your knight in shining armor will not be here in time to help you. Only God can save you now."

She bit her lip a little, thinking of James and what he was doing. Was he on his way? Was he killed? She worried and nervously tapped her feet while shooting looks at Khalim—her only hope, and a distant one at that.

Chapter 47

James had been fighting and swatting away bits of hay as it swirled up from the bed of the pickup truck and into his face. The smell of sheep dung, though largely swept away by the winds that coursed from the sides and over the top of the vehicle, still filled his nostrils.

He was still enamored by the expansive plains and farmland within the Jezreel Valley. He could scarcely believe that he was actually here. It was a place where armies of pharaohs, Joshua, and Napoleon all marched. Alexander had been there, and so had King David. He was viewing a land where Jesus Christ had once walked, and in fact, grown up just a short distance away in Nazareth. Moreover, he was now riding in that bed of a shepherd's pickup truck through the *Valley of the Shadow of Death*. He was casting his gaze upon the prophesized site of the Apocalypse, the end of days, Armageddon.

He was forced to look to the rear the whole trip, his back leaning against the exterior of the main cab. He always got frustrated when he could not look ahead of him on a trip. He liked to see what was coming next. He had to make do with looking to the sides for landmarks that he might know. And that was exactly what began to happen. He started noticing a familiar topography, though he had never been to this land. But he had studied this place enough to know the landscape. In the distance, a haze was creating a translucent veil around them, but he could see Mount Tabor and Mount Carmel. Mount Carmel was particularly recognizable. Unlike Mount Tabor, which rose into the sky like a lump; a pimple on the face of the earth, Mount Carmel was kind of a continuation of a small mountain range in the near distance that sloped downward to the fertile valley below.

The truck continued to sear the asphalt at an ungodly speed, and then slowed abruptly at the junction with a new highway. As it rounded onto the new route, James was exposed to the sight of the once fortified mount that had been the subject of his obsession for the last few days. A churning uneasiness appeared in his gut as he set his eyes on a place so important to Solomon and his successors. But it wasn't just the thought of where he was that was unsettling. Somewhere in that forgotten stronghold, Noelle was being held against her will, or perhaps her lifeless corpse was beginning to stiffen.

Sharply, the truck took another left into a gravel entranceway, and then pulled into the empty parking lot of the site. James immediately rose to his feet as the vehicle came to a stop, and leapt over the side of the bed, kicking up dust and gravel as his feet hit the ground. He slapped the side of the truck with is left hand, creating a hollow, metallic clang, and then waved to the men inside the truck with his right.

"Thank you," he smiled as the men smiled and waved back. The driver put the car into gear, speeding off, and filling James's face and mouth with a cloud of dust.

He drew a handkerchief from his pocket, his eyes squinting from the grit in the air. The dust had clung to the sweat on his face, creating a thin film of mud and grime. He used the handkerchief to wipe away as much of the sweat-mud concoction as he could, but there was nothing to rid him of the dirt in his mouth. It had coated every inch from his tongue to his pallet, and ground like sandpaper between his teeth.

The dirt and gravel ground popped beneath his feet as he pivoted in place. Returning the handkerchief to his pocket and placing his hands on his hips, he looked upward at the mount, sweat rolling into his eyes with a bitter sting. He wiped his brow with the sleeve of his shirt, and began stepping toward the steps carved into the stone ahead.

The heel of his shoe continued to squeak with every step as he embarked on the last leg of his journey. He saw the *borrowed* Honda parked across the way, confirming he was in the right place. Up the stairs he went, knowing that he was drawing closer and closer to fate. His stomach twisted with anxiety. He felt the shiver of fear and excitement blanket him as he walked along.

James did not know what he was going to do at this point. Each step to the summit of the hill he tried to procrastinate, but he knew time was wearing thin. The fuse was losing length, the sparks threatening to undo mankind and he wished time would somehow slow down. There was plenty of time to devise a plan of action, but when it came down to it, he had nothing. There was no plan. He reached the top of the mount, entering the ruined city through Solomon's gate, not knowing that this was the same way that Noelle had entered. It was quiet. Only the wind rustling the distant trees and flapping his sleeves provided sound. No one was there, not even tourists. He quietly walked past the rectangular spaces where once stood homes and soldiers' quarters to a place centered with a low, round structure made up of small stones with no mortar to reinforce it. This was an ancient Canaanite altar; testament to a time before the Hebrew conquest.

"Where could everyone be?" he spoke aloud to himself.

He looked around the ruins, pacing and searching for clues. He could not make sense of it. His mind was hard at work, trying to rationalize and find a starting point.

"I don't understand," he said, getting frustrated with his inability to think. "There has to be some hidden place around here. A big fucking machine needs a big fucking room! The tablet at Vesuvius was found buried, so the machine has to be underground! But where . . . ?" he paused to look around.

Stuck again, he continued to contemplate over what sort of underground space could exist at the site. He remembered something as he spied another set of stairs leading downward, seemingly directly into the mount.

"The spring," he gasped and moved in that direction.

The Israelites had identified a spring on the premises, and cut a shaft down instead of having to exit the city walls as they had previously. It was part of what made Har Megiddo such an important and special place. In ancient times, for an army to lay siege to a fortress was a virtual deathblow to its existence. They would cut off supply lines, block the ability to reach fresh water, and all inhabitants would starve and dehydrate. Eventually, an outpost such as this would fall to the invaders. But the Israelites had built their fortress here because of a source of fresh water within the confines. They, in the event of a siege, could hold out almost indefinitely against their enemies, and still maintain control of the mountain pass that they guarded with a shaft to the spring within the walls. It was no wonder that most of the versions of the fortress on this spot had fallen prey to earthquake and disrepair, rather than conquest.

"The tunnel to the aquifer is the only subterranean place that I've ever read about on this site," he spoke to himself as he reached the stone set of stairs.

He slowly and carefully stepped down the ancient stairs, making sure not to lose his footing and slip on the surprisingly smooth surfaces. As he descended, he took his eyes off of his feet and began to scan his surroundings. Immediately, he could see the apex of the tunnel's curve below him. He had only seen it in books and websites online, but those pictures did no justice to the real thing.

He looked upward to the top and ran his gaze along the curved outer rims to the ground. He then trained his eyes on the interior of the structure itself, both mesmerized and frightened, as if he were looking into a bottomless pit or into Hell itself.

As he walked down the tunnel, the boards creaking beneath his feet, complementing the squeaking of his shoe, he could see the sunlight shining in from the other end of the tunnel. His heart fluttered with anxiety at what he might find. He ran his right hand down the length of the wood railing as he traversed the entire tunnel, reaching the spot where the spring was below. Moving beyond, he came to the other opening of the tunnel, looking up at the blue skies above.

"Okay," he spoke aloud in a bewildered tone. "Where the hell is it?"

He gazed back down the length of the corridor in the direction of the shaft entrance, and back up at the sky above and behind him. He twirled around with his hands and shoulders elevated in a shrugging position.

"Okay, be more observant," he said aloud. "Let's do this again. It's gotta be down here."

He walked back toward the other end again, more slowly now and analyzing everything. He looked deeply at the tool marks and uneven places. As he walked along, he even noticed the point not far past the spring where the two digging teams met in the middle. His head moved up, down, and all around the sides, searching for something, but not knowing what.

His sense of sight was growing weary, but his nose picked up an odd scent. He knew what it was immediately, but it seemed strange and out of place. He did not expect the smell of burning oil and timber.

"Surely, I should be able to see it, right?" he said. "How did I miss it? How did I not smell it coming down the shaft?"

He looked around and then up, realizing that the smoke would rise to the top of the passageway, looking for an escape route to the open air. He followed a faint sight of gray smoke from near the far opening of the tunnel back down and began walking toward the shaft, trying to track it like a blood trail to a wounded deer. Past a certain point, he lost sight of it, as the sunlight did not reach that far in to illuminate the charred carbon particles that it consisted of. He continued to walk until he could no longer smell it.

It was at that moment that he knew he had gone too far, and stopped. He took a few steps back until he could again smell the smoke. He turned his head to the right to look down the corridor in the direction of the shaft, and then did the same in the direction of the other opening. Pondering for a moment, he concluded that the end of the tunnel opposite the shaft must have been elevated slightly, therefore causing the smoke to exit that way, rather than through the shaft.

At that moment, he saw it. It was directly in front of him. He was ashamed that he had missed it before—a crack in the wall of the tunnel that must have been about seven feet tall and three feet wide. There were many uneven places on the walls, providing the opportunity for what little sunlight reached that far to create optical illusions and hide the existence of any hidden area.

"Could this be . . ." he stopped, squinting his eyes and moving his head in for a closer look. "Could this be it? Could there really be something down there?"

He moved closer to the edge of the planked walkway and nearer to the crack in the wall. He could smell, and finally see the smoke gently flow like a river from the upper pitched top of the crevasse. This was the place, and his heart sank into his stomach, giving him a feeling like he had just been kicked in the testicles.

He knew what he had to do, reaching into his waistband at the small of his back. He gripped the pistol, sliding his right index finger through the trigger loop, and positioned it in front as he crouched below the wooden railing, stepping off the safety of the walkway. Slowly, he positioned himself to move sideways into the stony gash, grunting a little, as the jagged edges scraped his chest and knuckles.

James's mind raced as he squeezed through the narrow passageway. Growing increasingly uncomfortable with the tight space, an uneasy feeling compounded with his anxiety causing him to sweat and tremble with nervousness. He could faintly see the gun in his hand quiver and shake as he dreaded what lie ahead of him.

Seeing the glow of orange flickering on the jagged edges, he knew there was a room ahead; the place his mind had been fixed upon for days. For a moment, he could not move, as if his feet were embedded in concrete and his joints and muscles were experiencing lockjaw. Knowing what he had to do, he once again picked up his feet, and resumed inching closer to his fate.

Rounding the corner of the passageway, he could see the opening. At first, there were just flames, as if he really *did* descend into the bowels of Hell. But as he drew closer, the picture widened and he could see the expansive cavern.

It took a moment for him to focus, then he saw three people. A young man, and old man, and finally, Noelle. A sigh of relief silently exited his mouth to see her alive and sitting in a chair to the right, guarded, but alive. More remarkably, however, he saw the main attraction of the space, and his jaw slouched into a look of disbelief.

This was it—the ultimate weapon of mass destruction. It was a piece of ancient technology that the world could never imagine really ever existed, or even would ever exist. It was enormous, extending upwards to the high reaches of the cavern ceiling. Its wooden frame creaked under the weight of the rock, and the bronze container of water that operated the countdown device had nearly reached its full height. The time for action was growing thin and he had to make his move soon. He had no plan and he was terrified.

James caught Noelle's eye, and she was unable to conceal her expression of relief, alerting Khalim to the presence of the intruder.

The young man leapt to his feet, instantly raising his gun barrel in the direction of James. He jerked Noelle to her feet, pulling her backward away from the intrusive Tulane scholar. He needed not say a word, and James balked, unable to speak, himself. The Shaoshant saw what was unfolding, stepping down from his altar in a quiet and calm fashion.

"Ah, the other American," the old man walked a few steps in his direction, reaching into his robes for his pistol. "The hero of the day, I assume. And you've furnished your own weapon. Just like the wild west!"

"Actually, it belongs to that murderer you sent after us on the train, asshole," he spoke to the Shaoshant, but kept his gun trained sharply on Khalim.

"If you think it upsets me that you killed him, you're wrong," the Shaoshant remained calm. "He died for his cause, and will be rewarded. In a few minutes, we will all die as well, and the world will be cleansed in time."

"What, you're going to stay down here as the walls cave in?" James motioned upward. "You're not gonna run, leaving your boy-servant to die with us while you take shelter?"

"Of course not," he looked strangely at his adversary. "I'm the Shaoshant—the chosen savior. I'm the one who will carry out the will of God. I am to die a martyr, much like your Jesus Christ."

"You're nothing like Christ," Noelle muttered beneath her breath, causing Khalim to look sharply at her and back to James.

"You have to shut this thing down," James began to plead with the Shaoshant.

"Why would I want to deny the prophecy?" he replied.

"Because it's *your* prophecy!" he yelled, his words echoing through the cavern. "Not ours! Not the rest of the world's! What if I went around shooting people in the head because they were bad people or wrong in my opinion?"

"Yes, but that scenario isn't written in prophecy, so you are unfounded."

"Give me a break! I'm sure if I looked hard enough in the Bible, the Torah, the Qu'ran *and* your precious Avesta, I could find *something* that might be interpreted as permission to shoot people in the fucking head!"

"You Westerners are all the same," the old man scoffed. "Always have been. So violent and unclean. It was all my people could do to hinder your advancement as long as we could. Why do you think Europe remained so ignorant and ill-advanced for so long after Rome's fall? Had they continued advancement, their technology would have paired with their greed, and the rest of the world would have suffered for it. And today it finally has. Though the ages, machines like this one have created *natural* disasters throughout Europe. Earthquakes and volcanoes plagued the Greeks, Romans and medieval Europeans, continually setting them back centuries. Meanwhile, our brethren infiltrated your precious Christianity from its beginning. All of those laws, restrictions, and heresy charges were no accident. Keep people ignorant and they cannot trouble us."

"While your own ignorance troubles the entire human race," James angrily replied. He was awe-stricken by the Shaoshant's revelation, yet he was not surprised. After all, it offered proof to his theory on the course of western civilization.

"Drop your weapon," the Shaoshant quietly ordered, and as two guns were pointed at him, James decided to comply, throwing it out in front of him.

James paused a moment after his outburst, realizing that he was not going to convince the old man to abandon his beliefs or talk him out of ending the world by cursing and insulting his faith. He cooled his temper, and began again.

"Look, I think the world has become as evil as you do. There are a lot of unsavory people the earth can do without: child molesters, rapists, murderers, Tim Horn. But it's not up to us to bring about the end of days. Think of all the innocents who will die with the evil! Let God sort it out. Let God do His job. We are not gods! You are not God!"

"Khalim, please," Noelle belted, her eyes pleading with the young man to her left. "I know you understood everything I told you earlier. You know this is wrong."

Khalim shook and trembled as he looked around the room for guidance that would not come. He shifted his weight from one foot to the other, the gun in his hand unsteady. He began to move closer to the Shaoshant, keeping his eyes on the Americans.

"Shaoshant," he trembled and spoke lowly, "perhaps . . ."

He did not have the opportunity to finish his sentence. Before he could utter another word, the old man quietly and effortlessly pointed his gun to this left, squeezed the trigger, and discharged a round into the right side of young Khalim's body, sending him into a painful crouching position. There he tumbled to the floor, bleeding from the ribs and between his fingers as he tried to stop the flow. It was in vain, as he collapsed into the dirt.

Noelle gasped, her right hand covering her mouth. Tears began to roll from her eyes as she realized that she had just convinced a man to commit suicide. She wept uncontrollably into her hands as the anger welled up within her and was about to erupt from her mouth.

"You murderer!" she screamed in rage. "All he did is look up to you and do everything you told him! Is murder in your Avesta, too? Is that part of the prophecy?"

The old man said nothing, needing no vindication in what he had just done. He quietly stepped back a few paces, his gun pointed directly at Noelle. Without taking his eyes off of the two intruders, he reached back upon the altar, grasping the one thing that could stop the triggering of a worldwide earthquake storm—the scepter of Alexander.

"The will of Ahura Mazda will be done!" he raised it overhead as if it were the staff of Moses and he were about to part the Red Sea.

Terror fell over James and Noelle as they could see beyond the Shaoshant. The bronze mechanism was grinding and churning ever more closely to its end position. The water had nearly completely drained from the container high above and the heavy bronze bar that moved with it was dangerously close to the beam that it was to break.

"James," Noelle spoke frantically.

"What?"

"You see that huge crack in the ceiling?" she looked upward.

"Yeah."

"I've been studying that thing for hours, and I can tell you that if that machine collapses, the entire cavern is coming down."

"What about the earthquake storm? Is that possible?"

"Based on the location and the horrible fault line that runs through here, I'd say yes—a global earthquake epidemic. James, let's get out of here. The old man has what he wants. We can just go!"

"But what about the other people in the world? Your family. My . . . well, what about us later on? He's gotta be stopped!"

James then did something he thought he would never do. He began walking in the direction of the Shaoshant. He was unarmed and the old man was holding a gun on him. He finally made the decision to take his fate in his own hands and do something that would better mankind, rather than drink himself into oblivion. All he could do was think about the old man in the airport. He knew that he was probably going to die, but that would likely happen anyway, so what did he have to lose?

But a loud pop stopped him dead in his tracks. James could not tell if it was the breaking of the beam that held the mechanism together or the muzzle of the Shaoshant's gun. He instinctively checked himself for bullet holes and blood, and then looked up at the old man. He was bleeding from the chest, a torrent of crimson life fluid soaking increasingly into his snow white robes. His mouth hung open as the gun and scepter fell from his hand. Slowly, the old man dropped to his knees, and then, eyes wide open, he toppled face-forward into the dirt. The martyr was martyred for his cause, and young Khalim lay on his side, the smoking muzzle of his rifle still aimed at the Shaoshant.

Khalim was hurt, and still bleeding profusely from his wounded side. He was quickly weakening and falling short of breath as his gun finally fell back down into the dust.

"Khalim, what do we do?" Noelle ran to his side. "How do we stop the machine?"

"The key," he painfully uttered, pointing to the scepter on the ground before the lifeless old man.

James ran over to the symbol of royalty. He studied it, trying to figure out how the grooves at the end of it could stop the machine.

"You must insert it there," Khalim pointed to a circular hole on the front side of the mechanism near the altar. It was a bronze circle at the center of eight wooden crossbeams that fanned out from it to help form the structure of the machine. "Then turn." He seemed to utter these words with his last breath.

"I'm so sorry," Noelle stroked his sweaty forehead, sobbing. "I'm sorry. Thank you."

"Thank *you*," he gasped and smiled. "You have saved me," he said, emptying his lungs. His heart stopped and his eyes closed as his head rolled to the side, lifeless in the dirt.

James stood behind the altar, looking at the porthole in front of him. The mechanism was drawing to its terrible finish and there wasn't much time. He shoved the scepter into the opening, and twisted it clockwise, releasing a series of weights and bars that released even more. One bar turned clockwise, which released another that turned counter-clockwise below it. At the very bottom, a wide, bronze sheet shot out to the left beneath the fatal bronze bar, stopping it from crashing into the master beam and preserving the integrity of the structure as a whole.

They both stood motionless, staring upward at the mighty weapon as the ancient beams creaked and bowed. The bronze container dripped the very last of its water from high above them, an indication of how close the end really was. James and Noelle looked at each other, both sweating, but finally exhaling a sigh of relief.

They had finally come to a point when they could relax, when the cavern began to rumble and shake. The beams of the scaffolding swayed as small bits of rock and dust rained down from above. They both panicked, crouching down with their hands atop their heads in a futile attempt to shield themselves from the potentially imploding cavern. They squinted their eyes, silently praying that after their long journey, they would not meet their end this way, nor would the cataclysmic world destruction take place.

And then the shaking stopped. A few more bits of pebbles and dust fell, coating the two scholars, who slowly opened their eyes, wary that the quake would resume. It, however, did not, and the giant apocalyptic mechanism held true, the scepter still jutting slightly from the front of it.

James, finally feeling confident that the deed was done and the beams would hold, walked briskly back up to the altar and extended his hand to retrieve the priceless artifact from its keyhole.

"James," Noelle extended her hand outward with a concerned look, implying that the machine may start again if he pulled out the scepter.

"It's over," he turned his head over his shoulder, smiling warmly. He then tightened his hands into a firm grip around the shaft of the scepter, and pulled with a force sliding the artifact from the porthole. James held it with both hands, looking it over in admiration of its beauty and enormous historical significance.

He looked up at Noelle and smiled as he walked over to her, took her by the hand and began leading her back across the room to make their exit.

"James," she said as they were walking.

"Yeah?"

"Let's never do this again," she looked over her shoulder at the machine and smiled as it grew further away from them. James simply laughed as he allowed her to slip first into the crevasse, and followed close behind.

They exited the crag into the tunnel and turned right toward the opening that would lead them outside the original city walls on the other side of the mount. They stepped in exhaustion closer and closer in the direction of the sunlight—a light at the end of the tunnel.

Helping one another up the steps into the blinding shower of sun rays, they ascended to the surface, immediately feeling the heat from above and shutting their eyes almost completely as their pupils constricted and adjusted.

"Do you think anyone will ever find that place again?" Noelle stopped and looked back as she clung tightly to James's dingy shirt.

"Don't know," he looked back into the opening. "It's taken this long for anyone but the cult to discover it."

"But what if the cult goes back in and restarts the machine?" a look of worry came over her.

"Not without this," he smiled and held up the scepter. "This is needed to remove that bronze sheet."

"Even so," she continued to worry, "the beams will eventually rot and the whole thing will fall apart. That might set off the earthquake storm. Then all we will have done is buy time."

"Yeah, probably," he continued to look into the opening of the tunnel, and then back to Noelle. "But it's possible that the fault would have given away centuries ago. What if, in the end, all the cult did was *prolong* the inevitable end? What if they hindered the will of God? Either way, it's up to Him now."

"So," she smiled, "you're a believer now?"

He simply smiled, shaking his head in a way that implied a renewal of some sort of faith, but in God, rather than in man's perception of God.

"Come on," he nudged her to go. "I could use a shower," and they began their long trek home.

Chapter 48

Captain Qadurra sat at his plain and cluttered desk, poring over reports and paperwork. He looked exhausted and fatigued. He had not gotten much sleep in the past few days, having to explain to his superiors the events that had taken place, save a few details that he had to fabricate.

There was a rapping at his office door, followed by an almost intrusive subordinate who was carrying a rather long, rectangular package with both hands.

"Captain," he said in their native language. "A package for you."

"Who is it from?" he looked over his shoulder in perplexity.

"It doesn't say," he searched the exterior in vain, "but it's post marked from Tel Aviv."

Puzzled, Qadurra took the box from the sergeant's hands, and then motioned for him to leave. As the young officer exited, closing the door with a click, the captain turned the package over, examining it thoroughly. He had not been expecting anything in the mail, and the Tel Aviv postmark troubled him. Nonetheless, he pulled a letter opener from beneath the clutter on his desk and began breaking the seal of packing tape that bound the box together.

Reaching inside, he felt the coolness of metal on his fingers. Now he was even more perplexed as to what it could be. He enclosed his hand around the cylindrical object and pulled it from its cardboard sheathing. He smiled immediately as he realized what it was. He held up the exquisitely crafted golden scepter in wondrous admiration, examining it before he reached into the box once more to see if there was anything else.

Inside was a small, rolled piece of paper, which he flattened for a better look. The text was in hand-written English, and immediately, he knew who it was from.

Dear Captain Qadurra,

I first want to thank you for your help, and I assure you that everything is fine now. Your efforts were not in vain. I'm sure this beautiful artifact will make an excellent addition to the Alexander exhibit that your city is no doubt planning to construct. I'm sure it will find a SAFE home there in your government's care. Guard it. Take care, and thanks again.

My deepest gratitude,
James P. Beauregard

The captain smiled widely and uncontrollably as he reread the note, holding it before his face. He then turned his attention back to the scepter that was lying on his desk, gripping it with his hand and smiling.

In New Orleans, a phone rang in the study of the Beauregard home on Chartres Street. It rang several times before a hand finally reached over, gripped the receiver, and picked it up. James put the phone to his ear, saying nothing, as he seemed distracted.

"James? James?" the voice repeated. "It's me, Tim Horn. Look, before you say anything, I just wanted to apologize for everything. I was worried. You stormed out of here the other day, and I haven't heard from you since."

"It's okay, Tim. Oh, and I forgive you," James smiled.

"By the way," Tim changed the subject, "some colleagues and I at Yale think we have made some headway on the artifacts we found at Vesuvius . . ."

"Goodbye, Tim," James smiled and hung up the phone.

The smile on his face grew as he sunk back into his living room couch. Light was again in his eyes. He studied every inch of Noelle's face up-close, rubbing his hands across her willing cheeks. He kissed her and then melted with her into the cushions.

About the Author

J.M. Richardson is a native of southeast Louisiana where he studied education and social sciences, earning his degree from Louisiana State University. He has been writing for leisure nearly all of his life, wrote competitively in high school, and had intensive writing coursework in college. He now resides in the Fort Worth, TX, area with his wife and two daughters where he teaches geography, history, and sociology.

Follow J.M. Richardson:
jmrichardsonbooks.com
Facebook: facebook.com/J-M-Richardson
Twitter: @JMRichardson1

www.ingramcontent.com/pod-product-compliance
Lightning Source LLC
Chambersburg PA
CBHW060421180626
46817CB00007B/2608